4.6

OGRE
ENCHANTED

Also by GAIL CARSON LEVINE

NOVELS
Dave at Night
Ella Enchanted
Ever
Fairest
The Lost Kingdom of Bamarre
Stolen Magic
A Tale of Two Castles
The Two Princesses of Bamarre
The Wish

THE PRINCESS TALES
The Fairy's Return and Other Princess Tales
The Fairy's Mistake
The Princess Test
Princess Sonora and the Long Sleep
Cinderellis and the Glass Hill
For Biddle's Sake
The Fairy's Return

PICTURE BOOKS
Betsy Red Hoodie
Betsy Who Cried Wolf

NONFICTION
Writing Magic: Creating Stories that Fly
Writer to Writer: From Think to Ink

POETRY
Forgive Me, I Meant to Do It: False Apology Poems

OGRE
ENCHANTED

GAIL CARSON LEVINE

HARPER
An Imprint of HarperCollins*Publishers*

This book was inspired by the fairy tale "The False Prince and the True," adapted from the Portuguese by Andrew Lang in *The Lilac Fairy Book.*

Ogre Enchanted
Copyright © 2018 by Gail Carson Levine

Library of Congress Cataloging-in-Publication Data

Names: Levine, Gail Carson, author.
Title: Ogre enchanted / Gail Carson Levine.
Description: First edition. | New York, NY : Harper, an imprint of HarperCollins
  Publishers, [2018] | Prequel to: Ella Enchanted. | "Based on the fairy tale 'The
  False Prince and the True,' adapted from the Portuguese by Andrew Lang in *The
  Lilac Fairy Book.*" | Summary: "Healer Evora is turned into a hideous ogre by the
  fairy Lucinda after rejecting a proposal and has only a few months to find a love
  to reverse the curse"—Provided by publisher.
Identifiers: LCCN 2018004918 | ISBN 9780062561213 (hardback)
ISBN 9780062561237 (library edition) | ISBN 9780062889287 (special edition)
Subjects: | CYAC: Fantasy. | BISAC: JUVENILE FICTION / Fairy Tales
  & Folklore / General. | JUVENILE FICTION / Fairy Tales & Folklore /
  Adaptations. | JUVENILE FICTION / Fantasy & Magic.
Classification: LCC PZ7.L578345 Ogr 2018 | DDC [Fic]—dc23 LC record
available at https://lccn.loc.gov/2018004918

Typography by Katie Klimowicz
Map illustration by Diana Sousa
18 19 20 21 22   PC/LSCH   10 9 8 7 6 5 4 3 2 1
❖
First Edition

To my friend Joan, who proves that some transformations leave the essence unchanged

Spires

Giants'
Farms

Fens

Master's
Farm

Elves'
Forest

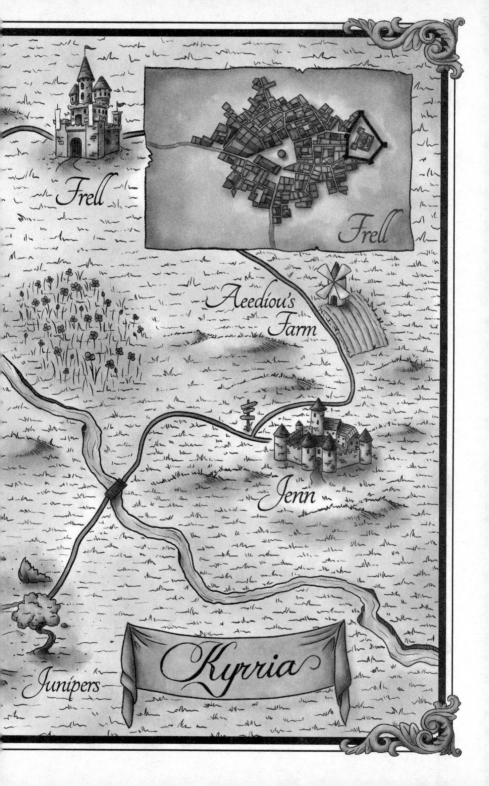

Frell

Frell

Aeediou's
Farm

Jenn

Junipers

Kyrria

OGRE
ENCHANTED

CHAPTER ONE

WORMY WAS DISTRACTED. I counted three symptoms:

- He kept forgetting to mash my inglebot fungus.
- He twice asked me to repeat why Master Kian's cough had seemed odd.
- Whenever I looked at him, he was wetting his lips, although—exasperatingly—nothing emanated from them.

Soon he'd need a remedy for chapping.

He was spoiling our daily companionable time, when we worked together in my apothecary (in a corner of Mother's kitchen) and chatted; we were old friends, though we were both just fifteen.

"Wormy, what did you notice on your way here?"

"Drag leg. Ferocious sneeze. Palsy. A gentleman who

tripped over nothing." He named streets: "Moorcroft, sorry—don't know where the sneeze lives—Ashton, Westover."

"You're a miracle." He never missed anything.

Wormy was a healer's best friend. He knew almost everyone and where almost everyone lived, and he had a fine eye for symptoms, as well as for beauty, which—shame on me—interested me less. He arrived midmorning every day, after working on the books for his parents' various enterprises. Not a coin remained unaccounted for when he was in charge.

Half my patients came from his observations. He told me about sufferers, and I tracked them down. Healing was my calling and my joy.

"Thank you." I patted his hand.

He blushed. He'd been blushing often. This blush seemed too brilliant. "Do you have one of your headaches?"

He shrugged. "Maybe." The blush faded.

I teased, "*Maybe* I'll treat you."

The blush flared again.

"Are you feverish?"

"No!"

Grimwood, my fever remedy, tasted bitter.

He smiled. "Grimwood cures as many patients by being threatened as swallowed."

I smiled back. "A good healer knows when to just mention a remedy and when to pry open a jaw."

A moment later we spoke at exactly the same moment. He said, "Evie?" and I said, "Wormy?"

Ah. He was finally going to reveal what had been occupying him.

But he insisted I go first, and I didn't mind. Unless an emergency case came in, we'd be together the rest of the day.

I reached into my cupboard for my darkroot salve. "Sit."

He sat on my stool and gazed up at me. I felt the satisfaction of an artisan surveying her good work. His chestnut skin glowed with health—and with his blush. His brown eyes were bright. "If you saw yourself on the street, Wormy, you'd have nothing to report to me. A headache is invisible."

"People are patients or nothing to you."

A mere dab of the ointment was all I needed. I began to rub it into his temples, my fingertips describing tiny circles, always going counterclockwise. "*You* are my friend. How lucky I am that you're also delicate, and you like my ministrations."

When we were eleven, I'd set his broken ankle. Before then, I'd treated only birds, rabbits, and mice. Afterward, I'd made his stomachaches vanish, his headaches recede, and his fevers fade, and I'd spooned unpleasant concoctions into him to convince him he was well when he merely thought himself sick.

Gradually, I'd garnered more human patients, but I'd always be grateful to him for being first.

He breathed deeply. Either that was the headache receding, or it was a sigh. If a sigh, why?

"What were you going to say, Evie?"

Oh, yes. "Wormy, am I peculiar?"

"No!"

"Who else my age wants nothing more than to take care of sick people?" I continued rubbing. "Who else reeks of camphor at least once a week?"

"Or worse," he said solemnly.

I nodded. "Pig bladder!" Stinky, but excellent when wrapped around a sprain. "I'll be an outcast! People will want peculiar me when they're sick and never otherwise."

He raised an eyebrow. "Some folk are friendlier at a gathering, a dance, even"—he stage-whispered—"a *ball*."

I kept to myself at such affairs. "I'd rather observe for symptoms than talk or dance." Although I liked dancing. I lifted my fingers. "How is the headache?"

"Better, but it's still there."

I returned to rubbing.

"You're not peculiar. You're remarkable." Wormy slid off the stool. "Evie?"

Finally.

Someone banged on the front door. Rupert, our manservant, would answer, but pounding meant an emergency.

"Wormy—"

"Go."

I put the salve on my worktable.

It was as well I went, because Oobeeg, a ten-year-old giant, couldn't fit through our door. Weeping, he gasped out his story. His mother, Farmer Aeediou, had had a brush with an ogre. She was alive because her hound, Exee, had sunk his teeth in the ogre's throat before it could say a word. Still, by the time the ogre died, it had lured her close enough to deliver a gash to her leg. With their honeyed words and irresistible voices, ogres could persuade people to do anything.

Calling behind me, I rushed back to the apothecary. "I'll get supplies. Don't leave. I'll be quick."

Untreated, the cut would kill Aeediou. Whatever Wormy had been about to say would have to wait.

Back in the apothecary, while I nested a pot of honey in my healer's basket, I told him what had happened. Where was my packet of turmeric?

There it was. Now I needed my flask of vinegar.

I smelled lilacs.

I turned to see and forgot everything in staring. A woman stood behind Wormy. How had she arrived without a sound?

She was a vision of health and beauty: yellow hair cascading to wide shoulders, garnet lips, blue eyes, and petal-smooth skin.

Wormy said, "Oh!"

She must have been dosed to create such perfection. What herbs? Periwinkle, for those eyes? Strawberry juice, for that skin? What else?

And what a smile. What teeth. I blinked.

"Young Master"—her voice rang out, as if her chest were as big as a castle—"speak your mind! Brook no delay!"

"Welcome!" I curtsied and wished my apron weren't shapeless and grease-stained.

"Thank you." She nodded graciously. "Continue, Young Master."

I remembered Aeediou. "Mistress, this must wait. Beg pardon. I have an injured—"

"I repeat: Continue, Young Master."

How dare she?

Wormy said, "Mistress, there's no hurry for what—"

Her voice gained volume. "Continue!"

Who was she? I gripped tight my manners and my temper. "I am Mistress Evora, called Evie by my friends, and this is Master Warwick." Wormy. "May we have the honor of your acquaintance?"

She drew herself up even taller. "I am the fairy Lucinda."

Really?

Wormy bowed.

I curtsied again. "Can you replenish my purpline? And give me a unicorn hair? Or sell both to me?" Purpline—dragon urine—cured almost everything, even barley blight, and lately there had been none in the market. Unicorn hair in a soup was nonpareil for fever. "I'd also welcome anything else for an ogre scratch, enough for a giant."

She seemed not to hear. "The young man will say his piece."

Wormy dropped to his knees, as a puppet might. "Evie, will you"—his Adam's apple popped in and out—"marry me?"

The woman clapped her hands. "So sweet!"

That was his secret? That he wanted to ruin our friendship?

"I relish proposals"—Lucinda jigged a quick hop-step—"and weddings and births. If I can, I come." Her hands embraced each other. "Proposals are the start—"

"No, Wormy, dear. Thank you for asking me, though." I put the vinegar in my basket with my next-to-last vial of purpline. "I must leave." But curiosity held me. "Why do you want to marry me?"

He stood up. "Because . . ." He shrugged. "You're you."

Did he think—being me—I'd say yes? He knew my ideas about marriage.

And I didn't believe he could truly be in love with me.

As his healer, I made him feel better. He'd confused loving health with loving me. That was my diagnosis: imaginary infatuation, which would clear up as soon as we got a little older.

"And you can stop working so hard." His family was rich. "But"—his blush returned—"pretend I didn't ask."

"Why won't you marry him?"

I picked up my basket. "He's Wormy." Yes, I loved him—the way I loved my pet rabbit. I didn't even know how romantic love felt. We were too young. If Wormy didn't think he was, I thought we both were. I didn't know if I'd ever want to marry anyone. But I didn't have time to explain. "Good day." I'd be two hours riding to Aeediou's farm. A few farms owned by giants covered the rolling hills near Jenn, though most lay in the west near the elves' Forest.

"I urge you to reconsider. If you persist in breaking this young man's heart, you will suffer the consequences."

Wormy's jaw hung open.

I picked up my herb basket. "If I accept him, we'll both suffer the consequences." No one should marry before they were ready—and certain.

For a moment she looked puzzled; then her face cleared.

My mind emptied. The kitchen tiles no longer seemed to be beneath me. Somewhere, fabric ripped.

My mind filled again. I held my arms out for balance

and felt the floor under my feet. My mouth tasted gamy and spoiled, as if I'd swallowed a three-day-dead squirrel.

Wormy's jaw was still unhinged. He extended my name. "Evie-ee . . . there's hair on your face."

Not what I expected to hear. I started to lift a hand to my cheek but stopped and held the hand out. Hair sprouted there. My fingernails were long and filthy.

My stomach rose into my throat.

"Evie . . . you're an ogre."

CHAPTER TWO

I **LOOKED DOWN** at further horrors. My bodice had ripped, but my apron strings held and were squeezing my stomach. Hastily, I untied them. The seams of both sleeves of my bodice had split. The hem of my skirt, which had hovered just above the floor, now fell a little below my knees. I had shot up a whole foot! My boots, which were visible now without raising my skirts, had come apart. When I lifted one foot, the sole flapped.

My stomach settled, though I didn't know how it could. And it rumbled. But I'd had a big breakfast.

How delicious Wormy looked: a little lopsided because he always hiked up his left shoulder, which just added to his appeal, and those rounded cheeks, those plump earlobes (the sweetest part), that flawless neck, that skin the hue of a goose roasted to a turn. How healthy I'd kept him, like a farmer safeguarding her livestock. How dear he was to me.

Aaa! What was I thinking?

The fairy Lucinda frowned. I sensed outrage, though I couldn't hear her thoughts. Her feelings buzzed, as if a quarreling crowd were packed inside her.

How could I tell? I'd never perceived feelings before.

She needed a dose of my bonny-jump-up syrup to calm her. Maybe she'd turn me back then. "May I treat—"

"Fairy Lucinda," Wormy said, "pardon me. Proposing was just a prank. We play tricks on each other, as friends do." I sensed his emotions too. He was frightened. Oddly, he wasn't in any pain, though he'd told me that his headache hadn't entirely gone away.

The fairy's outrage mounted. She glared at Wormy. What would she turn him into?

Had he really been jesting about the proposal?

"Yes," I said. "We have a merry time with our capers." My voice sounded husky, as if I'd been shouting. "We're never serious." Turn me back! And don't harm Wormy!

She surveyed us, her emotions still in turmoil. Finally, she decided. "No. I think he meant it. And you"—she poked a perfect finger into my large chest—"will remain an ogre until someone proposes marriage and you accept."

I gripped my worktable to steady myself.

Wormy went down on one knee this time. "Mistress

Evie, please accept my *sincere* offer. I think—I believe—I'm certain—we'll be happy."

I sensed his fear and desperation. Kind Wormy. Perhaps the first proposal had been a prank, and now he wanted to save me from its consequences.

He added, "You can work as hard as ever. As hard as you like."

I did feel love coming from him. But we weren't *in* love. I definitely wasn't, and I didn't think he could be, either.

Maybe I should accept him, become me again, and figure the rest out later.

It would be wrong to accept him just to be human and stop wanting to eat him. I couldn't do that to Wormy. Not to my dearest friend. Not to anyone.

Lucinda clapped her hands. "See how true his love is."

She didn't mind destroying a person's life? "Do you do this often?"

"Help people?" Her smile blazed again. "Yes, oft—"

"Turn them into ogres?"

"It's my latest inspiration."

She was insane. I turned back to Wormy. "No thank you." I was young. Eventually I'd find love with someone who loved me, too, someone who saw beyond the ogre.

"Oh." Now Wormy was sad as well as scared.

"But if you're ill, of course, I'll help you."

Lucinda's rage surged. I put my hands over my ears, which accomplished nothing.

I felt furious, too—at her and at Wormy for bringing this down on me, though he hadn't meant to. I doubted I'd ever been so angry.

"Then, foolish girl," Lucinda said, "if you don't receive a marriage offer and accept it, you'll remain an ogre forever. You have"—she tilted her head from side to side, deciding—"sixty-two days."

Barely more than two months!

"Counting today?" asked Wormy.

"Certainly, counting today."

"Might she have a little longer? A year?"

Thank you, Wormy!

"Certainly not! Sixty-two is twice twenty-eight."

"Er . . ."

"What, young man?"

Wormy, the mathematician, saw my face—and my fangs.

"Er . . . er . . ." He collected himself and thought better of pointing out her error, which, if she corrected it, would cost me days. "Then the last day will be November twenty-second."

"I suppose."

13

"At midnight?" I asked.

"At four o'clock in the afternoon."

Why then?

She went on. "Who else will want her anyway, even if she were human, defiant and contrary as she is?" She smiled. "You, young man, are exemplary. When you find someone who deserves you, I'll devise a marvelous gift."

"If I have to stay an ogre, will my human side disappear?"

"No. You'll always know what you lost." She disappeared.

And reappeared. "Do not think another fairy will come to your rescue, either, no matter how much you plead. The fools disapprove of me, but they fear their own magic too much to intervene." She vanished and this time stayed away.

A fly buzzed over my basket. I needed to eat. I wished the fly were a lot bigger, but I caught it and licked it off my palm. Tasted like venison.

"Wormy, why did you?"

He blushed yet again. "I thought we could spend the next few years discussing it."

A reasonable answer.

A fist pounded on our door, a large fist by the sound of it. Oobeeg! What would he do when he saw me?

"Wormy . . . Tell Oobeeg what happened. Tell him I'm me."

He left the apothecary. A bowl of late peaches rested on the kitchen table.

Ugh.

But I loved peaches.

No longer. I was angry they were even in my presence.

The stew for dinner bubbled over our low fire. I wondered if I could fish out the meat and ignore the flavor of carrots and onions.

Wormy returned and blushed. "Somehow I thought you would be you again."

"I am me." I forced my eyes away from his meaty thighs. "What did Oobeeg say?" The stew would have to wait. Aeediou couldn't.

"I couldn't tell him. The words wouldn't come out. I think the fairy won't let me."

Would I be able to say them? I grabbed my basket and left.

As soon as he saw me, Oobeeg screamed.

I tried to explain, but the words seemed to choke me. Oobeeg jumped on his enormous horse and spurred it. His terrified wail wafted back to me. I watched him grow a little less huge in the distance.

Aeediou would die without doctoring. Ogres are fast,

so I started running, clutching my basket to my chest and stumbling in my broken boots. Ahead of me, the streets of Jenn cleared, as if Lucinda had cast another spell.

Beyond town, I stopped to strip off my boots. Luckily, the soles of an ogre's feet are calloused, so the dirt and pebbles of the road wouldn't hurt. I ran again.

Aeediou's farm lay ten miles from town. I hoped ogres had stamina. Ahead of me, Oobeeg crested a hill. As he descended, his height, especially on his mount, kept his head visible until, finally, all of him disappeared into the valley.

My mind returned to Wormy. Blockhead!

Edible blockhead.

Ugh! I wanted to leap out of my skin, as if the ogre were just a covering. I let go of the basket with one hand to touch my face, hoping for a miracle.

No miracle. Still hairy. Nincompoop fairy.

Why did I keep thinking this one or that one stupid? Was being angry part of being an ogre?

A side of beef hung in our shed at home, untainted by vegetables. I'd eat it raw. Mother wouldn't have to see.

As I streaked along, a new feeling mingled with the misery and rage—pleasure in the strength of my legs, the energy in my muscles, the depth of my breathing.

By now, Aeediou's large leg had probably swollen to three times its size.

Again I thought of Wormy's proposal. As a healer, I had seen too much unhappiness in marriage. Stomach complaints and worse were the result! The commonest cause, I'd observed, was youth. So I had decided that no one younger than eighteen should wed, no matter how in love they believed themselves to be. Many married at fourteen, and then—for example—one or the other grew ten inches! And height was the least of it.

My calves were aching when I finally reached a stile for giants and had to boost myself up each step with my arms. When I descended the other side, Aeediou's bull, an acre away, pawed the ground and lowered his horns.

I heaved myself up the far stile with his breath on my neck.

There was Aeediou's vast farmhouse—made of boulders, thatched with a mountain of straw. I banged on the door.

No one answered, but Aeediou and Oobeeg had to be inside. Exee trotted to me, clearly meaning no harm. His back, which used to be as high as my shoulders, now came up only to my waist. He rubbed himself against me. Did he know me despite my form?

I wondered how dog tasted.

I wouldn't eat a dog!

The door didn't open.

"Exee trusts me!" I cried. "Uueeetaatii (*honk*) obobee

aiiiee." *I am a friend.* I knew a few words of the giants'
language, Abdegi, which includes sounds as well as words.

Oobeeg's face appeared in a first-floor window, right
above my head.

"I mean no harm. I'm—" The words *your healer, Evie*
wouldn't come. "I'm a healer ogre. Aeediou needs me."

Oobeeg's face left the window. Was he going to let
me in?

Five minutes passed.

Aeediou had to be in pain, which would soon rise to
agony, and shortly after that, she'd be beyond my remedies.

Now was the time for ogrish persuasion. A born ogre
would have had the door open before the end of her first
sentence.

"Oobeeg, I won't hurt anyone." I tried to soften my
voice, but it still came out rough. "I'm as kind as . . ." As
what? "As a good human." In exasperation I cried, "If I
were an ordinary ogre, wouldn't I have convinced you by
now?"

Nothing happened. I was furious. Two stupids.

I couldn't reach the door latch, which hung too high for
me even now. I saw nothing to stand on to get to it, either.

My rage melted as my own leg ached in sympathy
with Aeediou's. I backed away and put down my basket.
"Oobeeg! Aeediou! I'm leaving my basket and going away."
I told them what was in it and how to use the ingredients.

"Be generous with everything except the purpline. A few drops are all you need. I want the rest back. Aeediou, don't stand up—Oobeeg, don't let her stand—until the pain is completely gone. Coat every bit of the wound." Now I was just repeating myself. "If you wait another half hour, nothing will help. I'm going now." They'd pay me next week. You can trust a giant.

Please, Oobeeg, be brave enough to go outside for my basket. Aeediou, please let your son go out and save you. Be well, both of you.

CHAPTER THREE

DISCOVERIES:

- Ogre hands are blink fast.
- Squirrels are not quite blink fast.
- Biting through fur with fangs is easy.

I ate three squirrels by the time I reached the outskirts of Jenn. Mother and I had many times dined on squirrel ragout. Raw squirrel was chewier. Soon enough, I'd discover if it made me sick.

The September afternoon was half over. On Earl Road, Jenn's widest thoroughfare, I heard a *hisssss*. An arrow whizzed past my ear. Another *hisssss*. *Smack!*

An arrow bored into my right arm just above my elbow. The numbskulls were shooting at me! People poured out of houses and shops, making a mob.

I dashed into Rushy Alley and loped between fences that guarded back gardens.

- The ogre heart has a triple beat. Sped up, it sounds like a dancing three-legged stool.

No one in the alley yet. I stood still to look around. Nobody peering down at me, either, all probably drawn to the front of their houses by the ogre on the avenue.

I felt no pain, but I yanked the arrow out and hoped the tip wasn't poisoned. Human-looking red blood seeped through my sleeve. I wondered if the blood of born ogres was the same color.

Someone shouted, "That way!"

I vaulted a fence and landed on a woodpile, which avalanched, bringing split logs down on me. One rammed the side of my head but didn't knock me out. I lay still and clenched my jaw against the pain.

A crowd pounded by. Luckily, its own noise covered the rumble of the cascade I'd caused.

Gradually, my heart quieted. My arm throbbed, and my bones and skull ached from the log attack.

I wondered if Oobeeg had dared retrieve my basket.

Time ticked by.

When Aeediou smiled, her cheeks rounded into melons. A dose of an Aeediou smile kept me cheerful for a month. I couldn't help imagining her anguish if Oobeeg had been afraid to retrieve my basket. I got mad at both of them again.

Mother and I were toiling people. I was a healer, and Mother a learned this-and-that: scribe, reckoner for folks baffled by mathematics (though she wasn't as adept as Wormy), and go-between when the poor had to parley with the mighty. We earned enough to keep up a modest household and afford two servants, but without either one of us, we'd starve. With my new appetite, we might starve anyway.

Half an hour passed. Carefully, quietly, I restacked the firewood, this time two feet from the fence, providing myself a cramped hiding place. I'd be invisible even to a householder who came out for logs. Only someone peeping over the fence would see me.

I squeezed in. The pain in my arm grew.

Hours later, by following alleys and streaking across thoroughfares, I avoided the night constables. The lord mayor's clock chimed midnight as I climbed the steps to our front door. My second day as an ogre began. Sixty-one days left.

Inside, Mother and Wormy sat at my worktable.

Mother—my own mother!—tempted my stomach, too. Wormy couldn't have told her what Lucinda had done, but he must have said he'd proposed and must have communicated that some disaster had befallen me as a result. Perhaps he'd been able to say a fairy had been involved. When she saw my ruined clothes on my new body, she instantly drew the correct, dreadful conclusion.

She stood so quickly her stool fell over. "Oh!" She righted the stool and smile-grimaced at me. She sat again. "It's not so bad, Evie. You're just bigger."

What a dreadful liar she was. I smile-grimaced back, which, considering my fangs, must have been appalling, but, to her endless credit, I sensed just pity and sadness, no fear—

—until she saw my wound. "You're bleeding!"

Wormy cried, "Evie!"

"I've treated worse." Except I knew what I was about when my patient was human.

While they watched, I mixed the same ingredients from my remedies cabinet that I'd assembled for Aeediou, including a scant drop of purpline, so called because dragon pee is purple. The scent of camphor seared my nose. When I'd been human, I'd barely smelled it.

Mother stared down at her hands in her lap. With my new awareness, I felt her concentration. I believed she was running through solutions, as if I were a customer with an unusual problem. "Evie," she said, "can't you accept Wormy but stipulate you want a long engagement? Anything can happen before you have to get married."

"The fairy can hear you!" Wormy jumped up, and his stool capsized, too.

Mother said, "Good. Say you no longer want to marry Evie."

He nodded. "Evie, I no—"

"Stop! Who knows what Lucinda will do to Wormy when she hears." If she was listening—I had no idea. "She could turn him into anything." What would be worse than being an ogre? "Or do some other dreadful thing. And she'd punish me for trying to trick her if I delayed the wedding."

Using my left hand, I applied the remedy to my wound. Then, with my hand and my teeth, I wrapped a linen cloth around my arm and managed to tie a neat knot. "And she probably wouldn't change me back anyway. I still rejected a suitor, even if he decided later that he didn't want me."

No one spoke.

"I'm hungry!" burst out of me.

Wormy jumped in his seat. "We hardly touched the stew."

"No!" I didn't want the taint of vegetables with my meat. I ran out the back door, through my herb garden, where the scent of herbs disgusted me, and into our shed and the darling side of beef. Too hungry even to bring it into the kitchen to butcher, I lifted it off its hook and plunged my face into a haunch—

24

—and looked up, while still eating, to see Mother in the doorway, holding a candle in one hand, the other fist stuffed in her mouth, tears running down her cheeks.

I loved her so much—even if she made me think of food. She had deep smile lines around her mouth and equally deep lines of puzzlement between her eyebrows. Up-tilted chin. Brown eyes flecked with blue.

My tears welled up and spilled over, too. I couldn't bear to see her seeing me, so I closed my eyes and kept eating, more aware of need than taste. When I checked a few minutes later, she was gone. I devoured the entire side down to bones. Full at last and exhausted, I curled up on the straw.

- Ogres—or human ogres—dream in red, the color of anger.

Surrounded by a vermilion haze, I wafted spectrally in and out of the bedrooms of Jenn, where I stood over its sleeping citizens, some of them my patients, saliva dripping. Even in sleep I knew I couldn't eat them, but, oh, how I wanted to.

CHAPTER FOUR

AT DAWN, fresh hunger woke me. My arm no longer ached. When I untied the bandage, I found the wound not red, not swollen, not even needing another bandage.

- Ogres are excellent at recovery from arrow wounds.

I crossed to the house in a light drizzle. Inside, I crept upstairs and sat at my vanity table to consider the hairy, blotchy nightmare in the looking glass. I tried to make the small, bloodshot (still hazel) eyes sympathetic but couldn't judge my success.

Ogre hunger and human nausea warred in my belly.

If this was to be my shape, I had to ogrishly persuade people not to mind. "Friend . . ." Too raspy. I swallowed. "Dear friend . . . Beneath this . . ." This what? ". . . this *odd* exterior, I'm really—" I couldn't say aloud who I actually was, even to myself. "I wouldn't harm anyone."

Even *I* wouldn't believe me. I spent the next half hour practicing, until I thought I detected a scintilla of improvement. Then I stepped into the hall, though I should have listened at the door first. Bettina, our maid-of-all-work, was sweeping.

"Eeee!" Her broom clattered on the tiles.

Use a sweet voice. "Kind Bett—"

She flew down our stairs. I heard the front door thud.

Rupert, our manservant—big, young, bovine—gawked from the stair landing above. After an instant, his cry was as high-pitched as Bettina's. He stood frozen, afraid to pass me on his way down.

Honey voice. "I'm harmless. A healer, too, like your mistress."

His eyes bulged. He clutched his head. To save him from apoplexy, I backed into my room and stayed there until I heard his boots clumping down the stairs.

I reemerged into the silent hall. Last year, I'd hardly left Rupert's bedside when he was desperately sick with fever, and he'd lived, even though I'd had no purpline to dose him with at the time.

His decamping gave me an idea. In his room, I sat at his shaving table, poured water from pitcher to bowl, and applied his razor to my face and the back of my hands. That done, I took his pig-bristle brush and attacked my fingernails, succeeding in freeing them almost entirely of grime—which half of me missed when it was gone. Then I stripped out of yesterday's tattered gown and donned his spare breeches and worn linen shirt. The fit was fair, too tight here, too loose there. His boots, miraculously, pinched only a little.

Much improved, I told my ghastly reflection. My pores were vast, my lips thin, my forehead low. I wondered if another ogre would recognize me as female. I addressed my reflection. "You're not so frightening anymore . . ." I grinned. "If you don't show your fangs."

The grin turned down. Who could possibly love me?

Daily, before breakfast, I visited patients. My roster for today: Mistress Poppy, who had birthed her first child the night before last; Master Caleb, who was probably at his ovens, though I'd ordered him to rest his knee; and Master Kian, whose cough had alarmed me. I plotted a route to each one that would avoid the trafficked thoroughfares.

Mistress Poppy had a younger brother my age, whom I'd never met. Perhaps he'd be visiting the baby. Perhaps he had odd tastes in sweethearts and would like the looks of me. Perhaps I'd like the looks of him—not just as a meal.

I had to eat.

As I descended to the kitchen, I thought of the chunk of bacon in the larder, which was all the meat we had left. But a side of mutton rested on the table, and Mother stood behind it. She must have sent Rupert to the market at dawn.

I framed my face with my hands. "Better? I shaved."

She managed to hide her dismay, but I felt it. "You look distinguished." She took a step toward me and stopped. Her eyes watered, but I didn't sense sadness.

"Evie . . ."

"What's wrong?" Silly question. Everything was wrong.

"Dear . . . er . . . I'm sorry. You smell."

"Smell what?"

"Just smell, love."

Me? I smelled fine: squirrel, beef, sweat, blood.

Ugh! I'd thought to clean only my hands. The mutton, sadly, would have to wait. I pumped water from our iron sink into our biggest pot and hefted it over the fire, which I now could accomplish easily.

When the water was finally hot and off the fire, it was hard to bathe without looking at myself.

- Ogres have clumps of hair everywhere except on their bony knees.

While I washed, Mother butchered the mutton into chops and fried them according to my instructions—in suet, without any repulsive herbs or vegetables.

Finally I was clean, though my ogre side thought me dull and unsavory until I greased myself up eating the mutton with both hands. Then I ruined it all by washing them again. So it would have to be, or my patients would retreat when I approached.

Ordinarily, by midmorning I had at least five people waiting in the apothecary, but today my sole patient was Wormy, complaining of an itch behind his ear, which I dosed in an instant while resisting the temptation of his earlobes. I wondered if he'd invented the itch just to comfort me for having no patients.

He thanked me for the treatment and started for the door. Usually, he lingered.

"Wormy?"

"Evie?"

"Are you angry at me for saying no?"

"I'm not!" I felt his shock. "You had the right."

Then why was he leaving so soon? "We're still friends, aren't we?"

"I'll always be your friend, Evie."

"Thank you, dear. I'll always be yours."

He left—as it turned out, just to visit Mother in her study.

When I opened our door to the street, I discovered that, despite a light rain, a mob had collected. My stomach roared at the sight of so much food.

They were armed with bows and arrows, rolling pins, knives, pokers. I stared down at the humans from the top of our steps. They stared up at me. The rain seemed to pause midair.

I supposed the clothing and the shave made them uncertain. They were two-legged sheep!

A woman's voice wavered. "Is that the ogre?"

Not trusting my voice, I shook my head and began to descend our steps.

"It *is* the ogre!" I recognized Rupert's voice. "It's wearing my clothes!"

Everyone rushed at me. I ran up the stairs and threw myself back at the house. A hatchet whizzed over my shoulder and vibrated in our wooden door, which I cracked open and squeezed through. Once inside, I shot home the bolt.

Mother and Wormy stood in the vestibule. Mother was biting her lip. Wormy's eyes were enormous. Pounding reverberated through the door. They were going to break it down!

I had to flee.

Mother's thoughts must have followed mine. "They'll have stationed people behind the house."

I nodded. What then?

"Mother, Wormy, go to the back door. If you hear them come in *here*, run out *there*." I didn't think anyone would hurt them outside, but a mob indoors would be in a fever. "Go!"

Mother cupped my cheek, as if I were still lovable, then hurried away. With a backward glance, Wormy followed. After a moment, I flung open the door to find fists and weapons waving in my face.

But nothing landed. The pack drew back a few feet. I bared my fangs and roared, truth giving my voice power: "I'm hu-u-ungry!"

They retreated farther. Rain deadened the quiet.

I spoke softly, lying (I hoped), but they didn't know. "If any of you enter this house, people will die." Taking a chance, as if I were unworried, I turned my back and re-entered. In the vestibule, I waited a full five minutes, but the assault on the door didn't resume, a small victory for the ogre. Would they disperse?

Mother and Wormy were no longer at the back door. In the kitchen, Wormy said Mother had retired to her study. He stood at the iron sink, piercing a side of boar with a hook. Where had the treat come from?

I sensed his happiness. "Why are you happy?" My instant anger flared. Was he glad I'd been punished for turning him down?

His pleasure changed to confusion. "How do you know I'm happy?"

"I can tell what people are feeling. Maybe that helps ogres persuade."

"But you can't persuade, right?"

"No."

The hook was in the boar.

"Where did this come from?" I hoisted the roast onto the steam-jack, where it spun slowly on its own axis. In just a few minutes, pork perfumed the air.

"I got it at the market."

How kind of him! "Thank you."

"The butcher's boy helped carry it."

I nodded and remembered my question. "Why were you happy?" My tone was accusatory.

"Because nobody hurt you at the door. Because you're all right."

Oh.

Who could love such a creature as I had become? Soon even Wormy would stop liking me. "Sorry! Everything makes me angry. And I can't stop being hungry."

"I'm often hungry, too."

Which angered me. A human appetite was nothing like what I was enduring.

He added, "I wonder if the fairy knew."

Which mollified me. "I don't know whether it would be worse or better if she did it without realizing. Why does she care if I get married? Or if I turn down a hundred offers?"

"Do you think she's married?"

I shrugged.

"Maybe someone turned her down." As always, a good conversationalist, Wormy continued to speculate. He went on and on, and I stopped listening, though I used to enjoy his notions, but now the sizzle of boar fat had more significance for me than words.

And I had thoughts to think, plans to make. I couldn't remain here, a prisoner in our house, endangering both Mother and anyone, like Wormy or future patients, who came to me.

But where to go?

Even before that, how to leave?

The boar cooked. The scent made thinking increasingly difficult, but I forced my mind to work.

Eventually I formed the beginnings of a plan, one that turned even my stomach and tightened my chest with fear.

"Will you stay for dinner? My belly says it's almost noon." I wondered if the mob was still outside. Wormy might not be able to leave.

"Will there be carrots in cream?" His favorite dish.

"Do you see anyone cooking it?" I mastered my rage. "Sorry. No vegetables for the time being, dear."

We stood in silence until he said, "I'll stay."

More silence. Then I asked, "Wormy . . . will your

family help Mother and make sure she has enough money?"

"Where will you be?"

"We'll repay you." If I lived.

He waved the offer away. "We'll help." His Adam's apple throbbed. "I'll see she's all right. Where will you be?"

My answer would wait for Mother. I didn't want to have to say it twice and argue twice. "Thank you." I sat on the stool by my worktable.

Wormy sat on the stool next to mine, but his closeness made me uneasy, as it never had before—and hungrier. I moved to the other side of the table. I would have checked the front door, but if people were still out there, I feared that just twitching aside a curtain would bring on an attack.

Silence resumed. Ordinarily, I would have told him about the patients I'd seen, and he would have had lots of questions.

After a quarter hour, the human side of me had a question for him. "Are you used to seeing me this way yet?"

"When we're in the same room I am. But if I go out or you do and then one of us comes back, I'm surprised. And your voice is different, so if you haven't spoken for a while, I forget, and then I'm surprised."

He'd chosen *surprised*, not *shocked* or *horrified*. He was a kind person.

"When we're in the same room—tell me the truth!— now that I've been an ogre a while, do I still look as bad?"

He took a full minute to answer, and then all he said was, "I know it's really you the same as always."

Mother came in. The boar gleamed a beautiful brown, and I deemed it fit for humans to eat, so I put it on a platter. Mother followed me into the dining room, trailed by Wormy. In the back garden, which the dining room looked out on, the rain intensified. I wondered if the weather had dispersed the crowd outside.

But before I checked, I had to eat. Wormy carved while I restrained myself from ripping off a rib.

Hesitantly, Mother asked, "Is there anything else? Bread? Turnips?"

Wormy shook his head at her. Mother's eyebrows went up, but she said nothing. He served me a single slice.

"I'm an ogre!"

He gave me three more slices, and then, seeing my face, four more. I began by eating with a knife and fork but forgot after a few bites. Wormy and Mother directed their eyes elsewhere.

We ate in silence. When the meal ended, I went to the front parlor and peered out the window. No one remained.

I was hungry again—or still hungry. I returned to the dining room and devoured the last chop. Mother and

Wormy had waited to find out about the mob.

"They're gone. Wormy, would you get me an armful of dried meat from your father's smokehouse?"

He stood up.

"Take Rupert's greatcoat. I don't want you to catch a chill." Sometimes, or so it seemed to me, I was entirely the human healer.

After Wormy left, Mother followed me to the apothecary and sat at my worktable while I filled a carpetbag with clean cloth for bandages, my most needful herbs, a pot of honey, my surgeon's kit, a flask of vinegar, and my last vial of purpline. Finally, I added my gift from my only elf patient ever, a fist-size bust of me as I had been.

Wormy returned with a bundle wrapped in canvas and tied with string.

"Thank you, dear." I resisted tearing into it and added it to my satchel.

He sat next to Mother.

"Wormy, Timon on Earl Road is a decent healer. Consult him."

"Why?"

I took Mother's hand, which disappeared in mine. How I'd miss her.

"Mother, Wormy, I need to learn to be persuasive."

Mother cried, "No! They'll eat you!"

"I hope not!"

"Evie!" Wormy's voice cracked. "Evie-ee! Not the Fens!"

How I'd miss him, too.

Kyrria's ogres lived in the Fens. Ogres were the only ones who could teach me. I had to go.

CHAPTER FIVE

MOTHER AND WORMY argued with me, but my mind couldn't be changed. If I hoped to survive in this form, I had to have persuasion to help me. If I couldn't persuade, I'd never be able to live among people again. I'd have no chance of finding love. I'd be an ogre forever, guaranteed.

By the time I finally exhausted them, night had fallen.

Wormy took his leave. He bowed to Mother and then to me.

I curtsied, feeling absurd.

He turned to go, then turned back, took my hand, and shook it. My appetite mounted. Inexplicably, my ears felt on fire.

We let each other go. He gazed at me. I sensed his

sadness, and the tip of his nose reddened. He was fighting tears.

He wheeled on his heels and left.

I wondered if, after tonight, I'd ever see him or Mother again.

Mother kept silent vigil in the kitchen with me. Finally, the lord mayor's bell rang midnight. Mother hugged me, though my stink had returned. I left in a soaking rain and began my third day in ogre form.

As I'd hoped, the streets were empty. Outside Jenn, the city closest to the Fens, the road forked. I took the left branch, which would eventually abut a section of the elves' Forest and would lead to another fork. The road to the right would take a traveler to the giants' farms and then to the Spires, the dragons' craggy homeland.

Surprisingly, just thinking of the Spires caused my fists to ball. Still, I wished I were going there as a human among a party of healers, escorted by a squadron of soldiers. With luck, we'd collect purpline and wouldn't trouble a dragon.

But I would turn left instead. Then no more turns; Fens straight ahead, a journey, I estimated, that would use up in total three or four days, if I could make my frightened feet hurry and hardly slept—and wasn't murdered along the way.

People knew little about the Fens. Few traveled there

unless in an ogre's thrall, and none of those returned. Kings and queens over the centuries had tried to wipe out the creatures, but had succeeded merely in confining them somewhat.

Confining *us*!

The Fens' periphery was patrolled only when attacks on people and livestock became frequent. Soldiers inevitably died.

After an hour or two, I had to rest. I hid myself behind the hedge that lined the road but found that I was too distressed and hungry to sleep.

My thoughts went to Mother, who probably wasn't sleeping, either. On nights when we were both troubled—usually about money—we'd each go to the kitchen and find the other there. I'd brew my auntwort tea, which had calming effects, and Mother would build up the fire if the night was chilly. Then we'd sit by the fireplace with quilts over our knees and play guessing games until our yawns came quicker than our ideas.

Tonight my guessing game was: Who would brew the tea for Mother? Who would sit with her?

When my tears dried, I sat up and reached for my carpetbag and the meat sticks, then stayed my hand, refusing to serve my stomach, trying to be that much human.

Wormy was probably awake, too. He'd be worried

about me and about himself—because he knew sleepless-ness was bad for health, and I wouldn't be there to dose him in the morning.

He was my favorite patient, willing to try any experiment if I was administering it. For example, when I'd presented him with a new cold remedy, snail slime and hedgehog grease, he'd drunk it down. As soon as he could open his mouth again without throwing up, he'd asked me to flavor it with anise and honey next time. *Not snail and hedgehog!* became a joke between us.

But his cold had vanished.

Would I have said yes if he'd waited a year or two? I couldn't tell. At fifteen I could barely recognize my fourteen-year-old self. At sixteen, I'd be different again, especially since being an ogre was sure to change me.

I lay back down. Sleep still kept its distance.

As a human, I hadn't liked dried meat much.

It could wait. I ground my teeth.

Wormy was precipitate. Time would have faded many of his ailments, but he wanted them gone in an instant. He might have decided he loved me five minutes before he proposed.

If I'd seen ahead, I'd have told him I wasn't sure I ever wanted to marry. Now I'd have to if—in sixty days!—I came to love someone who loved me back. That is, if a miracle happened.

Without consulting my mind or my will, my fingers undid my carpetbag straps and untied the knots holding the bundle of meat. I sampled a strip.

Depth of flavor! Meatier than meat prepared any other way. Much better than the side of boar, lovely as that had been. I closed my eyes, the better to savor the intensity—the difference between a candle and the sun.

In a few minutes I finished the strip and reached for seconds. And held back. I should hoard this marvel for real need.

What would it be like to meet ogres as an ogre? I didn't speak Ogrese—unless the language would flow out of me when I needed it. How would I explain myself? Would they sense the truth? Would they be able to persuade me to do anything, as if I were still purely human? Would they be kind? Would I like them? Liking them would be awful!

And how was Aeediou faring? Had Oobeeg treated her?

My thoughts revolved from one question to another until, finally, exhausted, I slept.

And woke to shock all over again that I was an ogre.

Travel on the road proved impossible during the day and even at night. After the sight of me caused a man to capsize his cart, I kept to the woods that bordered the road. I was in no danger of tripping, because—

• ogre eyes are as keen in dark as in light;

- ogre noses and ears are sharper than humans'.

My only company was my hunger, always loud about its need. Still, I saved the dried meat, and, one moonless night, I borrowed more—*borrowed*, because I'd pay when I could—from a curing shed near a farmer's cottage. No one awoke. The dog in the farmyard rolled onto its back for a belly rub.

I didn't eat this plunder, either, but kept myself alive on the occasional squirrel or rabbit unfortunate enough to cross my path.

As I jogged along, I remembered the fairy tale "Beauty and the Beast." The Beast stays home, waiting for luck to solve his problem, which, fairy-tale fashion, it does when kind, sweet, and comely Beauty enters his palace. He loves her, and, miraculously, she grows to love him. The happy ending arrives right on time.

However, what if he doesn't love her? She could be sour and unkind. Or she might have even more virtues than the tale bestows on her, but he still might not love her. All people should have a right to love the one they love, no matter the person's perfections or imperfections.

I swore not to be the fairy-tale Beast. I still wanted to marry for love and to be loved. If I didn't, I'd have regained my human form but lost my self-respect.

Some people never meet their true love.

* * *

Gradually, during the fourth night of my journey, the ground became sandy, and the woods thinned to copses of low junipers. Fifty-six days left.

Six gone.

The next morning, barely past dawn, I trotted on the road itself, reasoning that few would be traveling this early and my progress would be faster. The air stank of Kyrrian clematis. How I used to love the scent.

What was that shape in the distance? I loped along on tiptoe.

The shape clarified into a donkey with a lump on the ground next to it. The donkey, loaded with saddlebags, was scrawny enough to alarm my healer side and thinner than my ogre side would wish for—if I ate donkeys.

A young man, probably a year or two older than I, lay with his cloak pulled up to his chin. When I saw his face, my breath caught in my throat. The ogre stopped appraising him as food, and the girl took over.

Handsome, even with his lower jaw hanging in sleep. Long eyelashes, tight curls below a blue cap, clear skin, flaring nostrils; cheekbones high enough to speed my heart. Tall, by the length of him under his cloak.

Might his character be admirable, too?

If only I were already persuasive. Then I could travel with him. We could become acquainted—

—and fall in love?

Even now, I could take him with me. I believed I could overpower him.

Take him to ogres? No.

Might Lucinda have arranged for him to be here to give me a second chance? Could a fairy do that? Would she?

He must have felt my scrutiny, because his eyes opened, brown eyes. I watched them change from confusion to terror. And I sensed the terror, too. In an instant, he was on his feet.

"Don't be afraid! I only look—"

"Eat my donkey." He ran down the road.

I could have caught him, though he was both fleet and agile, signs of excellent health.

The donkey nickered and nuzzled my arm. How did beasts know I wouldn't eat them, even though my belly shouted that I should?

I wondered if there was anything in the saddlebags to tell me where the gentleman hailed from or where he was going.

It was wrong to pry!

And wrong to even *borrow* meat sticks without permission.

The donkey stood still while I unbuckled a satchel that bulged oddly. Under a rapier in an embossed sheath, a copper saucepan gleamed up at me, rubbed to a high shine.

Next to it nested three bronze straight-sided bowls with bumps hammered into the metal. Several linen caps protected the saucepan and the bowls from scratching each other.

He was a peddler. A toiling person, as Mother and I were. I closed the saddlebag, not wanting to dirty his wares.

A saddlebag closer to the donkey's neck seemed stuffed but not lumpy. Papers? Or dried meat?

Papers. It would be another misdeed to read them. I pulled out the stack. The sheet on top was a promissory note from a Master Peter of Frell (the Kyrrian capital) to jagH, a gnome. The prodigious size of the debt surprised me.

"Ogres can read?"

Master Peter, even more handsome vertical than horizontal, stood a few yards from the donkey. My heart galloped. He must have decided he could approach, since I had neither chased him nor eaten his mount. I still sensed fear, but it was manageable now.

Lucinda! I might marry this man. Turn me back and give us both the choice.

She didn't. Heartless fairy.

I swallowed. "This ogre can read, Master Peter, peddler by trade."

He swept an elegant bow. "Master Peter, *merchant* by

47

trade. I have excellent . . ." He paused, doubtless wondering what he might sell to an ogre. Eagerness mixed with his fear. I sensed them both.

Despite my shirt and breeches, I curtsied with what grace I could muster.

He blinked. "Excellent . . . and large, er, gowns."

I might be less terrifying in female dress, but I had no coin. "I'm Mistress Evora, healer." I batted my eyelashes. "Friends call me Evie."

"Ah, Mistress Evie. You cure, so naturally you don't kill."

I smiled, forgetting my fangs. "Exactly."

His fear ballooned. "May I take my leave?"

I backed away. Of course he didn't want to linger with me.

He went to his beast, who switched its tail. The donkey seemed ill at ease with its owner. Master Peter climbed on and flapped the reins. The donkey proceeded at a walk, heading the same way I had been.

I left the road again. How much more alone I felt, though nothing had changed.

As I continued my journey, I thought about love. The two people I loved were Mother and Wormy. To be sure, I loved Mother because she was my mother, but also because she was good and kind and loved me, too.

Father had died of the gripes when I was four. He was

probably the reason I'd become a healer—to keep Mother from dying of the gripes or of anything else. By now I'd cured dozens of cases of gripes with a mash of cabbage, coriander, and rosemary. I barely remembered Father.

I loved Wormy because he was good and kind, too, and because we were such old friends, and because he often was ill or thought himself so. Early in her profession, a healer needs someone like him. Who but Wormy would consult an eleven-year-old?

And I enjoyed his company. He liked novels, and I liked them, too, as well as medical books. My cases fascinated him. He helped in the apothecary by pounding herbs, rolling bandages, and watching my decoctions so they didn't boil away.

But such love seemed dull.

About a year ago, Mother and I were in our parlor after Wormy had gone home. I was combing our bookshelves for a treatise I'd misplaced.

"You're like me," Mother said. "Your father never lost anything."

Impulsively, I asked, "Did you love him very much?" I thought she had, but she'd never said so.

She put down the quill she'd been sharpening into a new pen. "Evie, just the sight of him lifted my spirits. He had only to touch my hand to make my heart and my head giddy."

I had herbs that would do those things. "But did you love him?"

"Look at me."

I turned away from the bookcase.

"Evie, sweet, I loved him. I honored him. We were best friends. Our friendship glowed brighter than the gold in his smithy. He made me tingle."

Wormy had never had that effect on me.

In our brief encounter, Master Peter had.

CHAPTER SIX

MASTER PETER could be traveling to trade with the elves, so we might meet again on my way back to Jenn as an ogre who could persuade.

A year ago I'd dosed an elf boy named Agulen, who'd visited Jenn with his parents and had developed a rash. (Elf skin color changes with the seasons, which sometimes causes itchy patches.)

He spoke no Kyrrian, but all he had to do was point at his elbows and neck. I spread a paste of galingale, zedoary, and ginger on the spots, while his eyes never left my face. He came back three days later, minus the rash, plus a gift of the bust I carried in my satchel: a carving in gray stone, a likeness of me as I was then.

The sculpture maiden looked solemn, as I'd never seen

myself in the mirror. Mother said it was an excellent portrait, and I was a pretty girl. I'd had to admit he'd gotten the little bump on my nose exactly right. Now a cluster of hair sprouted there.

By midafternoon, the barren landscape had softened, and forest had grown up again. I lost sight of the road, so I veered right, but after fifteen minutes, no road.

I stopped short. Ahead I sensed a volcano of terror covered by a thin lid of trustfulness. The trust meant someone captured by ogres.

Ogres! I didn't sense their feelings, just the captive's.

I started out again, struggling to control my own volcano of fear.

Was the fright coming from Master Peter? Might I save him? Earn his gratitude?

The fear was a beacon. I followed it, stepping quietly. Soon I stood in shadow at the edge of a small clearing, where an elf man faced half a dozen ogres, who seemed not to sense me as I had failed to sense them. I was aware of only the elf's emotions.

The ogres had arranged their faces to look benign, as much as they could. The elf tempted my stomach—in early adulthood, slender and tall as a grown human, his green skin tinged with gold for early autumn. He wore a patterned robe and tilted his head up at an ogre, who addressed him in Elfian, which I didn't speak.

"Aff ench poel?" The ogre ran a hand along the elf's sleeve, from shoulder to wrist. Its voice was honey.

The ogres wore bearskins, tied at the shoulders and belted to make rough tunics. Their feet were bare.

I heard a promise in the ogre's tone: *Submit and you will be oh so glad.*

"Dok ench Grellon, ote hux Zaret," the elf said in a soft, unworried voice. "Aff ench poel?"

I recognized the repetition and got the meaning. The ogre had asked the elf his name, and the elf—Grellon— had reciprocated. Polite conversation!

"Grellon, dok ench SSahlOO, ote hux HeMM."

Ah. The ogre's name was SSahlOO.

It lifted Grellon's sleeve and licked his upper arm. My hunger surged, and the squirrel I'd eaten earlier threatened to rise.

Grellon didn't stiffen, but I felt his panic mount.

SSahlOO bared its fangs. The other ogres did, too.

Run, Grellon!

"Er . . ."

They all turned. I saw the elf wake up. He pulled away from SSahlOO and fled—a few steps. But then the ogre spoke sweetly again, while glaring at me, and Grellon slowed, turned, started back, face rapt again.

This elf would *not* be eaten. I roared, "Get away, Grellon. Save yourself." I had no idea if he spoke Kyrrian, but I kept bellowing advice over the chorus of sweetness coming from the ogres, even as SSahlOO lunged at me.

It tried to stifle me with its hand, but I wrenched my head free and cried, "Grellon! Think! They just want to eat you."

He ran.

SSahlOO scratched and punched me, and the others joined in.

Rage flooded me. My muscles tightened; my fists balled. I struck—punched!—head butted!—scratched!—elbowed!—kneed!—kicked! Broke free. Crouched—all ogre—ready for the next onslaught.

I kept my carpetbag slung around my neck. They would not get my dried meat.

Or my healer supplies, but I thought of the meat first.

As one, they jumped up and crouched, too, all of us tensed and ready.

A few seconds passed. My mind returned, and my first thought was: How alike we all look.

One stood up and slouched. "LyOO."

Was that its name?

The others rose into slouches, too. Bad posture. I could fix that.

Blood seeped through my shirt and breeches. I felt

54

bruised, and the cuts stung. Ogre scratches wouldn't kill ogres, would they? A few of the others were bleeding, too, and seemed unalarmed.

The one who'd said *LyOO* was taller and broader than the others, with sprouts of gray in its chin hair. They all had chin hair. I had chin hair. That didn't make it male.

The speaker continued, in Ogrese, of course. I understood nothing. Lucinda, couldn't you have given me that?

But the language was beautiful, as liquid and smooth as my honey-and-oil syrup. The sounds ran together. I couldn't determine when one word ended and another began, though I could tell they weren't trying to be persuasive.

Was the fight over? I rose out of my crouch, too, shoulders back, posture perfect.

SSahlOO started toward me, open hands raised, meaning, I hoped, no harm. When it reached me, it stroked my cheek.

I jumped back. Was it testing my plumpness? Did ogres eat other ogres?

This caused laughter and amused head-shaking.

I felt myself blush, which I didn't know ogres did. Had I given myself away?

Seemingly not. They laughed harder, rocking from side to side. The ones laughing the most hopped from foot to foot.

SSahlOO said something that, by tone, had to be a question. Another question followed. Then it waited.

"Er . . ."

Eyebrows—well, facial hair above the eyes—went up all around.

I addressed SSahlOO: "Er . . . I don't speak Ogrese."

Its expression grew vaguely pleasant. Its voice softened our bumpy Kyrrian. "I merely welcomed you. We want you to feel as at home with us as with your . . ." It looked puzzled in a kindly way. "Your own sort, your . . . friends."

The girl in me was lulled, but not the ogre that surrounded her. They *would* eat me!

Could I eat them?

How could I think that? Ugh on me!

They'd be tough and stringy.

I tried to imitate it. "I'm sure you all welcome me, and I'm hoping you'll be my new friends." I reached out to touch the ogre's face. "You seem—"

They were laughing again, but SSahlOO grabbed my hand and held it, not hard. The hand bounced with its laughter. I could have broken away, but I didn't know what would happen if I did. Its touch made me uneasy, though not terrified anymore.

Then, seemingly for no reason, a different ogre knocked SSahlOO's arm away from mine. SSahlOO whirled, snarling. The two glared at each other. The second ogre lunged.

Both rolled on the ground. The others laughed harder.

Should I do something?

After a minute, before either combatant finished off the other, the big ogre—apparently the leader—said the word I'd heard before: "LyOO." Maybe it meant *stop*, because the skirmish ended, and the two stood, flanking me, but neither took my hand.

When the others finally stopped laughing, I said, "I think you asked me two questions, SSahlOO."

It told its seeming enemy, "See? She recognized my name." It knew I was female. How could it tell?

The enemy said, "My name is EEnth."

SSahlOO said, "Before, I wanted to know if you don't like elf. Or was something wrong with that one?"

Another one chimed in. "Why don't you speak Ogrese?"

I swallowed. What could I say except part of the truth? "The elf looked delicious, but I don't eat elves or humans or giants or gnomes. Or horses." Or a lot of other animals.

SSahlOO's jaw hung slack. If it had been Wormy, I would have told it to close its mouth for the sake of its throat.

The leader gestured with its hands. "You'll take the elf's place."

They all advanced on me, baring their teeth.

I ran, though I knew it was hopeless.

They must have expected me to fight, because they

didn't spring after me instantly. The rage I'd felt earlier returned, and fury speeded my legs. My satchel bounced against my thigh as I crashed through low branches and caromed off tree trunks. Soon, I heard pursuit.

Another few moments and the chase ended. Arms circled my legs. I was down.

An ogre pinned my shoulders and opened its mouth. The others crowded around, watching. I thought my heart would burst out of my chest.

Mother, this is the end. Wormy, I hope you find love.

It lowered its head. I closed my eyes, giving up.

CHAPTER SEVEN

I SMELLED ITS BREATH. Oh, the stink! My eyes popped open. I gasped out, "You have a toothache!"

The mouth came closer, then stopped. The ogre sat back, straddling my torso. "How do you know?" it asked in Kyrrian.

"All your meals know."

It grinned.

Its cheek looked puffy. "The last odor they smell comes from your . . . er . . . teeth." It might be rude to call them fangs. "I can make you feel better." Maybe.

The leader said something in Ogrese. My captor answered. Other ogres spoke.

I noticed repeated sounds in their speech. The syrup

separated into distinct words, though I still didn't understand.

Finally, the leader gestured. "ROOng hyNN. HyNN haZZ vAAnur."

I noticed the repeated word, *hyNN*. Double *n*, I thought, because it said the end of the word through its nose. What did *hyNN* mean?

My captor stood up. The leader must have said to let me go. Which words meant that?

Out of the blue, SSahlOO said in Kyrrian, "You're a beautiful mare."

Mare? Was that what they called a female? A horse?

Lucinda made me a beautiful ogre?

Maybe *hyNN* meant *girl* or *she* or *her*. Or *mare*. Yes, I thought. One of those. I could have a knack for Ogrese.

An ogre who hadn't spoken yet said, "UNN eMMong jOOl."

I didn't understand then, but this was the sentence I would hear and say myself and think most often: *I am hungry.*

The one with the swollen cheek returned to the subject of teeth. "You can make it stop hurting?"

"Yes." Because of the swelling, I expected I'd have to pull it. I stood. "Let me see."

It crouched, pointed to its left cheek, and opened its mouth.

60

I swallowed to keep from throwing up. There. A bright red lump on the gum and a black fang. "Your tooth has to come out."

"HaZZ!"

I'd heard the word before. *HaZZ* had to mean *no*.

It jumped up. Backing away, it said a few sentences in Ogrese that I thought myself fortunate not to understand. The others laughed.

"If I don't pull it, your mouth will hurt more."

"I don't mind. Ogres keep our teeth." It scratched its scalp. "I'd have used mine on the elf."

Were they going to return to attacking me?

SSahlOO said something menacing in Ogrese. No one advanced on me.

"Eventually the tooth will kill you." Eventually could take a year.

The ogre shrugged.

Why did I care? A few humans might live if it died.

But a thorn of irritation grew. This ogre had become my patient, and I made my patients better.

Might the others help? Friends and families often persuaded my human patients to be sensible. Did ogres have friends? They had to have family. Did they feel for each other? I addressed them all. "If you care about . . . er . . ." I turned back to it. "Excuse me, what's your name?"

It didn't answer, but SSahlOO did.

"HyNN riLL eMMong AAng. Her name is AAng." It pointed at each ogre and announced its name. In addition to the two I'd already learned, there were ShuMM, FFa-nOOn, and IZZ. The leader was ShuMM.

AAng was a *she*. And *hyNN* did mean *her* or *she*. SSahlOO was teaching me Ogrese.

I scrutinized AAng. What made her female? I supposed she had fewer hairs on her face than some of the others had. She was shorter than SSahlOO, as I was, too. Was SSahlOO a *he*? Probably.

"She won't know what killed her." I looked at each of them in turn. "Her chest or her head will hurt terribly. Then she'll collapse and die." I'd seen that happen to people, and the corpses had a black tooth. "Please tell her to let me pull the tooth."

ShuMM, the leader, yawned.

Two ogres said at the same time, "UNN eMMong jOOl." Just as people do when they speak in unison, both grinned.

No one spoke to AAng to encourage her or make her feel better.

I said, "Dead ogres can't eat, AAng."

She said, "Fangless ogres can't chew."

"One fang!"

She thought about it. I wondered if others in their group had died in the way I'd described.

SSahlOO asked, "EMMong szEE riLL?"

I understood. "My riLL or my eMMong?"

SSahlOO said, "RiLL."

"Evie."

"EEvEE?"

I nodded, though it had stretched out the sound of the *e*'s.

"Pretty—"

"Pull it." AAng crouched again and opened her mouth.

What an opportunity! Who else had ever operated on an ogre? I lifted my carpetbag strap over my head and set it on the ground.

Silence fell. I think they all were holding their breath. So was I.

I undid the laces on my surgeon's kit and opened the flaps. My tools glinted up at me, among them my tooth key with its wooden handle and iron shaft ending in a hooked claw. "It will hurt when I pull it and go on hurting for a few days, but then it will feel better." If ogre mouths reacted as human mouths did.

"If it doesn't—"

"You'll eat me with your remaining teeth."

She smiled. "Fangs."

I picked up the tooth key. AAng's eyes locked on it.

"Open wide."

She did.

I appealed to everyone. "When I say so, please make noise to distract her."

Steady . . . I held the handle in my right hand and used my left to bring the hook toward the rotted tooth. AAng's eyes crossed, watching the key wend its wobbling way to her mouth.

"Don't bite."

The others chuckled.

There. The key was ready. I ground my own fangs together and rocked the tooth back and forth to loosen it. "Now," I said, "noise."

Only SSahlOO and EEnth complied, but their shouts were deafening. AAng's eyes went to them. I yanked so hard I tumbled backward. The fang and its enormous root came out in my hand. Howling, AAng clamped her hand to her cheek. She glared at me.

SSahlOO and EEnth continued to yell until ShuMM gestured.

I scrambled up. "AAng, I can give you something for the pain."

She walked away.

"Don't chew on that side until it stops hurting." My stomach grumbled.

ShuMM squatted, slid my satchel along the ground, and took out my precious medicines, the little sculpture of human me, and my beloved loose meat sticks.

I cried, "Don't spill anything!"

ShuMM sniffed my herbs. "LahlFFOOn!" It spat. "Vegetables!"

"Herbs," I corrected, putting them back in the satchel. The dried meat from Wormy was still wrapped, but the strips I'd borrowed were loose.

It held one to its nose. "HaZZ lahlFFOOn." Not vegetables.

"Beef or mutton or pork." I barely kept myself from ripping the meat out of ShuMM's hand.

The laughter stopped. ShuMM nibbled, looked astonished, stuffed the strip in its mouth, chewed energetically, grabbed the rest, and ran—

—to be tripped up after a few steps. Fighting, fiercer than before, broke out. I kept my eyes on my satchel with Wormy's bundle inside. Could I hide it?

They had no right to Wormy's meat. He was my human!

CHAPTER EIGHT

OH! HOW COULD I think that? Wormy was his own human.

As I was mine. I'm human, I told myself, and repeated: human.

The skirmish ended. Each ogre wound up with a meat strip, although ShuMM had three.

SSahlOO broke his stick more or less in half and held out the smaller bit. "For you."

His rival broke his strip in half, too, and extended the bigger portion. Instantly, SSahlOO switched hands. My mouth watered.

I'm human! I thought.

What would happen if I took from each of them? Another fight between them, or would they attack me?

Was I supposed to take from only one, and what would it mean if I did? Would that be like accepting a proposal? Would Lucinda turn me back?

My patient moaned.

The end of a meat strip stuck out of her mouth. She had bit down on the wrong side.

SSahlOO said, "Choose one of us."

I dived on the satchel and ran, pulling out the meat packet as I went, tugging off the string, stuffing a strip in my mouth, tossing another behind me to slow the chase, gobbling one more, imagining how I looked, picturing both the merchant Master Peter and Wormy watching me.

This time I raced for half an hour, eating and dropping meat strips every several minutes, alternately hearing panting and fighting behind me. Finally, pain in my legs slowed me, and the others caught up. I held out the remaining meat strips in surrender. ShuMM took them and made me empty my carpetbag to prove there were no more.

Then it stuffed the strips into the neck of its bearskin tunic and let me have everything else. It set off through the forest at a less bruising pace.

SSahlOO took my elbow and pulled me along. "I never tasted anything as good, EEvEE." He smiled at me, his wooing continuing. "Or felt so full."

EEnth said, "Beautiful *and* useful."

We trotted into the night, ending my seventh day as an

ogre. Fifty-five left. So few! And yet, mixed with dread and fear was hope. Now I might learn what I needed to know to return to Jenn and to Mother. And, maybe, even to find love and release.

Eventually, the trees thinned. The ground softened and would have slowed my feet if SSahlOO hadn't been tugging me on. We emerged into a flat landscape of reeds and an occasional stunted tree.

The Fens. I saw no one, but I knew more bands must live here. We continued another quarter mile and stopped. Though nothing looked homelike, this seemed to be home.

"Can you get more sticks?" ShuMM asked me.

"You should say *yes*," SSahlOO prompted. "You can stay with us if you say yes."

I doubted I'd survive here on my own, and I could do it. All farmers smoked meat. "I want two things in return." I named my first condition: they give up killing creatures that had speech—humans, elves, gnomes, and giants. I'd be a thief, but I'd save lives.

"Not the creatures' beasts, too?" ShuMM asked. "Not everything you don't eat?"

EEnth said, sounding smug, "We don't eat adult gnomes, either. Too tough."

Somebody said something with the word lahlFFOOn in it.

"No." I knew they wouldn't agree if I reduced them to

eating squirrels and rabbits. "Just talking beings."

ShuMM considered. "All right."

I wondered if they kept their promises. "And teach me to be persuasive, especially to humans."

No one expressed surprise that I couldn't persuade. Evidently, my oddness had ceased being unexpected. We struck an agreement, and thus began my sojourn with the ogres.

The band's territory covered an area about the size of Mother's house and backyard, cramped for seven creatures (including me) who couldn't abide one another. If I crossed the border—marked by gnawed bones—someone always pulled me back in, because bands attacked other bands for trying to expand their plots. We could leave only to hunt.

Our bit of land was distinguished by a stunted willow tree and a broad stump that stood almost as high as my waist. No grasses or reeds grew, defeated by our feet and our skirmishes. Under the tree, the ground dipped into the shape of a shallow bowl—our shared bed, because, much as we despised each other during the day, we craved closeness in slumber.

I was no different. I remember waking in the middle of the first night and relaxing back into sleep only after feeling someone's foul breath on my cheek.

We had no shelter. When it rained, as it did for an hour

or more daily, we huddled under our tree, which was losing its leaves. We rarely had a sunny day. A mist that rose from the soggy ground kept us swathed in fog.

It was a meager existence, but I didn't pity my fellows or hate them any less than I had when I was in human form. They stayed together purely to hunt. Friendship didn't exist. Words turned into squabbles and squabbles into brawls. SSahlOO and EEnth were the ogre equivalent of polite to me, but only because each wanted a mate.

Worst of all, I was only slightly less combative than the others. If they rolled on the ground in combat six times a day, I rolled five. In two out of five of the skirmishes I was fighting to keep SSahlOO or EEnth away. The rest were my temper getting the best of me. The cause could be anything or nothing.

They used no weapons, although I was sure they could have taken an arsenal from the human soldiers who were sometimes their victims. I asked SSahlOO about this.

"We should use swords?" he said. "But when I beat EEnth—as I always do—I gloat, which is the best part. If I ran him through, he'd merely die, and I'd eat him. He wouldn't be there anymore for me to thrash again."

The only good aspect of being with them was that I could still be a healer, or at least a dentist. AAng's tooth pain vanished in a day, sooner than it would have in a human. The two others with toothaches let me treat them, and neither needed to lose a fang.

By the second day, I learned to tell male from female, and I discovered the personality of each ogre, generally by noting who was most horrible in some way or other: who constantly mocked the others, who started the worst fights, who was greediest. ShuMM, a male, was cruelest in a fight. We all went limp when he attacked.

After a week, and with forty-eight days left to change back, I became fluent in Ogrese, effortlessly, as if the words had always lived in the back of my mind. Persuasion, the skill I needed, they called zEEn, both noun and verb. The meaning was closer to *herding*—herding emotion—than to persuading, though persuasion was part of it.

Ogres couldn't zEEn one another, but ShuMM, the leader, wouldn't even let me try. I was unusual, and, if it turned out I could do what nobody else could, he feared I'd oust him as leader. However, because of our bargain, he told the others they could answer my questions.

SSahlOO and EEnth were the only ones who would.

SSahlOO pushed down with a hand. "You sense their fear and find the right tone to make them lower it. They do all the work."

"Tone is the only persuasion we use." EEnth yawned. "UNN eMMong jOOl."

"But how?"

"You felt the elf's fear, right?" SSahlOO said.

I nodded.

EEnth asked, "Did you feel the air in him around the fear, too?"

I shrugged. I supposed I had. The elf was more than his terror.

SSahlOO smiled as if I were a prize student. "That's the part you persuade with your voice. You make the air bigger."

"But before, you said I should push the fear down with my voice."

His smile widened. "Same thing. Then you tell the human what to think."

It sounded strange and impossible. And horrible. Nothing belonged to people more completely than their thoughts.

Alas, EEnth's and SSahlOO's explanations were just a lecture, like a teacher describing reading without showing the pupil a word. However, ShuMM maintained he'd kept his part of the bargain.

I thought of leaving, but I'd be giving up on ever learning, which was the only route I could think of to be with people again and maybe find love, so I stayed—while counting off days in mounting desperation.

At night I stole from farms and did so alone despite the risk, because I didn't want ogres to learn about smoke-houses or grow used to being indoors.

The first farmhouses began just a half hour's trot from the Fens and clustered together for safety. A few miles farther, they spread out, arrayed along the road, usually a mile or more apart. Prosperous farms had separate dry-ing sheds; humble ones cured their meat in a lean-to that shared a wall with the back of the cottage.

Every night I had to range farther. Soon I'd have to stay away for more than a few hours, even be absent over-night or longer. I feared what the others might kill in my absence.

Silly to worry, though, because if—when!—I learned to zEEn, I'd leave for good and they'd return to eating what they'd eaten before. This was a troubling argument in favor of deliberately staying an ogre, because I might save more people than as a human healer.

I thought of Wormy, who did his parents' accounts. Wormy, which side of the ledger, human or ogre, weighs more for the good?

Near the target of my theft I always grew afraid. With-out persuasiveness, an ogre had no better defenses than a wolf, and I had several close calls:

- A farmer came into his shed for an apple while I hid,

crouching between a plow and a wheelbarrow. He
left muttering about stinking dead mice.

- On a return to the Fens, I was taken for a bear by
  hunters hiding in brush. Their arrows went wide
  and I outran them.
- A farmer had guests. From the lean-to, I could
  hear their conversation. Starved for human voices, I
  listened until, lulled, I fell asleep and woke shortly
  before dawn.

On the occasion of my slumber, the sky was already
bright when I reached the Fens. No one, not even SSahlOO
or EEnth, asked if anything had befallen me. They just
took my meat sticks and began chewing.

During the day, we hunted either in the elves' Forest—
without seeing an elf—or along the road, hiding from
large parties, because SSahlOO said a single ogre couldn't
persuade more than three elves, gnomes, or humans at
once. "We can't sense their individual feelings when there
are more."

"The six of us," EEnth said, "can zEEn eighteen." He
didn't include me, who couldn't persuade even one.

It dawned on me that even if I learned to zEEn, I'd still
be unable to live in a city or a village, because there would
be too many people to pacify at once.

A lump filled my throat. What could I accomplish here? If I couldn't live among groups of people, how would I ever find someone to love? How many charming and honorable hermits lived in Kyrria?

Yet I kept trying, because I could think of nothing else.

In that first week we killed a deer and a boar, of which I partook, because I'd dined on such animals when I'd been human. The band also slaughtered three donkeys, but I stood aside from the killing and, despite my longing, the eating.

Naturally, to take the donkeys, the band had to zEEn their owners. It pleased me to imagine their relief when we left and they realized they were alive.

After I returned from my stealing forays, I slept and often dreamed of healing Master Peter of a dread disease.

On October 10, a cool morning for early fall, I woke up in a panic. This would be my nineteenth day as an ogre. In less than a month and a half I'd be unable to turn back!

I told ShuMM I wouldn't steal more dried meat until a better method to teach me to zEEn was found. He nodded and sent SSahlOO and AAng off to find a human for me to practice on.

"Don't eat it," I called after them. Not *it*! "Don't eat the *person*."

EEnth said, "UNN eMMong jOOl."

I was, too. We each took a meat stick. I bit down and remembered—

Wormy's birthday! He was turning sixteen today. If I were home, I'd close the apothecary and we'd have an outing. Last year, Mother had packed us a picnic lunch, and we'd climbed the Jenn clock tower to eat it. Wormy has an eye for beauty, a knack for describing it, and a deep knowledge of Jenn. We sat in the window embrasure and ate while he talked.

Now, from my changed perspective, I noticed how alike we were, both neat eaters but glad Mother had tucked extra napkins in the basket, both admiring the contrast between the orderliness of Jenn's streets and the unrestrained countryside beyond.

Our mood—mine, certainly—hadn't been romantic, just companionable. I treasured the memory.

Wormy—more sociable than I was—had many friends, while my few were patients or former patients. Was he spending today with his friends? Had he visited Mother at all since I left? Certainly he had. He was a kind person.

I hoped he didn't have a headache or stomach trouble on his birthday.

I hoped he hadn't forgotten me.

Where were SSahlOO and AAng?

In midafternoon, I finally saw them take shape through

the Fens' mist: two large, blocky figures on either side of a more slender one. I stood at attention, barely breathing, my bones seeming to hum with anticipation. *Come. Come closer, human. Teach me what I must learn.*

Gradually the forms clarified, and there was Master Peter, dashing as ever, his shoulders burdened with his saddlebags, walking trustfully between them.

CHAPTER NINE

WHEN HE SAW ME, Master Peter put his things down, smiled as if we were great friends, and swept his elegant bow. "We meet again . . . er . . ." He gave up trying to remember my name. "Mistress Healer."

How disappointing that he'd forgotten.

"Mistress Evie." I turned to SSahlOO and AAng. "Let me try."

Instantly, Master Peter's fear mushroomed. He ran.

I thrust my arm out and caught him. "You"—I tried to soften my voice—"have nothing to fear from me." I felt around his terror for the air SSahlOO said would be there.

Ah, yes. I tried to make it bigger. "I would never hurt you."

His fright didn't diminish. He swallowed, tried to push

words out, swallowed again. His eyes bulged, which diminished his good looks.

I glanced over my shoulder. The others were baring their fangs at him, having fun at my expense. I lunged at them, jerking Master Peter with me.

As a group, they drew back and laughed.

"Beg pardon! Master Peter, did I hurt you?" If I'd pulled his arm out of its socket, I could put it back.

No answer. His eyes were unfocused. I moved his arm around. It went smoothly, and I didn't sense pain, just terror—

—which brought on my ogre anger. How dare he be terrified when I meant him well? I could yank his arm out on purpose and heal it. He'd find out then that I'd take care of him.

Fie! What was I thinking?

I drew him to the edge of our plot, pushed his shoulders down until he sat, and squatted before him, sideways to the pack, so I could see them, too. They'd returned to their usual occupation, chewing meat sticks slowly to make them last.

"Greetings." I tried for a sweet smile.

His fear didn't lessen.

Keeping his distance, SSahlOO coached me in Ogrese. "Tell it you want it to be happy."

I did so. Master Peter just tried to pull away from me.

"I won't let anyone else eat you, either. They haven't, have they? You know you'd be in their stomachs by now, ordinarily."

The shred of reason he had left understood. I felt it expand and the fear shrink, a little.

"You're doing it," SSahlOO said in Ogrese. "SzEE eMMong AAh forns."

EEnth said, also in Ogrese, "In a way. Not our way." He softened his voice. "But very good."

I wanted to do it their way, the fast way.

For the rest of the day, I experimented. I spoke softer, louder, higher in pitch, lower in pitch, singsong or with clipped words. I had SSahlOO and EEnth demonstrate, and I imitated them perfectly to my ear, but without their effect.

Evening came. Eventually, Master Peter relaxed, but not because of my efforts. I was furious. I knew my failure wasn't his fault, but he became increasingly edible.

Three meat sticks finally calmed me.

I stole more dried meat that night and spent the next day, my twentieth, trying to zEEn again.

Master Peter became entirely unafraid of me and only a little uneasy with the rest of the band. Midmorning, he asked why we hadn't eaten him. "Am I too stringy?"

We all laughed.

I jested, too. "Lean but certainly not stringy." Or was I flirting?

"Make him scared again," EEnth said. "ZEEn can either calm or frighten."

But I couldn't do that, either.

I didn't give up. I believed I wasn't wasting precious time. Master Peter had intelligence, humor, health. In his presence I was always atingle. Did he have goodness? Might I love him already? Could I reveal enough of myself to make him like me and disregard my appearance? Already I seemed to amuse him.

On the third morning after his arrival, I asked him to show me his wares.

As the rest of us crowded around, he pulled a canvas cloth from a saddlebag and spread it on the ground before taking out his goods.

How deft he was. Cloth and apparel seemed to fold themselves to their best advantage. He spread his jewelry pieces with a flash of hands—jumble one moment, artful display the next—and grinned at my surprise.

I saw again the saucepan, the bowls, more cookware and tableware, the rapier in its sheath, a flute, and three pairs of shoes.

He stood next to me just beyond the canvas. His nearness opened a pit in my stomach. Hunger? Yes, and an ache, a yearning.

"There's something else." He lowered his voice, adding drama. "Shall I reveal it?"

"Please!" I sounded breathless.

Master Peter plunged his hand deep into another saddlebag, the one that held his papers. "This is a treasure. I keep it separate for safety." He drew out something long, covered by burlap.

Unaccountably, the hairs all over my body prickled. I felt the whole band tense.

He made room on the canvas for the new thing and unwrapped it.

A dragon's tooth! Orange, as long as my arm, its point sharper than a sword.

Instantly, I dropped into a crouch—we all did. My body heated up. My ears felt on fire.

As one, we chanted, *"Ack nack! ZuZZ!"* I was furious, wanted to kill someone—anyone.

Around me, everyone glistened with sweat; everyone's fangs were out in a grimace of rage.

Master Peter ran. The others charged after him. I took a step—

—but my human half wrested control. I wheeled and, with shaking hands, wrapped the tooth and hid it in the saddlebag again. My hairs relaxed. My body cooled.

Master Peter! I dashed after the band.

But they were returning anyway. Master Peter, zEEned again, ambled among them.

"Where is it?" ShuMM demanded of me in Ogrese.

"I put it away. Don't eat him!" I ran to the sack I kept the meat sticks in and pulled out four.

ShuMM took the peace offering and shrugged.

Master Peter returned to his wares. The others must have stopped zEEning him, because I felt his distress. "Mistress Evie, why did you all crouch and seem terrifying?"

I appealed to SSahlOO and EEnth in Kyrrian, so Master Peter would understand. "Why did we?"

I sensed Master Peter's surprise that I didn't know.

SSahlOO said, also in Kyrrian, "Do *you* like dragons?"

No! I hated—loathed—despised—them.

My human side didn't understand. Yes, dragons were dangerous, but they didn't seek people out, as ogres did. And, without them, there would be no purpline. "Do they attack ogres?"

"Not anymore. They have their Spires to live in and the giants' land to hunt in." EEnth pulled back his shoulders and puffed out his chest. "We have everywhere else."

SSahlOO stood as straight as EEnth. "We think there was a war a long time ago. Ogres won."

"Dragons died," EEnth said.

SSahlOO spat. "You can't even eat them. They stick in your throat."

"They're gummy," EEnth added. "But we'd fight them again."

"Fascinating," Master Peter said under his breath, but ogre ears could hear.

"What do the words mean?" I asked. "'Ack nack. ZuZZ.'"

"I don't know." EEnth took a meat stick. "There are more words, too, that we don't understand, either."

"Is this written down anywhere?" I asked, still in Kyrrian. Did ogres have writing?

EEnth slumped back into his usual bad posture. "No, silly mare."

I balled my fists. "Don't say that!" I hated for Master Peter to hear what the ogres called me.

EEnth just laughed.

But SSahlOO added, "I think the words start a spell." He held up a hand to prevent more questions. "I can't remember the rest of it." He snatched EEnth's meat stick, though he could have taken one from the sack.

The two rolled on the ground. I couldn't think of any more words, either, although *ack, nack,* and *zuZZ* had erupted out of me, too.

But I did know a little about dragons, who, for one thing, lost their fangs every five years and grew new ones. I asked Master Peter, "Did you buy the tooth from the giants, or are you going to sell it to them?" If the second, he'd gotten it direct from the dragons, a feat of daring. "Might you have purpline?"

"No purpline."

Too bad!

"I got the tooth from the giants." Master Peter frowned. "It would have been a fool's errand to go to the dragons myself."

I approved. "Cautious people rarely need a healer."

He chuckled. "Reckless people often don't need one, either."

Oh! "Because they're dead!" I couldn't help laughing.

He nodded, smiling.

Giants used the fangs to punch holes in leather, in wood, in almost anything. Dragons let giants take their teeth—they never flame at them—and the giants allow the dragons to hunt a share of their herds of sheep, cattle, and goats. Humans prized the fangs because they were rare. A single fang cost as much as a manor house.

Clouds blew in on a brisk breeze, fall beginning in earnest.

"Mmm." Master Peter stared down at his wares. "I know!" He picked up four wooden spoons and four wooden spatulas and ran his finger along one.

He wasn't touching me, but I felt that finger as if he were.

"See the design the grain makes, Mistress Evie. Artful, isn't it?"

I swallowed. "Yes."

"If they were strung, perhaps with beads between each implement, they would make a charming necklace for you."

"You'd have me wear *utensils*?"

He drew back. "Not many can carry such bold jewelry."

I blushed in spite of myself.

"The necklace would turn utensils into art. The beads would be lapis lazuli because the blue would complement your eyes."

Which were amber. My face was about to burst into flames.

"People would think of a ballroom, not a kitchen."

Did he really believe something would become me? He knew we had no money, so he couldn't be trying for a sale. Might he be sincere? I sensed pleasure in him. Pleasure in my company? In my looks because I could wear bold adornments? Or only in showing off his goods?

"The nights will be cold soon." He pulled a green wool shawl out of a blue linen sheath and held them next to each other. "Elegant, no, the two hues together?"

My human side had little experience with elegance, and ogres didn't heed beauty other than the beautiful-mare kind.

Master Peter draped the shawl around my shoulders, which trembled.

He stood back. "This shade brings up the color in your cheeks." He called to SSahlOO and EEnth. "Isn't Mistress

Evie prettier than ever?"

He must have noticed their longing for me.

That infuriated me. I removed the shawl. "I'm aware of how hideous I am."

SSahlOO and EEnth protested gallantly in Ogrese that I was a beautiful mare.

Master Peter murmured, "You improve on acquaintance."

Oh, my. Oh! My heart triple fluttered.

He was excited and happy. Happy because of me? Was he beginning to care for me? And I had forty days left!

The rest of the band left to hunt. I didn't have to go, since I was learning to zEEn, or trying to learn.

"Why is it you never leave with them?"

Did he want to be rid of me? Irritation sharpened my voice. "If I went, a human alone in the Fens doesn't need a healer, either."

He smiled. "Dead, eh?"

"Just bones." I gestured at our ghoulish border.

"You are my protector."

My heart's flutter quickened.

He held up a jug. "Pewter. Gnome-made. It never leaks."

When I left the Fens, I'd need a jug. If we departed together, perhaps he'd share it with me.

If he proposed, it would be mine, too.

Embarrassed at my thoughts, I picked up a cap,

bleached linen with a design of embroidered flowers.

"It would become you," Master Peter said, "but I'm afraid it's too sm—"

"The stitches are uneven." I knew it wouldn't fit me.

"You have discernment." He executed a small bow.

His voice or his words kept weakening my legs, but I curtsied without collapsing.

He produced another square of canvas from his sack and spread it in his quick-fingered way. "Will you sit with me?"

I couldn't, unless I ate something first—or I might nibble on his delectableness. I went to the sack that held last night's theft, already two-thirds diminished. As I returned, his eyes were on the meat strips. He was starving! I held one out to him. He took it, and I returned to the sack for two more for me and two more for him. When I sat, I left space between us for the sake of my heart.

But he moved close!

And when he did, when he wanted to be near me, I succumbed to the besotting power of love. I loved—cherished, adored, relished—Master Peter. He was my delight, my treasure, my happiness.

CHAPTER TEN

HE CHEWED on the meat stick in a way that combined fastidiousness and gusto. I ate more slowly than I would have if he hadn't been there, and kept my lips together.

I wondered if he delighted in buying goods and selling them as much as I adored healing. "Do you like being a merchant?"

"I love beauty, like that shawl paired with its sheath."

He gave me an idea. "I have something you may admire." I stood, though I disliked moving away from him. From my satchel, I took out the bust of me.

He reached for it, and I let him hold it.

"Heavy," he said. "Made by a greeny?"

"Greeny?"

"An elf." He looked closely at the real me.

See a resemblance! Guess the truth!

"A pretty face but not extraordinary or memorable."

That hurt, to be forgettable.

Master Peter went on. "But the artist is extraordinary to have caught the model's character: lively, intelligent, single-minded. I see humor, too. Do you know who made it?"

"An elf boy named Agulen. I treated his rash, and he carved it for me." Guess!

"I'll remember that name. I know some who would love this." I felt his mood change, become careful. "Mistress Evie, the shawl and the sheath can be yours."

Even he couldn't have my memento of me! And he'd get the better of the bargain. I snatched back the carving and returned it to my satchel.

I sensed his regret, and I was disappointed, too, though it would have been a feat of intuition if he'd divined that the not-extraordinary face was mine. Forgiving him, I sat at his side again.

"You asked if I like being a merchant. I enjoy finding the perfect object or bit of apparel for everyone." He shrugged. "Apparently, the little sculpture already has its ideal owner." He told me about selling a fiddle to a young man. "When he touched the bow to the string, the noise was worse than six cats caught in a sack, but he wanted it. I came back the next year, and his playing was so marvelous that the six cats would have waltzed along with it. He taught me a lesson."

Healers constantly learned from our patients. "What did you learn?"

He laughed. "Never discourage a sale!" He added, maybe seeing that his answer hadn't pleased me, "I also learned that thinking creatures choose the items they need, whether I see the need or not."

How, I wondered, did he—stuck here with us—manage to look fresh, as if he'd just awakened from a peaceful sleep?

"People don't choose their illnesses, to be sure." A surprising thought struck me. "I wonder if diseases choose the people they need." I used to have this kind of conversation with Wormy.

"Fascinating!" he said, and changed the subject. "You're a puzzlement, Mistress Evie. There's something in your eyes."

Tears. I blinked them away and tried flirting again. "What might it be? Something you alone can see?"

He brushed the hair on my scalp away from my forehead, which also had hair. His touch was light as a leaf.

"What I see in your eyes is tenderness, a sweet spirit. How improbable that we've met. How fortunate for me."

I sensed it. He was feeling love. He loved me!

I gasped out, "I'm lucky, too."

"Have you visited the many marvels of Kyrria?"

My throat was so tight I could barely breathe. Why was he asking? "I came here from Jenn. I haven't been anywhere else."

He smiled fondly, either at a memory or for love of me. "I can show you mountain waterfalls, the lakes, the flower farms, the—"

"I'd be delighted to see them." With you.

He went on. "I never wanted a companion on my journeys before, but I think you and I would be happy together. Would you—"

The band returned. I'd have heard them if I hadn't been mesmerized.

Had he been about to propose?

They brought a deer carcass. I didn't want to leave Master Peter's side, but hunger won out. I gave him three more meat sticks and feasted with the others.

We had to escape the Fens so he could propose, if that was his intention. If I accepted him here, we'd both be eaten. Tomorrow, when the band left again to hunt, we'd go. I'd fight any ogres who tried to stop us.

Meanwhile, I had to steal meat sticks.

How delicious he looked in the dying daylight, which hollowed his cheekbones and brightened his lips.

"Farewell." I touched his hand—and stumbled backward as the thrill ran through me.

"Till you return. Hurry back, love."

The band heard and roared with laughter—except EEnth and SSahlOO, who glared at Master Peter. I rushed at them. "If you so much as sample one of his ears, you will never eat another meat stick, and you will have no chance with this beautiful mare."

EEnth touched my cheek. "Beautiful but foolish."

SSahlOO stroked my upper arm. "It may love you. You're a beautiful mare. But when you learn to zEEn, loving it will seem like loving a puppet."

I ignored them. "I'll be quick, Master Peter." Oh, my. "I'll race."

Clouds lowered, but the storm held off. I ran until my breath gave out and I had to slow my pace. Why hadn't I called him *love*, too? Did he worry that his love wasn't returned?

Wormy, dear, I thought, the affection I feel for you can't compare with this . . . this . . . I searched for the word: *blossoming.*

I'd never believed love could come so fast. I didn't even know what books Master Peter liked or where he grew up. He might like puns. He might actually make them. He might admire the word *puce!*

Didn't matter.

I hugged his words: *I think you and I would be happy together.*

A thought slapped my mind. Had he been pretending admiration just so I'd take him out of the Fens?

But he'd still be with me then, and I could overpower him, even without zEEn. He knew that.

I'd sensed his feelings. His happiness could have been at the prospect of leaving, but the love had to be for me. There had been just the two of us.

Finally, after four hours of trotting and running and sometimes, or so it seemed, skimming above the ground, I reasoned I was far enough from the last farm I'd robbed to make my visit unexpected.

The farm I chose was prosperous, the house more manor than cottage, with actual glass and not oiled parchment in the windows. There must have been dogs, but none woke up. Still, my anxiety mounted. I had more to lose now than I had last night.

I trotted to the drying shed, which stood apart from the house. Wealth meant bounty. I would eat some of what I took before I started back.

Mums grew in urns on either side of the door, an unexpected nicety for the entry to a shed. The door didn't creak when I eased it open. Someone kept the hinges oiled, a well-run place.

I should have paused on the threshold, but I went directly in, reassured by the mums.

Instead of a dirt floor, I stepped on a plank, which cracked.

Bells clanged.

Ohhh! I plunged.

CHAPTER ELEVEN

I LANDED perhaps a dozen feet down, on straw, the air pounded out of me. As the bells subsided, I caught my breath and took stock.

Curious. Pit traps were generally used against foxes, wolves, or boar. The beasts landed on spikes—caught and killed in the same stroke. Here there were no spikes. I felt bruised, but that was all. The pit was so narrow I was half sitting up.

What might this mercy mean?

That the farmers thought they knew their robber. They meant to teach a lesson, not to kill.

The bells must have awakened the sleepers. My throat tightened. Soon I'd be among humans again.

And me unable to zEEn.

I heard people stirring, probably dressing, lighting lamps for eyes that weren't sharp in the dark, combing their hair in mirrors that didn't hate them.

Rows of dried meat dangled above me. My rage bubbled up. Food, near and unattainable.

Terror joined rage. If I didn't return to the Fens, the band, of a certainty, would eat Master Peter.

The sides of my prison pit were packed earth. I tried to climb, but there was no purchase. I fell back, tried again, fell again.

From the house, I heard feet on the stairs, going down. In a frenzy, I attacked the dirt with my hands, digging in with my long, curving nails. A few inches loosened and dropped away.

No time to dig myself out. What else? I could hardly think over my heart.

I heard them on the path to the shed.

Ogres had strength.

I raised my arms and crouched, then jumped. Not high enough. I fell back, jumped again, and fell back.

The door swung open. "We've caught you, Dill, you rascal!"

In the light of a grease lamp, four people peered down at me and gaped. I gaped up at them.

Terror was stamped on their faces. In my narrow confines, I curtsied.

They stood frozen: an elderly man, a middle-aged gaunt man, a plump woman about my size, and a girl my age.

Hunger locked hands with my fear.

I tried to soften my voice, but four were too many for any ogre to zEEn. "I'm pleased to make your acquaintance." I sounded like a goat with a sore throat. "I happened by, hoping for shelter on my journey to the Fens. I mean no harm."

Their faces relaxed a little, only, I was sure, because I wasn't leaping out of the pit and attacking.

The old man tilted his head at the plump woman, who backed away slowly. Out of sight, I heard her feet thudding.

She would return with weapons and, possibly, more people.

As soon as she was gone, I felt their emotions—each of them afraid but not locked in terror, the old man the least frightened, the most capable of thought.

Lucinda, I was close to getting a proposal!

If one of *them* would propose, we'd all stop being afraid. I burst into panicky laughter. I had, I guessed, three minutes before the woman returned.

The old man became preoccupied and sad and angry as his fear lessened. Angry, as if he'd been ill-used. He had dignity, revealed by his erect stance and the upward tilt of his chin. I thought he might be their leader and the owner of the manor.

The younger, exceedingly thin man had a busy mind. I couldn't read his thoughts but I sensed their buzz. In the girl, fear mixed with exhilaration, probably because she was in the presence of an ogre and not dead.

Patients were often afraid of what I might do to them, and I had to heal their fright before I could heal their bodies.

A measured tone. "You've heard . . ." Too harsh. I swallowed. "You see an ogre . . ." Truth calmed patients more than promises. I managed to sweeten my voice. "You believe we're all alike, but you know already that I'm different."

The air around their fear grew. The other feelings—distraction, eagerness, worry—dulled, and the terror shrank into a tight fist.

Not small enough. The elf Grellon's and Master Peter's fright, when they'd been zEEned, had been the size of a pea. I listened for the absent woman and heard her faintly.

Why was she tarrying? Was she too afraid to come back and save her fellows?

If I could zEEn the old man, I thought the others might follow along, and the key to him was probably his melancholy and sense of ill use.

In my new, honeyed voice, I said, "There is solace for

everyone." There would be for me if I could get back to Master Peter. "For some it's in a poem."

No response.

"For some in a fine meal." Not that, either, though a meat stick would relax me. "For some in a garden."

The man's air grew. His shoulders relaxed. Being reminded of the garden eased him. The others breathed more easily, too. As I succeeded, they seemed more edible.

I heard a muffled clatter. The woman had dropped some part of the arsenal she was carrying.

Be slow picking it up! Drop more!

I said, "My favorite flowers are roses. In our—"

In an age-roughened voice, the old man said, "I like the red rose best."

I heard the woman's labored breathing. She was carrying weapons for them all, and no one was with her.

"On my way here," I said, forcing myself not to rush, "I happened across a cluster of night daisies, late for the season."

"Where?" the old man asked. "Would you show me—us?"

Ah. "If you help me out, I will."

The gaunt man disappeared from my view. Using my new voice, I said something about flowers. The woman with the weapons was closer.

The man reappeared with a pole, which he extended

to me. I took it and planted it in the earth beneath the straw. Hand over hand on the pole, my feet climbing the dirt walls, I rose, reached the top, and hauled myself out.

The people smiled at me, which made them look even more delicious. Beautiful puppets, as SSahlOO had predicted. Offering themselves. Wanting to be eaten.

Of its own, my hand moved toward the girl's cheek, to stroke it and feel its tenderness. I pulled the hand back and started to reach for meat sticks.

The door burst open.

The zEEning shattered.

CHAPTER TWELVE

THE WOMAN STAGGERED IN, bearing an axe, a scythe, a rake, a spade.

"Would you . . ." But my honey had fled.

Farewell, Master Peter!

Hastily, the woman passed out weapons.

If I ran, they'd pursue me on horseback and catch me.

We faced each other in momentary uncertainty.

Run!

And leave the meat sticks? No!

With ogre speed, I grabbed the old man's elbow, pulled him close, wrested his rake from him, and flung it on the ground. Using my free hand, I grabbed meat sticks, many meat sticks, and shoved them inside the man's shirt and mine. Not trying for honey, I rasped out, "If you wish to see your friend again and not just his bones, do not pursue me for two hours."

The girl cried, "Don't hurt the master!"

Brave.

"We'll come after you," the thin man said.

My captive—the master—said, "Listen to it. Give it the two hours. I'll be all right." *It*. My fury flared, but I backed out, keeping him facing them. Outside, I picked him up and ran on the road in the direction of the Fens. Rain still threatened.

Master Peter, I will see you again.

As much as he could, the man craned his neck away from me. I remembered how rank I smelled. He smelled meaty.

I expected him to be terrified, but he wasn't. And he was no longer under the influence of zEEn—I sensed no dullness, no dense pea of fear. Instead he was curious and thoughtful.

He said, "I think you won't eat me. Are roses actually your favorite flower?"

"To look at. They're not as useful as lavender."

He said no more. I plucked a meat stick out of his shirt and managed to chew it while galloping. My hunger for him lessened to wishfulness.

When should I let him go? I might have already covered three miles. If the rain came, he would be soaked. The night was cool. He might get chilled, which could lead to fever. I wouldn't be here to treat him. Who knew what sort of healer he had? I didn't want him to die.

I stopped, set him down, and took the meat sticks I'd stuffed in his shirt. "The other man—your servant, I think—is too thin." I shook my head hard. "Not too thin for me to eat! That's not what I meant. Disease hunts people like him. See that he drinks sheep's milk flavored with ginger." I added, "I'm a healer."

"This has been the strangest night of my life." The man's chest rose in a deep breath. "You should stop stealing."

I couldn't! A realization broke over me. I didn't need the band anymore. "I'll steal less." I had to feed only myself and Master Peter.

The man raised his eyebrows. "Now that we know you're an ogre, even though you're an odd one, people will kill you—or try to—and I won't be able to prevent it. By now my servants will have sent for help, but I won't let anyone go after you tonight."

"Thank you." With a little luck, I wouldn't be an ogre much longer.

He called after me, "Farewell."

I started to run again but discovered I was too tired even to trot. Merely walking called for reserves I'd used up. I left the road and curled up on the far side of an oak. The threatened rain fell.

Happiness deepened my sleep, which, untroubled by the downpour, was sweeter than it had been since before Lucinda entered my life. I didn't awaken until late the next morning. My clothes were damp, but the day was sunny, and they soon dried. As I ran, I satisfied myself with meat sticks from the night's plunder.

By early afternoon of my twenty-fourth day as an ogre, I reached the Fens. Near home, an unusual quiet reigned. For once, I heard no snarling, no thumps as bodies slammed into one another. The band seemed to be at peace, as I was.

No! The only times they were quiet were—

Master Peter!

I raced.

My love!

They heard me and looked up from their prey—

—which wasn't Master Peter.

A young female giant, still alive, still zEEned, bleeding but only nibbled so far, smiled at me. "Oooayaagik (*honk*)." *Welcome.*

SSahlOO raised his head. "Beautiful mare, we thought you weren't coming back."

AAng said, "I missed giant. Nothing else is this tender." She returned to eating.

They all did, taking turns to keep up the zEEning.

I shouted at the giant. "Wake up! Run!" Even if she didn't understand Kyrrian, my tone would break the persuasion.

Where was Master Peter? Had they already eaten him?

I didn't see fresh bones. Master Peter's wares were scattered. There lay the utensils that were to be my necklace. There lay his rapier.

The giant sat up and brushed away two of the band. AAng bit into her leg and hung on, like a badger with a hedgehog. ShuMM began zEEning again. Her face relaxed. The others resumed feeding.

Now she was really losing blood.

My rage dwarfed anything I'd ever felt.

But my human side intervened. "Meat sticks!" I cried, running to them, waving meat sticks in their faces.

They pushed me off, though SSahlOO made room for me at the belly. The two who'd been swept away by the giant ate again.

I roared, snatched the rapier, and pulled it from its sheath. They'd have to kill me before they killed the giant.

Unless I killed them.

The giant, roused by my bellowing, rose on one elbow.

"Run!" I shouted. If she still could.

AAng first. With a healer's certainty of where to thrust the sword, I stabbed the base of her skull. She slumped forward.

SSahlOO lifted his head. To lull him, I smiled—and then pierced one of his eyes, which were blue. He fell on his side.

A hand seized my arm and yanked me away. I slashed.

EEnth howled in pain, jumped back, and faced me in a crouch, his side bloody.

They all faced me, the four that were left. ShuMM's mouth moved, but I couldn't hear him over my own blaring.

I held out the rapier and waved it from side to side. "Let it go." *It!* Her. "The giant. Run, giant!"

As one, the band rushed me. I stabbed. ShuMM groaned. Then they were all on top of me. Someone bit my shoulder. I lost the rapier, but I writhed, wriggled— couldn't get free. AAng's toothache wouldn't save me this time. I hoped the giant had escaped.

Mother and Wormy wouldn't know what had become of me.

CHAPTER THIRTEEN

THEN THEY WERE GONE. I opened my eyes. IZZ and FFanOOn sprawled on the ground near me, their faces blue.

But EEnth and a bloody ShuMM were already at the giant again, zEEning her between bites. I yelled, and her hands, in an instant, circled the throat of each, squeezed, then tossed them aside.

"Uueeetaatii (*honk*) obobee aiiiee." *I am a friend.* I hoped she knew Kyrrian, because I'd just used up most of my Abdegi. In Kyrrian, so she'd know I spoke it, I repeated, "I am a friend."

Carefully forming each word, she said, also in Kyrrian, "Thank you. You saved me."

"Not yet." She was bleeding from many wounds.

Luckily, none were gushing, but ogre bites were even more poisonous than their scratches, and she'd endured both. Untreated, she'd certainly die. I bled, too, though I wasn't as badly cut, and ogre bites and scratches—unless they were severe—didn't kill ogres. I reached for my satchel.

Luckily, I hadn't used any purpline on AAng.

Whom I'd killed.

I couldn't think about that now.

I found my carpetbag and shook out its contents.

The giant backed away. I felt her gigantic fear.

ZEEn! The air around her fear was also bigger than in a human. I honeyed my voice. "I mean no harm. I helped you before, didn't I?"

She nodded, her face relaxing, the air expanding.

I kept zEEning. As I usually did with patients, I explained what I was doing. Meanwhile, I worried. I didn't have nearly enough bandages.

Why hadn't I prepared for a wounded giant, when I'd just left Aeediou behind in Jenn?

"A drop of purpline is all you need," I repeated again and again, telling her and reminding myself. And keeping at bay thoughts of my dead band and my Master Peter, who was almost certainly dead, too.

A drop in each wound was almost all I had, with a drop or two left over. My bandages were enough to bind only one of her legs. While I worked, I worried that another band might attack, which would doubtless finish us off.

But none did, perhaps prevented by respect for the boundary of our—now my—land or by the certainty that some of them would die.

When I'd done what I could for her, I used the last of the purpline on my shoulder, where the wound was deepest. I stopped zEEning and said in my ordinary rasp, "I'm finished. Please rest." If the purpline did its work, her wounds would be healed enough by morning for us to attempt to leave. "Don't move." If she remained still, the need for binding the cuts would be less.

I walked our perimeter, looking for a sign of Master Peter among the bones.

Human ulna, femur, many finger phalanges, two skulls. I saw nothing distinctly Master Peter. Every skull has high cheekbones. None have noses or lips. Or eyes that softened when they looked at me.

I asked the giant if she'd seen a human when the band had brought her here. She said she hadn't.

Even if my band hadn't eaten him, he couldn't have gone far. He was dead.

However, if the giant and I lived, as soon as I delivered her to safety, I would, against all reason, search for him. He'd do the same for me, I was sure of it.

Night fell, and I was grateful to the dark for concealing the bodies. I sat near the giant, whose name was Udaak, and let myself feel my grief, despair, and fury. I sobbed noisily. Udaak put a gentle, huge hand on my back, but I moved away from the comfort and continued weeping until I was empty and exhausted.

Then the thoughts started. I'd never killed any being who could speak. Even though they were ogres, I loathed myself for not having saved them and for not preventing Master Peter's death.

How could they have done it? They knew I cared about him and didn't want anyone killed.

EEnth and SSahlOO! Why didn't you wait for your beautiful mare?

Because they were ogres. Like me.

We survived the night. By morning, my wounds were trifling, and I deemed Udaak well enough—barely well enough—to travel. I was more than eager to leave both the Fens and this grisly scene, but we waited several hours, while ogre bands, dimly seen through the perpetual fog, passed by on their way to hunt.

I gathered my meat sticks and had the forethought to stuff Master Peter's jug into my carpetbag, too. I should have taken someone's bearskin against the chill, but I couldn't bring myself to.

The weather cleared beyond the Fens. Even limping, Udaak's long legs forced me to trot to keep up. By early afternoon, we reached the fork and turned toward the giants' farms, beyond which lay the dragons' Spires. Automatically, my hands made fists, and I needed a meat stick to calm myself.

As we went, Udaak thanked me repeatedly for saving her and for being unlike other ogres.

Giants' farms are vast by human and ogre standards, but the beet harvest was in progress, so we didn't have to walk to a farmhouse. In about an hour, we came to a fence, which Udaak was tall enough to see over. With honks, whistles, and words, she called to someone.

I heard thudding footsteps. The chest, shoulders, and head of a male giant appeared at the fence. His enormous smile vanished at the sight of me.

Udaak explained me in Abdegi and, at the end, with a tap on my head. I'm sure she didn't mean to force my feet half an inch into the road.

The farmer's face softened. In Kyrrian, he thanked me for saving Udaak.

I described Master Peter and asked him if he'd seen such a person. He hadn't.

Udaak, who had learned something by observing me, invited me for a meal.

Denying my stomach and infuriating my ogre half, I said no. I had to search for Master Peter.

I devoted three days of my dwindling store to looking, hope against hope, for him. Anyone who could have watched would have seen a hideous, distracted creature—sometimes sobbing, sometimes shouting at herself—dashing through the elves' Forest, running near the roads that went by both the giants' and the humans' farms, listening, sniffing.

But I was always aware that, if he lived, he could be where I wasn't. When I was *here*—say, near the road—he could be *there*, in the elves' Forest or a farmer's kitchen.

Master Peter had been unique in the way he'd understood me, appreciated me. It couldn't happen again. Two humans couldn't fall in love with such a one as I was.

As a memento, I had only his jug, which I filled from a stream in the Forest.

I missed the band at night, when I longed for their snores, their restless sleep, the stink of all of us.

On the third night, while lying awake in a woody dell on a giant's land, the healer in me woke up. I was my own patient now, and this search for my dead love would destroy me. I didn't let my patients die if I could help it.

Forgive me, Master Peter! I gave up seeking him and considered where to go next. After an hour of indecision, I chose my destination.

I wouldn't endanger anyone else in this quest. I'd go alone. If I succeeded, I'd be welcome anywhere, at least for a while, even as an ogre. I could live at home again and wouldn't have to eternally miss Mother and Wormy.

When I rejoined humanity, I might save someone

whose gratitude would progress to love. Then, if I could set aside the memory of Master Peter, I might return the feeling, because saving someone's life was almost as good as drinking a love potion.

Yes! I would go to the dragons' Spires. I'd try not to, but if I died seeking purpline, my end would sadden only two people, neither of them myself.

CHAPTER FOURTEEN

I SET OFF for the Spires on my twenty-eighth day as an ogre. The morning was cloudy with a brisk wind, but I warmed as I followed the road from a distance. I would have to travel for the next three days at least to reach the end of the giants' property.

During the first morning of loping along while munching a meat stick, I surprised myself by marveling at this thrilling (and miserable) adventure I was on. The dragons' Spires were said to be thin rock towers, resembling knotted rope that impossibly stood on end. They sprouted in a basin so deep that they didn't poke above the surrounding flatlands. The ogre didn't care, but—dragons aside—the girl in me could hardly wait to see this wonder.

My mind veered to Wormy, who, of the two of us, was

the greater admirer of beauty. I wished he could be with me when I reached the Spires—and that we'd both be safe there.

I began to plan. It might be true that the ogres had once defeated the dragons, or it might be nonsense, but it was certainly true that a single ogre hadn't overcome them all.

Besides, I didn't want to kill dragons. I just wanted purpline.

Did dragons hunt during the day or during the night? Might I slip in while they were away, fill Master Peter's jug, and leave? Purpline was occasionally for sale in the market. Someone had to get it and return.

The final day of the journey, October 22, marked a miserable milestone: I had been an ogre for thirty-one days, and in thirty-one more, unless the improbable occurred, I would be an ogre forever.

I set out at dawn, shivering in the frosty air. After half an hour or so, I heard a faint *whoosh*, and every hair on me stood up. Despite the cold, my body heated.

A black shape winged its way west, toward the farms, too high for even my ogre eyes to tell if it was hawk or dragon—but my body seemed to know. Sweat beaded on my face. Could it see me? Would it dive? I was ready.

It flew on.

Gradually, I relaxed . . . until the next dragon appeared. Singly—never in pairs or flocks—twenty-one dragons passed overhead, spaced about three minutes apart. I didn't respond as strongly to the succeeding twenty as I had to the first dragon, but I still reacted—warmed, felt my hairs rise. When the flow finally stopped, I was as tired as if I'd been in a fight.

But I continued on my way. Gradually, the farmland's loamy ground gave way, first to sandy dirt and then to hard-packed earth.

I doubted I'd meet other travelers, because only the Spires lay ahead, so I ran on the road.

Three hours later, the stream of dragons reversed and my symptoms started again, only worse, because the creatures were lower in the sky. I saw irregular shapes bulging from their snouts. Luckily, I still seemed to be too distant for the dragons to make me out, or they'd already had a meal and, unlike ogres, didn't want more.

I counted the returnees, too. Twenty-one out, twenty-one back in.

Late in the afternoon, craggy formations of gray boulders popped up, as if the giants had planted stone seeds that had yielded a tall crop. Some of the rocks arched to create bridges over air; some boulders balanced on other boulders to make doorways and windows. The Spires had to be close.

I stopped for the night under a rock bridge, hoping that it would hide me from view in the morning when the dragons left to hunt—and when they were hungriest.

The next day, I woke when the sky was still dark, my mind buzzing with questions. Were there no more than twenty-one dragons in the Spires? Or didn't all of them hunt every day? Would throngs be waiting when I entered?

How good were their ears? Their noses? Were they already aware of me and merrily looking forward to ogre for lunch?

I ate a meat stick to comfort myself.

The first dragon rose out of the pinkening east. I endured the agitation I'd felt yesterday, and then endured it twenty more times. Were these the same dragons as yesterday, or did they take turns?

I hefted my satchel and left the shelter of the rock bridge, but I hadn't gone more than fifteen yards before another black shape appeared above the horizon. I raced back to the hiding spot.

Had I miscounted?

I waited to see if more would fly over.

Master Peter had called it a fool's errand to go to the dragons. How frightened for me he'd be.

After about half an hour without more dragons, I set out again.

I passed a tall thin stone topped by a short fat one, an arched rock, and three straight ones shaped like candlesticks.

Then the earth plunged. I stood at a cliff's edge, the Spires below.

The ogre in me yawned. Nothing edible, and I saw no smoke plumes or tail tips to suggest the presence of dragons. My stomach growled.

The human in me gasped. Nature had made a bowl and filled it with a city of ironstone castles with knobby turrets and lumpy walls. Purely for decoration! The dragons didn't live in the castles, which were arranged in wandering rows to make alleys where a few spruces grew.

There had to be a way in. I started around the perimeter and found a narrow path, which I followed carefully—and loudly to my ears, where the blood was already drumming. After only a few yards, waist-high miniature spires cropped up.

As I wound downward, the spires grew. When they exceeded eye level, I lost the vista. If a dragon sat on its haunches straight ahead, I wouldn't see it. I wondered how dragons smelled. I wondered how their hunting was progressing. Might they have caught their prey especially quickly today?

Did dragons pee wherever they were when the need

possessed them? Or were there special spots, like humans' privies? Or something else?

The path widened. Ahead of me, the ground hollowed to form a wide basin about two feet deep. I wondered if it had formed naturally or if a dragon had made it, possibly by peeing here, and the pee had evaporated in the dry air.

The path narrowed again and then forked. As soon as I took the left fork, the right one looked safer, but I continued. In perhaps ten minutes the way forked again. Right this time.

Five minutes later, I smelled camphor, an ingredient in purpline.

My hairs began to rise. A dragon was here—ahead or to the side, above or below. I should retreat.

But my ogre side filled with fury, like a pillow stuffed to bursting. The ogre half forced all of me forward, toward a stout spire. I had never felt so alert and alive.

Around the curve, a dragon slept, its soft slumber breaths puffing diagonally and fading before rising much. No wonder I'd seen no smoke plumes.

Between the dragon and me lay the half-eaten carcass of a giant sheep. My stomach roared. The dragon looked and smelled too metallic to seem edible, but the sheep—well-muscled, threaded with fat—looked delicious. I would fight for it.

No! Kindly dragon. Has a right to eat. Don't fight!

Back away slowly. I gripped my ogre self, willed it down, and inched away. The dragon's eyes flipped open. Its pupils were crimson.

I felt hot enough to be burning already.

The dragon raised itself onto its back legs.

My sheep!

Beyond thought—lost in rage—I faced the dragon.

From claw to skull, it lit up and glowed like a stained-glass window. Flames licked its snout.

I widened my stance, stood on my toes, pushed out my chest.

It glowed brighter.

I stepped toward it and my carcass.

It leaned toward me.

I planted my right boot on the sheep's ribs. Mine!

The dragon pushed out a tongue of flame.

I'd go for its wings first. It wouldn't fly off and escape me.

The fiery tongue lengthened.

I screamed—roared—howled, *"Ack nack! Moyz flegum smEEnoy! SquEEng zuZZ! ZuZZ!"*

CHAPTER FIFTEEN

THE DRAGON'S EYES PALED. It swallowed its flame, and its mouth curled in an apologetic smile. It lifted, flew above the Spires, and disappeared over the lip.

My chest heaved. I could hardly stop panting. Sweat poured off me. The words had just appeared in my mind. Must have been a spell, as SSahlOO had said.

Would the dragon return? I doubted I had the energy to face it again.

I scanned the sky. No dragon. I looked down and saw what the dragon had blocked: a huge but shallow puddle of violet purpline.

Eat the sheep first or take the purpline first?

The healer won. I emptied Master Peter's jug, then half

filled it with enough purpline, if used sparingly, for at least a year of ordinary ailments.

Next, never too tired to eat, I devoured the sheep.

When I finished, still worn out, I dragged myself up the narrow path, out of the Spires, and back to the rock bridge where I'd spent the night before. Once there, I waited for the dragons to fly back to the Spires. Whenever one went by, my symptoms started again, though diminished by distance.

While I waited, I wondered about my victory. If the words I'd said were a spell, how had the ogres come by them? Why did they spring from my lips automatically?

Did Lucinda have anything to do with it?

When all the dragons had passed, I made myself start out again, though I was too tired to travel at my usual pace. If I could return to living among people, I wanted to begin as soon as possible.

By late afternoon, however, I could go no farther. I stopped and slept in the shadow of an arching rock.

In the morning, restored, I woke up with a question. Could purpline, a remedy for almost everything, cure me of being an ogre?

I dosed myself with a drop on my tongue and waited, feeling no different. I looked at my hands, which were still hairy.

Purpline was useless for transformations.

Twenty-nine days left.

Three days back to the fork and another four to Jenn and Mother and Wormy would leave me just twenty-two days to find romance.

If I reached Jenn alive. Archers might—likely would!—wound me mortally before I had a chance to show my purpline. If they killed me, they'd have it all.

I couldn't go to Jenn! Or to any city or town.

Best, I thought, to be a hermit. As long as it lasted, I'd supply humanity—and elves, giants, and gnomes—with purpline, but I'd live alone. Word of my goodness would spread. People would flock to thank me for their cures. They'd bring meat sticks.

And would halt a mile from my cottage in the woods, driven off by the stench, because why would I bother to bathe?

I sobbed, and as I wept, my next destination revealed itself. It had to be the master's farm, where I'd taken the master himself hostage. If I was going to be human again, I needed to be among people as soon as possible. There could be no second Master Peter, but maybe there could be someone.

More likely, I'd remain an ogre forever, but Mother could come. Wormy could visit. Eventually, he'd marry and have children. His whole family would visit. I'd be Auntie Ogre.

I didn't want to be Auntie Ogre! And why did I feel a pang about his marrying when I didn't want him for myself?

I sheered away from that question. The tears kept coming. I stopped and squatted in the dirt.

When I'd cried myself out, I felt more cheerful. At the master's farm, I'd find out if he had followed my advice to feed sheep's milk and ginger to his skinny servant. Also, I might help lift the melancholy of the master himself.

Maybe, since I hadn't stolen meat sticks lately, no one would kill me before I could reveal that I had purpline.

I stayed far from the road and no one troubled me. Finally, on a winter-cold night, under a bright three-quarter moon, I arrived at the master's farm.

Before approaching the front door, I peered through a side window into a drawing room that was crowded with people. My stomach rumbled. The master had guests, two dozen or more, far too many for me to zEEn out of their fright.

Hungrily in the ogre way and longingly in the human, I took in the scene.

Half or more of the guests seemed not much older than I was. They couldn't all have been comely, but at first sight they seemed to be. My stomach rumble rose to thunder. I tingled.

It felt just like the tingle I'd experienced with Master

Peter! Had I been merely hungry? Had it been brought on only by his health and comeliness? I didn't love these delectable people!

The drawing room was lit by dozens of candles—on the buffet and side tables, and on the decorative chest, and in the chandelier. My human side drank in the warm hues of furniture and patterned rugs against the cool, creamy walls.

How civilized! A different kind of appetite opened in me. A book lay on the writing desk along with a sheaf of paper, ink, and a pen. Vases of dried broom and baby's breath on several tables recalled summer. Portraits adorned the walls. Between the windows that faced the road hung a round mirror with an ormolu frame.

I felt as if I were watching a play. In human form, I could have been among the actors. I might have stood at the side of the young woman closest to my window, whom I saw in profile, whose bloom of youth and health wouldn't have made me want to stroke her arm to test its tenderness. We could have exchanged pleasantries.

Her gown had been turned, though skillfully done, to make it look new again. I wondered how pressing her poverty was.

I scanned for signs of illness, but the people all seemed hale, though a young man had pimples, which I could treat. A year ago, I'd cured my own—and now a constellation of blackheads pocked my cheeks.

Four men and a woman clustered around the master. My sharp ears heard even the softest-spoken of them. They discussed weather, the harvest, and news from the city of Frell, where King Imbert held court.

Though he said little, the master's expression was cordial. I wished the guests gone so I could sense his inner state.

Clearly, they respected him. Even when his opinion hadn't been sought, they waited in case it might be forthcoming.

As I watched, I decided the young people were there in hopes of finding their future. Many of the couples might have become acquainted in the master's drawing room. Two young men and a pretty young woman tarried, chatting and laughing, at the table that bore the teapot. Could I find my future here, too?

The woman I'd watched earlier left her place near my window for the fireplace, where a man stood warming himself, his back to me. The hitch in his left shoulder reminded me of Wormy, and, if he were here, Wormy would have been at the fireplace, too, since he shivered from October to May.

But this man stood with his legs apart in a firm stance, while Wormy tended to shift from foot to foot. And this young man seemed taller, though that was hard to judge.

Might he become my love? Might his resemblance to Wormy please me?

Where was the real Wormy now? Did he haunt someone else's apothecary? Did he still comfort Mother with his familiar presence? Did they often talk about me?

The man's cloak, which he hadn't removed—another similarity—fell in soft folds, bespeaking fine wool, bespeaking wealth. The young woman, smiling, tilted her head up to him.

Were they childhood friends, as Wormy and I had been? Or had they just met? Was she hoping he might make her rich?

"Sir," she said, "I appeal to you." Her expression was saucy. They must not be well acquainted if she called him *sir*. She went on. "There is such a crowd around the tea, I don't like to be bold and shoulder my way through."

Three people a crowd?

"I appeal to your gallantry." How bold!

He bowed and turned toward the tea table.

I burst out, "Wormy!"

CHAPTER SIXTEEN

LUCKILY, THE MASTER'S WALLS were thick. No one rushed to the window.

How could it be Wormy? Why was he here? Had something befallen Mother? Was she ill? Was he looking for me to bring me home to treat her?

I squeezed my hands together. Let Mother not be sick!

Wormy made his way to the tea table and, without having to shoulder anyone, reached the teapot, where he poured two cups. More of the young people ambled to him. A young man asked if he was staying long in the neighborhood.

"I'm off in the morning." He didn't reveal his destination.

But first he was staying the night. I had to talk to him!

"I see." His questioner was too polite to probe further.

I wished he'd been rude!

The man added, "Some of the young people would have liked to become better acquainted with you. I admit I would have."

Wormy bowed and blushed, but not as hotly as I'd have expected. While I was gone, had he grown used to such attention?

Another young gent chimed in. "City folk rarely journey here. They don't discover how welcoming we are."

A maiden nodded eagerly.

Wormy was a catch!

Someone else spoke. The tea would be cold by the time he escaped. The bold young woman returned to the window and gazed out.

I had forgotten how bright the night was.

"Someone's watching!" she cried. "Big! A bear!"

I ran. They'd know from my boot prints that I was no bear. Would the master guess who I really was?

People exited the house. Cries followed me, but no pursuit. They seemed to be satisfied with scaring me off.

Where to go?

Not to the drying shed and its meat sticks, where I'd been before, where I would be sought if anyone realized my identity. Not to the stable, where the guests' horses would be. Not to the barn, where overflow steeds might be.

The pigs were kind enough to let me in their sty. I liked their scent, and they seemed not to mind mine. Best of all, they were warm. Snuggling with them reminded me of the nighttime comfort of my band. Soon, I slept.

"Evie-ee?"

SSahlOO was dragging Wormy away, and I had to save him, but I was trapped in a morass of leather pillows.

"Evie?"

I woke. Still night, still bright. Still an ogre.

"Evie?"

Wormy! There he was, only a few yards away, facing the barn, his back to me. The master and the servants I'd encountered before were beside him, also facing away. Two of them held lanterns, but they carried no axes or scythes or rakes.

They all wore cloaks. I couldn't tell if the too-thin man had put on flesh.

I hoped to get out of the sty before anyone saw me in here, but the hogs didn't cooperate. They made noise moving, and they squealed and grunted.

"Evie!" Wormy hurried to the pigpen, then drew back as the combined stink of them and me reached him.

The bold young woman at the party hadn't wanted to shoulder through a few people, and here I was, shoving through pigs, holding my carpetbag over my head.

"I'm smelly, Wormy." Defiantly, I added, "I don't mind

it." The healer took over. "The stench may scratch your throat."

He touched his neck and kept his distance. I wished the others weren't here so I could tell what he was feeling.

"Is Mother ill?"

The master frowned. I supposed he was thinking, This man knows an ogre's mother?

"No, but she's worried."

When Mother worried, she forgot to eat. "Tell her to drink auntwort tea. That will soothe her. Don't let her get too thin, and tell her I'm fine."

"She keeps saying she misses her healer girl."

"You're female?" the master said.

"Does anyone else in Jenn miss me?"

He shrugged.

"My patients have found other healers?"

Another shrug. Of course they had.

"*I* haven't, Evie."

"Are you sick?"

"I'm as ever."

But he looked better than that. My stomach growled. I tingled my confused ogre-girl tingle.

"Why are you here?" Oh! "Did the fairy tell you where to find me? Did she transport you?" Did fairies do that?

"The fairy?" the master echoed.

"I haven't seen her. She didn't tell me anything. I came

on Biddable." His horse. "Evie, you have only twenty-four days left."

He'd kept track! I wondered if he was going to propose again. What would I say? "Why are you here?" Then I rushed to explain it. "On business for your parents?"

He squared his shoulders, a gesture that looked less absurd than I remembered. "I came in hopes of finding you or at least getting word of you."

"For Mother?" Or for yourself?

He nodded.

Oh. For Mother.

He shivered and hugged his cloak.

The master and the others clutched their cloaks tight, too. The master proposed continuing the conversation in the house, then thought better of it, considering my odor. At his suggestion, we went to the barn, and I saw him notice that the beasts were untroubled by me.

I asked him my most important question: "Master, has a trader been by, a Master Peter?"

"Tall?"

I nodded.

"Rakish?"

Jaunty. "I suppose."

"He was here half a year ago. I'd send him packing if he came again. Our last kitchen wench sighed over him until her wedding day to another fellow."

133

He was lovable, so naturally I wouldn't be the only one to love him.

Wormy frowned. "Who is Master Peter?"

"I met him on the road." I didn't want to explain the rest of it.

"Oh." He waited for me to say more. When I didn't, he asked, "Are you still on your way to the Fens?"

"No. I lived there for a while." Why did I feel ashamed?

"Did you learn persuasion?"

I nodded. The master and the others already knew.

"Then you're coming home?" He sounded eager.

"I can't. Persuasion doesn't succeed if there are more than three people and only one ogre. In Jenn, they'd kill me before I could persuade anyone."

"Oh."

The young girl servant stifled a yawn, which set off a round of yawns among them, except for Wormy.

What was he feeling toward me? What would I say if he proposed again? I continued to grieve for Master Peter. At bottom, Wormy was still just my childhood chum.

But now he made me tingle, too—as almost everyone did.

He didn't propose. Had he stopped caring for me?

CHAPTER SEVENTEEN

I TOLD HIM my great news. "I have half a jug of purpline." I grinned. "Fresh from a dragon!"

He grinned back. "You'll heal dozens with that. Congratulations!"

"More than dozens." Oh! How could I have forgotten? "Did Aeediou survive?"

Wormy said Aeediou had used my remedy and was fine. "You're welcome at her house."

The master mentioned the lateness of the hour and offered me a stall in the barn, but I preferred the pigs, and he didn't mind.

Before dawn, Wormy woke me again. "Evie?"

I struggled out of the sty. He was alone, his saddlebags over his right shoulder. I wished I'd had time to hunt before he called me. He wasn't plump, but he wasn't lean, either. Lucky for me that he couldn't read my thoughts.

"I wanted to see you before I left. I wanted to say—"

"What?" I felt his fear. *Could* he read my thoughts?

Or was he going to propose and was afraid I'd say no again.

"If I hadn't asked you to marry me, you'd still be yourself."

He was afraid I was blaming him. "It's Lucinda's fault, not yours."

"Will you stay here?"

"Here?" I laughed, not happily. "The pigs don't seem to mind." I added, "The master may."

"Last night, I told him how good you are—what a good—" He struggled to get a word out, put his lips together as one does to say a *p*. He was trying to say *person*. "Ogre and healer you are. I couldn't say what happened. She's stopping me."

Lucinda. "She won't let me, either. It hasn't been all bad. I have the purpline." I wouldn't have met Master Peter. "No one else has ever lived among ogres."

I sensed love coming from Wormy, but it could have been love for me as his friend or as his healer. I couldn't tell if he tingled. Who would tingle at an ogre? "Are you well?"

He raised his shoulder. "I miss your fenuce tonic."

But he *was* well, better than well. I sensed no discomfort. His usual complaints weren't complaining.

He returned to his earlier question. "If the master doesn't mind, will you stay here?"

I shrugged.

He waited.

"Stop staring! Your eyes look like they belong on a dead fish."

He directed his gaze over my shoulder.

My anger drained away. "I'm sorry, Wormy, dear. I'm horrible. It's been mostly bad. No one will want me."

"Can I do anything?"

"Here." I opened my satchel, emptied two vials, and poured in purpline from the jug. "Tell Mother to keep one and sell the other. Your family won't have to help her any—"

"Evie! We don't mind."

"Tell her I miss her. I miss you, too. I mean, I will, as soon as you leave." But, really, I did already. "Be careful. If you catch up to any large parties, join them. They'll keep you safe from an ogre or two. If there are more . . ." I trailed off.

"How will I find out where you are?" His anxiety rose, either over the prospect of ogres or of not knowing my location. "How will your mother?"

"I'll write to her if I stay here or find another place. I

want her to come if it's possible." I wanted him to come, too.

In the stable, while Wormy saddled his horse, I caught and downed four mice, which I wouldn't have done in anyone else's presence. I walked with him as he led his mount to the road, where we shook hands.

The master came out, and together—a few yards apart—we watched his horse diminish to a dot. Would I see my friend again?

Might I be human if I did? Probably not.

I forced my attention to the master, who was still melancholic, peevish, and bitter.

He said, "Your friend speaks well of you, and word has spread that you rescued a giant. You're spoken of as 'the good ogre.'"

Ah. I could remain in the region. Soon, I could send an address to Mother.

"Where does your mother live?"

"In Jenn."

"In a house?"

"Of course." Where else would she live?

"You— You—" His mouth worked, but no words came out.

An ogre mother wouldn't live in a house. He knew. I nodded, smiling broadly, alas showing my fangs.

"Can you— Will something—" He smiled helplessly and pulled his cloak tight.

Turn me back? I tried to say yes, but couldn't.

He was shivering.

"I'll bathe. Then I'll be bearable indoors."

A servant brought out soap and a towel. I hastened to a pond behind the house, where I scrubbed myself and laundered Rupert's clothing. An hour later, disgustingly clean, with my apparel still damp, I sat at the master's dining table, upon which rested the absurdities of table-cloth, napkins, and cutlery. I quivered just looking at the master—elderly, yes, but healthy. I clenched my jaw.

The large woman who'd gone for weapons when I'd been trapped in the drying shed emerged from the kitchen, carrying a tray on which rested two plates. The food was hidden by domed silver covers.

I drooled.

She whipped the cover off the master's plate and I almost wept. He breakfasted on oatmeal cake and onion pie.

He said, "Thank you, Dosia."

When she removed my cover, I saw that it had been crammed with dried meat sticks. Such kindness! Several tumbled onto the tablecloth. I thanked her and the master, and, with a full mouth, thanked them both again—thanked the woman's back as she fled to the kitchen.

The master's eyes avoided my face.

"Purpline will cure that nausea. I can dose you, if you'd like."

His choler surfaced. "A knife and fork wielded by you would cure it, too."

I apologized.

"How did you know I was nauseous?"

The silverware felt strange in my hands. The meatsticks were hard to cut, but I did. Fork to mouth. Chew. Swallow. Now speak. "Ogres sense people's moods."

Surprise, then discomfort. He stopped eating.

"It's how we persuade." Cut. Fork to mouth. Chew. Swallow. "We feel the fear, which is what we usually sense when we're with people. To keep them from fleeing, we use our voices to make the air around the terror expand. Then, to the victim, the fear seems less important, hardly there." Ogres were fascinating. "We pile pleasant feelings on top. I spoke to you about flowers, which soothed you."

His attention faded. Whatever was on his mind was more interesting than ogres!

"I know you're sad and fretful."

That captured him again. He defended himself. "I never snap at anyone."

Except at me just now. "You rein your anger in." As I tried to.

His eyes locked on mine. "You know that?"

"You don't want others to suffer from your unhappiness."

"You can read my thoughts?"

I cut a meat stick in as long a piece as would fit whole
in my mouth. "Just emotions. I guessed the rest." I changed
the subject to give myself time to think. "Did you give your
man the ginger sheep's milk I said to?"

"Yes, and he's adding pounds." His mind was elsewhere
again.

I thought of worms. When people had worms growing
in them, nothing could distract them from the gnawing in
their bellies. A healer could coax out the beasties with a
mash of honey, beets, and saffron. I'd done it.

The master's secret reminded me of a worm, which,
I believed, was poisoning him. Maybe ogre honey could
coax its head out, and it would talk to me.

I sweetened my tone. "My mother and I try to be first
to spot the ear lily. Then we believe spring will finally
come."

His expression softened. Air buffered his sadness and
anger. "I start checking for lilies in February. We have
three colonies."

I nodded and made more air. "We don't even mind if it's
cold again after we see one."

He took a spoonful of oatmeal. "A wondrous bloom,
both delicate and hardy."

I tested the zEEn by picking up a meat stick in my hand and eating it without the cutlery.

He didn't seem to notice. "It's pleasant to think of lilies this time of year."

"In Jenn, we call them the bashful flower." I'd made this up, but the flowers did hide under the plant's leaves.

"I can see why."

My voice dripped with sweetness. "People would be poorer in joy if they didn't search for lilies."

"I agree."

I had him! "You know my secret. It's only fair that you tell me yours."

"True." He put down his spoon. "Jerrold, my grandson, is the king's son."

CHAPTER EIGHTEEN

KING IMBERT, a widower, didn't have a son. The succession when he died was uncertain.

He repeated, "The king's son." Real happiness overlaid the pleasure I'd zEEned him into feeling. "He's at court, but he's coming here to visit. He must already be on the road. I expect him the day after tomorrow."

"I see." But I didn't.

The master added, "Jerrold doesn't know the truth about his birth, and neither does the king. Those are my secrets, which I swore to tell no one." Horror blew the zEEn air away. "What have I done?"

I could zEEn him back to calmness, but not forever. What could I say? "Er . . ." I began in my ordinary ogre rasp. "Er . . . Did you promise not to tell an ogre?"

That surprised him. After a moment, he laughed. "Aveece would despise me for betraying her, but I feel better for it."

Queen Aveece had been his daughter?

"How did she die, if I may ask?" She had left the court three years after the wedding. There had been a state funeral, which I knew about, but I hadn't been born yet.

"You don't know? It was printed in the gazettes." His sadness returned. "She fell off her horse. The injury was so severe that she died."

Oh! "I'm sorry."

Mistress Dosia came in for our plates. I grabbed mine, because three meat sticks remained. Happily for me, the master waved her away.

"I've begun. I might as well go on." He stood and went to the fireplace. Facing me, with his back to the heat, he recounted the tale.

With an effort, I ignored my food to listen.

The master said his family was ancient and noble. His daughter had been a respectable match for a king.

"However, I worried they were too much alike—both headstrong, stubborn, energetic, lively. Aveece would have done better with a more serene character, but they loved each other and were happy and merry for three years."

Their bliss, the master said, had frayed as the queen noticed that she was never consulted in affairs of state. She wanted a say, which hardened into wanting a seat on his royal council.

I imagined marrying an important healer who somehow managed to keep me from healing, too. I wouldn't stay in love with him for long.

"Imbert is king and has the right to rule as he pleases," the master said, "but Aveece was clever. Her opinion was worth hearing. I sympathized with her—and with him. He may have wanted her to be the one person he could be with and not think about the kingdom."

The royal feud had sizzled for a month, and then the queen had returned to her father's manor.

The master's voice rose in exasperation, as if these events had occurred last week. "Why couldn't they both bend a little?"

The separation had happened two years before I was born. To me, it was Kyrrian history.

"We lived between Bast and Frell at the time." Messengers had galloped from the master's home to the castle and back, continuing the quarrel. "She kept telling me, 'If he wanted a stupid queen, he should have married someone else.'" He smiled wryly. "I always had a headache."

He sobered again as he continued. When Queen Aveece realized she was pregnant, she refused to inform the king. "She said, 'Now, more than ever, he won't let me on the council.'"

I felt uncomfortable, hearing the secrets of my king and late queen.

"Before Jerro was born, she extracted a promise from me not to notify the king if she didn't survive childbirth and never to tell him about her baby if it lived and she didn't. She said she wanted the child to grow up away from its father's influence."

But both had lived, and then, a year later, she'd died. The master hadn't promised anything about revealing her death other than from childbirth.

"I wrote to Imbert. If he'd come to the funeral, he would have seen his son and I would have been released from my absurd promise, but . . ."

I felt a surge in the master's sense of ill use.

"The king merely sent his royal regrets, two ministers, and three jugs of mead to serve after the ceremony. I like to think *his* death would have melted *her* anger, but I'm not sure. I didn't let the ministers discover Jerrold."

A month later, the master had moved here, as far from court as could be. "I wrote to my acquaintances that Jerro had sickened and died without his mother"—he smiled— "but the boy never had a sick day in his life. Would you like to see him?"

Now?

The master started for the door.

I stood, torn. Then I tucked the three remaining meat

sticks in my shirt and followed him out, gnawing on one while his back was to me.

The dining room opened into the parlor I'd peered into the night before. He marched to a portrait that hung next to the window I'd stood outside.

"The likeness is excellent. It was painted a year ago, shortly before he left me."

Prince Jerrold was as deliciously handsome as Master Peter, though they were as different as cat and dog. Master Peter had been sleek and sinuous, while Prince Jerrold seemed sturdy and vigorous. I swallowed. "A fine-looking young man." I wished he were already here, so I could eat—meat—meet!—him.

Ignoring both my stomach and my heart, I considered the rest of the painting. According to custom, females in portraits were painted sidesaddle on horseback, though they actually posed in a chair, with the horse painted in later. Males generally posed standing, with one leg on a footstool, which, like the chair, would be changed to something heroic. In this painting, the imagined corpse of an ogre replaced the footstool. If there had been as many slaughtered ogres as paintings of them, Kyrria would have been a safer kingdom.

"The ogre is absurd." My voice rose. "Am I that big? Do I have a wolf's ears or a shiny black nose? We may not clip our nails, but we don't have claws. People know what we look like." Some survived an ogre encounter. "It's heroic enough to kill an ordinary ogre. Why did the artist have to make us more monstrous?"

The master chuckled. "I had hoped your attention would stay with my grandson."

I checked the master to trace a resemblance between him and Prince Jerrold, but beyond the square jaw, I saw none. The master's lips were thin, the grandson's fleshy; the grandfather's nose was beaky, Prince Jerrold's wide and straight; the master's eyebrows arched, the grandson's ran straight across. The master's cheeks and nose were freckled, the prince's clear.

"He takes after my wife, as Aveece did."

Except for the cleft chin, I didn't see much likeness to the king, either, whose face was stamped on our KIs, our coins.

A resemblance to the master was evident in other ways, however. Prince Jerrold had pulled his shoulders back for the portrait, and his hands hid behind him as the master's did right now. The young man gazed out of the painting as frankly as his grandfather now regarded me.

I thought of Wormy, whose gaze was more confiding than pointed. "How does he come to be at court if his mother wanted him to live away from it?"

"Because he wished to go, and I wouldn't stop him. Aveece hadn't foreseen that. Mistress Evie, he was made to be king. His judgment has always been careful, unlike his parents'. He has all their virtues and none of their faults. He may be a bit overserious."

An excellent trait in a monarch. And his face would look well on a coin.

My stomach rumbled. I wanted the meat sticks in my shirt. "He isn't headstrong, like his parents?"

"He's brave. There's a difference."

An enormous difference, so why did he bring up *brave* when I said *headstrong*? Was the master less willing to recognize his grandson's faults than he had been to see his daughter's and son-in-law's?

"He's athletic, sits a horse well . . ." The master recited all the virtues a paragon of a king would have. "He has shot birds that my old eyes couldn't even see, but there they were, falling out of the sky."

My neck ached from nodding. Perhaps Prince Jerrold could be the man to dethrone Master Peter in my heart.

But he'd be unlikely to see beyond the ogre, as my love had.

Maybe he would. His grandfather had.

Alas, the distance from not fearing someone to loving that person was long.

The master said, "Whether he's ever acknowledged as royal, I'd like him to be happier in marriage than his parents were."

I wasn't stubborn, except about how to treat my patients. I'd be perfect!

"He's hoping to win a knighthood, unaware he's already a baronet through me." The master explained that he'd left his history, his title (Lord), and his name (Niall) behind when he'd moved here. "This close to the Fens," he said, "people welcome new neighbors and don't ask questions."

"What does Prince Jerrold believe about his parents?"

The master put a finger over his lips. "*Squire* Jerrold. No one here knows." He went on. "I told him the truth about his mother's death—that she fell off her horse—and said his father died in a hunting accident. He thinks they were both magistrates who judged disputes with Ayortha." The master's smile was mischievous. "Imbert does judge when the disputes are serious."

I noticed he never said *King* Imbert.

"Come! Follow me."

I thought the master the source of his daughter's imperiousness. He led me back to the dining room and on to the kitchen, where I found out that the man whose gauntness had alarmed me was the master's cook. In the two weeks since I'd seen him he had noticeably gained weight—and had become tempting.

He stirred a smelly porridge in a clay pot on a brick stove—a new invention that even Wormy's family didn't have. What a wonder it would be in an apothecary. He smiled at me and bobbed a bow. "Thank you, Master Ogre. They called me Twig until you came. Now I'm making them call me Trunk."

I congratulated him. "Please call me Mistress Evie."

"Ah. I'm sorry for not guessing. Mistress Evie it is, Mistress Ogre."

The master had no guests but me at dinner. Mistress Dosia served me a quarter of a roast mutton and a slice for him, with a mucky mess of broad beans and onions. Though I could have eaten twice as much meat, my belly was comfortable when I finished. The master was comfortable, too, his melancholy barely there.

"How does Squire Jerrold fare at court?" I asked.

The master's irritation reawakened. "He was doing well—made friends, won a tournament. He's a squire because a young knight, Sir Stephan, took him on."

"But he's no longer doing well?"

"In his last letter he spoke of a new arrival at court, a hero who'd killed several ogres and had their heads to prove it, which are now displayed on pikes."

"Do you know how they died and how many were killed?"

"Jerro didn't mention how. He said half a dozen heads."

CHAPTER NINETEEN

I TOLD MY RACING HEART it couldn't be Master Peter. A skilled and lucky archer could pick off several ogres. Probably such a one was the hero.

"I killed two of my band of six, and the rest are dead, too. That's when I saved Udaak, the giant you heard about." I told the master what had happened. "I stole the meat sticks for the band. Master Peter must have been eaten. I should have prevented it."

"A healer yet again."

That brought on my anger. "Healers don't kill."

"Could Master Peter have survived somehow and taken the heads?"

"He'd have had to sever them from the bodies, slow work with only a rapier. Then he'd have had to take them out of the Fens. He'd have been eaten himself." I hated imagining it all. "Did Squire Jerrold mention the name of the hero?"

The master frowned. "No, though he didn't trust the fellow. He wrote, 'My doubts will seem to arise out of envy, so I'll keep them to myself.' But in the next paragraph he added, 'Grandfather, I *am* envious. I would emulate the deed if I knew how it had been accomplished.'" The master blushed. "After a day or two, I know each letter by heart. He'll tell us more when he comes."

"May I stay until then?" Please don't cast me out.

"You can live here as long as you like. After sharing my secret, I feel lighter than I have in years, and I have you to thank. What's more, the closest healer is thirty miles away."

I hugged his words. A home. And being a healer again. I really could send for Mother. Soon we could set up our own household. "How long will Squire Jerrold stay?"

"His knight is kind enough to spare him for a month." The master chuckled. "I'll take an hour of the time to accustom him to the idea of you. Then I'm sure he'll be happy to meet you."

He'd be extraordinary if he were happy.

I didn't have a full month left, but if we were often in each other's company . . . If we esteemed each other . . . If I tingled with more than hunger and could tell the difference . . . If . . . If . . . Perhaps.

Following dinner, the master and I talked all afternoon and late into the night. We ranged over many subjects: the monarchy, healing, farming, my childhood, and even his. I doubt he would have conversed so long with a girl my age, but my shape hid my youth.

Afterward, I retired to the pigsty, where I wasted sleep time in wishing that Wormy had stayed longer. He'd hardly told me anything of home or Mother or himself.

In the morning, I set up an apothecary in the master's kitchen, with my dried herbs and a vial of purpline on a small table between the shiny copper sink and the marvelous stove, where I kept a kettle of ginger tea simmering.

My first patient was Mistress Winnet, the kitchen wench, who consulted me at Trunk's urging. She was the young girl who'd come to the drying shed on the night I'd taken the master hostage, and she suffered from a wart on the bottom of her foot. "I thought it was a stone in my shoe, but it's a stone in my foot, Mistress Ogre."

"Mistress Evie."

"Mistress, if you don't mind, what is your price for one foot?"

As I spoke, I scrubbed my hands in the sink. "This foot is free. If the other gets a wart, too, we'll decide between us." I spread a paste of corn-cockle seeds and warm water on the spot and covered it with a thin bandage. "The wart will collapse in a few days."

"Thank you, Mistress Ogre."

I swallowed my anger.

Trunk brought me the master's weasel terrier. "Moozy has a desperate cough." Trunk, holding the dog in his arms, looked desperate himself. "He's stopped eating. He can't stand up. Look at his ribs, Mistress Ogre."

"Mistress Evie."

The entire dog rattled with each cough. I put my hand on his chest and felt his laboring heart.

"He isn't afraid of you! Brave puppy!"

"Beasts are smarter than that."

My elecampane would take a week to work, but Moozy could be dead by then. I shook a drop of purpline into a tablespoon of cream. Trunk opened the dog's mouth and I poured in the concoction. Moozy breathed deeply.

"Look at that!" Trunk brought meat scraps.

The dog gobbled them, and my stomach rumbled so loud that Trunk fetched me some, too.

The master's groom suffered from dizziness, a serious affliction in someone often on a horse. I gave him a packet of hartshorn powder and told him to inhale it when he felt unsteady. He asked, and I told him, too, that there would be no charge.

Just one person—Mistress Dosia—had anything I wanted, and I worried that she might be healthy, but at dusk she came forward, reeking of cleanliness and confessing to a boil behind her ear. She agreed to my fee. I washed my hands again. Ogre hands, and especially fingernails, seemed to be magnets for dirt and grime.

While Trunk looked away, I had her remove her voluminous unbleached apron and the faded mulberry gown beneath it. Then I lanced the boil and cleaned the wound. When I finished, I gave her herbs to add to the baths she was to take thrice daily for a month. Finally, I held her gown up, near enough to me to get an idea of the fit but not so close it would absorb my odor.

Mistress Dosia said, "It should do, Mistress Ogre."

"Mistress Evie." I asked her to fetch the second gown and the shifts she'd agreed to pay me with as well. As soon as she left, I slipped out for another bath.

The second gown turned out to be faded brown. I put it on and saved the mulberry for the next day, when Squire Jerrold was expected. The gown was tight in the shoulders and loose around the waist and hips, but it declared that I was female.

When Mistress Dosia served me supper, she said, "It becomes you better than it ever did me, Mistress Ogre."

I nodded graciously. Lies infuriated me.

In the morning, after my bath, I shaved and endured the sight of my face: mottled, pitiless, savage. Afterward, I proceeded to my neck, my ears, and the back of my hands. The ears required the light touch of a healer. I managed without gushing blood.

Temporarily clean and temporarily shaved, I donned Mistress Dosia's mulberry dress. Then, hoping that Squire Jerrold might not arrive until I was ready, I boiled rose hips and rosemary in water and let the brew cool while I mashed bergamot rind and added walnut oil. Everything mixed together gave me a perfume, which I dabbed behind my ears and in the hollow of my throat. I struggled not to gag.

Trunk said, "You smell as sweet as a maiden, Mistress Ogre. Fancy that!"

Half the morning was over by the time I joined the master in his library, which looked out on the road.

He raised his eyebrows at the sight and smell of me but said nothing. I went to his shelves. The books about gardening didn't interest me, but I was drawn to a novel, *Daniel the Foe*.

The master said, when I opened the book, "I confess, Mistress Evie, the sight of you reading is no less fantastic than if my oak trees began to waltz."

I swallowed my irritation and wondered if I already needed another shave. My nose announced that my ogre smell had begun to encroach on the perfume. My stomach rumbled. I read:

In childhood I was called Daniel the Friend, but, after the murder of my beloved, rage possessed me. I hungered for revenge.

Promising.

The master peered out the window. I continued reading. An hour later, I bathed again.

Soapy—naked!—I heard hooves.

I stifled my alarm. The visitor might not be Squire Jerrold, but if it was he, he'd go in the manor, not around it, and the master wanted time to introduce the idea of me. I massaged soap into my scalp. I'd shave again, too.

What was that? I heard wood crack and splinter.

Something heavy—a body?—thudded to the ground.

"Mistress Evie! Come! Hurry!"

CHAPTER TWENTY

I SURGED out of the pond, ran toward the house, reversed. The towel was too small! Back at the pond, I pulled on my shift, which clung wetly.

The master cried, "Jerro! Wake up!"

I rounded the building. A riderless horse stood between the house and the smashed gate. I burst through a knot of servants and crouched over the still form. The master had Squire Jerrold's head in his lap.

I leaned close. My sharp ogre ears heard life. "He breathes."

"He breathes!" the master echoed. Everyone else took up the words.

Over them, I cried, "Look at his eyes!"

Delicately, the master raised Squire Jerrold's right eyelid.

The brown eyes of his portrait had paled to a faint yellow. His gaze was unseeing. I checked his fingernails and saw the telltale bumps. Barley blight!

I dashed into the house. In the kitchen, I poured half a cup of the ginger tea from the kettle and added three drops of purpline.

If Squire Jerrold didn't die in the next two minutes, I would cure him, and—if I could bury my grief for Master Peter—purpline might be our love potion. Who could resist the (ogre) maiden who'd saved his life?

Back outside, the master held up his grandson's head. I pinched open his mouth and dribbled in the tea, waited for him to swallow, tipped in more, gradually emptying the draft. "Three drops of purpline in the tea should be enough."

While we waited for the effects to be known (I was already confident), the master, Trunk, and I carried him into the parlor and laid him on a sofa. By the time we set him down, the wax had left his cheeks and his breathing had strengthened. His faint passed into an easy sleep.

My stomach woke up. How handsome he was.

The master said, "Trunk, tell Dosia to paint the double *B*."

Houses with barley blight warned visitors away with a two-letter sign on the door.

Squire Jerrold's mouth fell open, revealing a small gap between his front teeth, which were otherwise white and straight. The little imperfection added to his deliciousness. I could hardly catch my breath.

I rushed into the kitchen and cut three ribs from a side of beef that Trunk had been planning to roast.

Squire Jerrold may not have realized he was ill. Barley blight was stealthy, beginning mildly with a headache and tiredness. One accustomed to good health, as the master said Squire Jerrold was, might dismiss the first symptoms. The serious ones came in a rush. The squire might have felt merely indisposed until an hour ago and might even then have expected the spell to pass.

Back in the parlor, a blanket had been tucked around him, and Trunk had returned. I thought of what should have occurred to me instantly. The master and I said the words in unison: "Did he catch it in Frell?"

Trunk gasped.

Or he might have been infected at an inn on his way here. If in Frell, many thousands would likely die. There had been a shortage of purpline, and unicorn hairs were rare.

The master paced back and forth. "Imbert could die,

could be dead by now." He added, "I don't know if he ever had it."

If the king died without naming an heir, Kyrria would be in turmoil.

You couldn't catch the blight twice. I'd never had it, and I had no idea if I was susceptible now. Elves and gnomes were immune. Ogres or half-human ogres might be, too. In any event, I had purpline.

"I have to go to Frell." I wouldn't have time to discover if I could love Squire Jerrold and he could love me.

If he'd caught the disease in Frell, I had to bring my purpline there. If he had contracted it on the way, I had to find the source and the other victims—probably a quicker process—treat them, and hasten back.

If an arrow didn't kill me before I had a chance to cure anyone.

Barley blight varied from person to person. Illness could show itself in two days or in two weeks. Everyone's fingernails bumped up, but their eyes didn't always pale. Some lingered; others went quickly. A few survived even without medicine.

But people who'd never had it always caught it. We didn't know how—whether by touch or by breath or even by the speech or thoughts of the infected. And we didn't know what started an epidemic, with everyone healthy on a Monday and people starting to die a few days later.

"Trunk and I have had it," the master said. "No one else has."

As soon as Squire Jerrold began to stir, I fled. Outside, I bathed yet again.

When I entered the empty kitchen, I heard from two rooms away, "An ogre? An *ogre!*"

"Lie back, Jerro. She saved your life."

I packed my things in my satchel, leaving out a vial of purpline for the master's household. Then I began to shave.

From the parlor, Trunk said, "Look how plump I'm growing, Master Jerrold. She said to drink sheep's milk with ginger to keep from wasting away. I call myself Trunk now."

"She's fattening you up!"

The master spoke in such a quiet voice, even ogre ears couldn't hear what he said next.

"I drank *what*? Dragon *urine*?"

I finished my face and moved the razor to an ear.

From what Squire Jerrold went on to say when he stopped shouting, the blight must have begun in Frell, because he hadn't stopped at any inns on his way here—had slept the six nights, as Master Peter had, on the road, wrapped in his cloak. "No one was ill when I left—no one I knew of."

This was good news. The blight had been in its early stages, so more people would still be alive when I got there. I began shaving my hands.

I should have set out immediately. Squire Jerrold would recover without me. But I wanted to be presentable when I bid the master farewell and met the grandson.

In the parlor, Squire Jerrold said, "Grandfather, Sir Stephan may be sick. Even if he isn't, he'll need his squire."

No! He should rest, not travel.

"What use is an iron constitution if I'm made to stay in bed?"

The master said, "Blight isn't to be trifled with."

Correct.

"I won't die just riding to Frell."

If he'd been weakened enough, he might. Was this the willfulness the master had called bravery?

"Must I fear for you again? You'll go in the carriage."

I heard jubilation in the grandson's voice. "I'll rest all the while."

Ah. I saw how the master's daughter, Queen Aveece, had extracted foolish promises from him. He was undone by love.

"Mistress Evie will ride with you. If you sicken, she'll dose you."

"With urine? Ride with an ogre?"

"You'll like her."

I splashed perfume on myself and poured the remainder into a flask, which I added to my carpetbag. Then I stuffed in the razor wrapped in linen.

We'd be alone together. A wicked idea came. If I thought I might someday love him and he might love me, I could zEEn him into a proposal.

But if love didn't come to Squire Jerrold, I'd have ruined his life.

When the master called me back into the parlor, I curtsied from just inside the door, hoping distance would improve me.

Squire Jerrold bowed from the sofa where he now sat up. His expression was neutral.

A few minutes later, an hour before sunset, Trunk drove the master's glass carriage—*glass* because the windows were glazed—to the front of the house. He hoisted in supplies for the journey and helped Squire Jerrold climb up. That done—because it didn't occur to him to help *me* in—he mounted behind the horses: four of them for speed. Next to him on his bench were his basket of victuals and a jug of ginger sheep's milk.

On the way, we'd stop at inns only to change horses and replenish our provisions. I'd remain in the carriage.

The master took me aside. "If Imbert isn't ill or will live, please don't reveal the truth about Jerro. If he's dying and there's time, yes, do tell him. I don't have to mention that you must keep the secret from everyone else."

Yet he had mentioned it. I nodded. "Of course. Master?

Please write to my mother and say where I've gone and that there's blight there, and she mustn't come, and Wormy mustn't, either." I gave street directions for the letter.

"It will go with the post." He swept me a bow as if I were a great lady and, gently, ceremoniously, handed me in.

Squire Jerrold slumped against the cushions and closed his eyes. We rattled away.

The squire faced forward as his rank deserved, and I rode backward. A coal brazier sat on the floor between us, smoking the air as much as heating it. Next to the brazier rested a basket of fresh coals. Blankets were stacked on the seat beside the squire. Next to me were the bag of carrots and sweet onions I'd requested, a second jug of sheep's milk, and a hamper of the dishes I said would speed Squire Jerrold's recovery: stews and chicken-and-lamb meat pies stuffed with carrots, turnips, garlic, and onion. The vegetables, which would have soured the air, were neutralized by the enormous sack of meat sticks at my feet.

I spread a blanket over Squire Jerrold. "A chill could make you sick again."

His jawline squared—he was clenching his teeth. What definition that gave his face!

When I sat back, he closed his eyes and slept. His lips curled into a smile. Such a look of innocence he had, as if he'd never done a single wrong thing. If the master could be believed, he hadn't.

I chewed dried meat and looked around the grand carriage, which I saw perfectly in the dimness. My girl eyes appreciated the arched ceiling and the violet-and-gold fleur-de-lis pattern painted there and on the walls. A braided rug in pinks, purples, and greens complemented the paint.

The next time Squire Jerrold opened his eyes, I would make myself eat a carrot, for whatever harmlessness the crunch would suggest. I wondered if carrot was his favorite vegetable. We'd be together for days. I could ask. Our courtship could begin with carrots and onions.

My mind turned to our destination. When we arrived in Frell, how would I reach the king despite crowds and guards? I needed a plan, but no ideas came. I rested my free hand on my satchel, which held the jug of purpline.

When the winter sun went down, I applied more perfume and woke Squire Jerrold. "You should eat." This was true, but I also wanted to be just a voice in the dark until he'd grown accustomed to me.

Obediently, he ate stew from a crock. "My grandfather says there's a mystery about you that he couldn't tell me though he tried. He said I shouldn't misjudge you."

I sensed little fear. He did have courage. "I can't tell you, either."

"You could tell him but not me?"

"I didn't tell him. He figured it out."

Now I sensed resentment. Accusingly, he said, "What did you do to him? He seems happier."

"You're not glad?"

"I'm glad!" I didn't sense gladness. "I just want to know what you did."

He had tried to make his grandfather happy, and I—a stranger and an ogre—had succeeded.

I remembered to take a carrot. I used to love their sweetness. I bit in decisively for the sound. Faugh! As quietly as I could, I spit it into the napkin that the vegetables were wrapped in.

How to explain the change in the master without revealing his secret? "He talked about your mother. I think that was a relief. He doesn't to you, because he doesn't want you to be sad. She sounds extraordinary."

He burst out, "Are some ogres good?"

"I'm the only good one, and I have my faults." He might as well be told I wasn't perfect if—at the least—we were to be friends. "I'm always hungry and often angry. I'm furious when people don't listen about their health." I added, hoping to make him laugh, "Or their posture. I hate slumping."

Wormy would have laughed, but Squire Jerrold just looked earnest, his most regular expression, as I was to learn. He said, "I don't slump."

"Your posture is admirable."

I sensed his pleasure in the compliment. On a long

breath I said, "The master told me you wrote in a letter about a hero who came to Frell with six ogre heads."

"Sir Peter."

Peter? My chest felt tight. "A knight? From a noble family?"

"King Imbert knighted him for the feat."

My voice sounded more hoarse than usual as I described my Master Peter. "That man?"

"They sound alike."

My love lived.

I sat back. Oh, joy.

But had the blight taken him? Was he dead again?

The horses were trotting and could go no faster if they were to go far. I wished Lucinda had given me wings.

If he'd had the blight before, he lived. If he hadn't, he might be in the early stages and I'd save him. I'd be so happy if I could save him.

A question reared its head, but I pushed it down and listened to the horses' hooves, the breeze outside, Squire Jerrold's soft breaths. I added coals to the brazier.

Still, the question waylaid me and refused to be ignored. Had Master—Sir—Peter searched for me after he escaped from my band?

If he had, he would have found me searching for him.

Maybe he'd thought me dead, as I'd thought him. He may have been grieving, too.

But I'd had reason to think him killed. He had no such reason.

The next question sprang up. Had he just pretended to love me?

Or had I pretended he did?

No. I'd sensed love. I hadn't been deluded in that.

Did the heads belong to my band, or had he killed six other ogres?

He couldn't have. He'd never declared himself to be a warrior, and nothing about him had suggested he was.

Squire Jerrold said something, but I couldn't pay attention.

How did he get the heads out?

Why did he take them?

That answered itself. To be thought a hero. For gain.

Was he dishonorable?

Oh! Had the love I'd sensed been self-love?

I took a deep breath. Very likely. He'd spoken of touring Kyrria with me, but he'd probably merely wanted me to escort him safely out of the Fens.

I hadn't felt this much shame since becoming an ogre— or ever.

How had I convinced myself anyone would ever propose to me, even if I had a thousand years?

CHAPTER TWENTY-ONE

MY TEARS FLOWED. I sobbed.

Then my anger woke up. If he was still alive when we reached Frell, I'd dine on him.

No. If he was sick, I'd cure him. Sobs broke out again. I quaked with them.

Squire Jerrold shifted on his bench. "Can I help, Mistress Ogre?"

I choked out my name. "Mistress Evie. No. You can't." I hated my love.

Finally, I calmed. "Squire Jerrold, I killed two ogres, and a giant slew the remaining four. I told the master about it." I repeated the story.

"Sir Peter's heads may not belong to the same ogres, Mistress Evie."

At least he called me by my name. "You wrote to the master that they're on display. Where? I would recognize them."

"They're on pikes on the road into Frell."

"For people to gloat over." I'd never pitied my dead band members before.

"They're ogres!" He realized what he'd said. "Apologies. I don't mean *you* should be killed."

"And have my head exhibited."

"Certainly not, but if they were the ones you knew, they were trying to eat a giant."

"They're thinking creatures with speech. They don't show off the skulls of their victims or boast of the numbers they've killed." I didn't mention that they didn't distinguish in kind between, for example, a meal of human and horse.

"You say *they*, not *we*."

Guess the truth, Squire Jerrold. Guess it!

But he just waited for me to answer.

"Because *I* never killed any people." I went on more calmly. "Or elves or giants or gnomes. The only beings I killed were the two ogres." I chewed a meat stick. "I've murdered many fleas."

He smiled, showing the adorable gap in his teeth. "Did you eat them?"

"Too small. Not worth it."

"Do most ogres have a sense of humor?"

"The ones I knew did."

I felt his confusion. "Are you joking?"

"No." I went back to Sir Peter. "How did he say he killed his ogres?"

"He hardly knows me, but I've heard from others that he climbed a tree and watched their movements. Then he set traps."

"They would have smelled him."

"He said he rubbed himself with mint leaves to cover his scent."

"That's silly! Our noses are sensitive, and we know mint doesn't grow on trees. We would have looked up and seen him."

"He could have lied about his method and still have killed them."

How fair he was. And correct. I should delay judging Sir Peter until we knew. "Do you like him?"

He hesitated. "I don't usually speak ill of people—but he's too . . ." He searched for words. "Too good at saying what people want to hear."

People and ogres.

"Especially what the king wants to hear."

That was more troubling than deceiving me.

I said, "You should sleep."

He leaned back, exposing his straight, robust neck.

I tingled. How I hated my treacherous tingle.

He opened a window. My stink! Hastily, I dabbed on perfume.

His breathing evened out. I cried myself to sleep.

In the morning, I woke before Squire Jerrold did. Twenty-three days left. Tomorrow November would begin.

Squire Jerrold's breathing was even deeper than it had been last night, and his skin looked brighter. Again I dabbed the disgusting perfume here and there.

I took stock of myself. No blight symptoms that I could detect.

When Squire Jerrold stirred, I asked to see his fingernails, where the blight bumps had flattened. His eyes, however, were still paler than I liked. He ate well—two meat pies, devoured with his head half out the window despite my perfume.

Afterward, he questioned me about ogres, and I told him what I knew, concealing only that I'd been thought a beautiful mare.

Was Lucinda watching? Did she notice I'd gone on as a healer and hadn't eaten anyone? Did she care about a person's behavior?

Some of Squire Jerrold's questions were beyond my knowledge. Most strange to him was my ignorance about ogre health and ogre diseases. "You're a healer!"

My mouth worked, but the words *I'm not entirely an ogre* wouldn't come out.

"Grandfather looked the same when he tried to tell me about you. Are you both under an enchantment?"

I shrugged, unable to say that I was the enchanted one. If he thought the master and I were both under the same spell, he'd never get to the truth.

"Will the spell harm him?" Considerately, he added, "Harm you both?"

I assured him the master was in no danger. The best I could do to explain my knowledge of healing was to say that most of my patients had been human, which just added to his bewilderment.

He napped when he finished interrogating me. If he let me, it would be my turn next to interrogate him.

When he opened his eyes, breathed deep at the window, stretched athletically—beautifully—I said, "Now may I ask you a few questions?"

"Yes. Of course you can." But he was uneasy.

I began anyway. "What do you do to be honorable?" I had to know if I hoped to love him. This was something I should have asked Master Peter.

"If you don't mind, I don't boast."

I pushed down my irritation. "All the same, please educate this ogre."

He nodded. "I'm courteous to everyone, no matter their rank." His discomfort rose. "I tell the truth, and, truthfully, I hate to talk about myself."

Modesty. Another virtue. Or not. I said, "It's as much a lie to hide virtue as to flaunt it."

I felt his astonishment, either at this idea or at my elegant turn of phrase.

"Would you let me use my ogre persuasion to ask the questions? Then you won't feel embarrassed."

He hadn't been much afraid of me, but now his fear swelled. Yet he said, "Yes, if you promise I'll remember." I must have looked surprised, because he explained. "It may be a useful experience."

How thoughtful and noble he was.

I promised. Meals didn't remember only because they were, well, eaten. I softened my voice. "You don't mind my questions, do you?"

His fear shrank. "No. Not much."

I grew hungrier and took a meat stick. "What else do you do that's honorable?"

A list of virtues followed. He helped the feeble, gave to the poor, listened to people . . .

I yawned.

I wondered what I'd think of him if I were all human. To this half ogre, he was honorable, yes, intelligent, yes, but uninteresting—lovable only because he was edible.

"Do you consider yourself cautious? Or brave?" I asked.

He didn't hesitate. "I hope I'm courageous and not overcautious."

I hadn't said *over*. My healer self couldn't help saying, "*Caution* would have kept you home to recover." Wormy wouldn't have ventured out so soon.

Good manners and zEEn stopped him from arguing. I asked him to continue listing his virtues, and, naturally, he complied. I noticed how gracefully his lips made words.

He did his duty without delay, was kind to his horse and hound, remembered the birthdays of his friends, practiced his fencing and archery even when he preferred to do something else.

"What would you rather do?"

"Sleep an extra hour, just do nothing, play dice, which is a vice, so I never let myself. I played only once, and I liked it too much. I never let myself sleep longer or do nothing, either."

"You must be pleased with yourself for resisting."

"I wouldn't be pleased if I did what I disapprove of." I felt his annoyance. "Isn't that obvious?"

"Yet many people do those things."

"It's their right. I don't think there should be a law against them." He paused. "Maybe there should be a law against dicing or a way to stop people from losing all their money. It's something to think about." He smiled charmingly. "Thank you."

What else did I want to know that I could learn only

by zEEning? Nothing came to mind, so I changed my tone. "I've finished."

Alas, I failed to think of the question that—with or without zEEning—would have yielded the most important information.

"Why are you interested in my honor?"

What to tell him? "The master fondly thinks you perfect." I smiled.

He recoiled at the sight of my fangs.

Hastily, I added, "He seems to be right."

"If I'm good it's because I was taught by example."

"Your grandfather is extraordinarily kind. Not many people would take in an ogre."

We rode in silence, and I pondered love.

My recipe for a love potion called for mashing together periwinkle leaves, marigold petals, leeks, and an earthworm, and then thinning the paste with cherry juice. I'd administered it twice, to good effect, according to my satisfied buyers. What was love, really, if swallowing earthworm pulp could produce it?

CHAPTER TWENTY-TWO

MOTHER SAID she loved Father because of their friendship and her tingle. But my tingle was universal. The more delicious someone looked, the stronger I felt it. Tingle was useless!

ZEEn had enlightened me as thoroughly about the honorable Squire Jerrold as long acquaintance would have. Sir Peter was, by contrast, clever, crafty, amusing, mysterious, indistinct as fog, slippery as wet moss. Alluring.

Wormy, whom I knew best, was sensitive, sweet, sympathetic, kind, thoughtful, loyal, devoted, trustworthy. Impossibly, both helpful and helpless. As amusing as Sir Peter, but more gently so. Nervous, delicate. Always underfoot—until now.

Squire Jerrold asked, "Will everyone in Frell get sick?"

I smiled and remembered to keep my teeth together. "Anybody who hasn't already survived the blight will catch it."

"Will they die?"

"Your grandfather and Trunk lived. I don't know if they were treated with purpline or treated at all. Can you tell me how many healers and physicians ply their skill in Frell?"

He couldn't. Wormy would have known.

What was I to do here, now, in this carriage, with Squire Jerrold?

In the common way of becoming friends, I introduced the subject of books. He liked to read almanacs; I preferred novels and medical tomes. But I smiled and nodded at his preferences, so he'd know I respected them and was open-minded, and, above all, friendly.

Neither of us enjoyed poems, which made me think again of Wormy, who loved them. And Squire Jerrold and I were alike in disdaining fairy tales, upon which I now considered myself an authority. The fairy wasn't always good!

Squire Jerrold answered my questions but didn't expand on them or question me in turn. If he were ever to become king, he'd have to learn the art of conversation.

Or he might know it and not want a long discussion with an ogre.

But I wondered why he wasn't more curious about the oddity that I was, beyond those aspects of ogres that might lead to their defeat.

My amiable expression firmly in place, I moved us on to music, dance, gardening. His lovely, big eyes became bigger when I said I relished performing a galloping gavotte. He said he made a fool of himself if he tried anything quicker than an allemande, and, for music to listen to, he also preferred stateliness. He enjoyed the outdoors for athletic pursuits, not for gardening.

"We both pursue what we value," I said.

"I'm a little tired." He closed his eyes, but his breathing didn't deepen to sleep.

Tired of me, not tired.

If I zEEned him into a proposal, which I accepted, he'd witness my release. As noble as he was, he would stick with it to save me. Heal myself and harm him? I thought about it.

Eventually, he did sleep—and slept through the night.

I imagined my ogre self as a rowboat that held the real me. The shore was humanity, but no matter how hard I rowed, it stayed exactly as distant as it had been thirty-nine days ago, when Lucinda cast her spell.

In the morning—when I had twenty-two days left—Squire Jerrold awoke and I dabbed on fresh perfume, but my nose told me it accomplished little if I didn't bathe first.

He asked me to judge his recovery.

"Hold out your hands."

He did.

"Palms down."

No sign of bumps.

"Open your eyes wide."

Dark brown again. I felt a healer's satisfaction. "I declare you cured."

"Thank you!" He reached past me and pounded on the carriage wall that separated us from Trunk. "I'm sure Trunk would like to come inside a while. He can't sleep soundly behind the horses."

The beasts slowed.

ZEEn him! I might not have another chance. I blurted, "Do you like me?"

He blushed, and I felt his embarrassment.

I plowed on. "If I were—" Would Lucinda let me say it? No. *Human* wouldn't come out. "If I were . . . an elf, for example, might we be friends?"

The embarrassment lessened. "You saved my life!

I'm grateful." He thought about it. "You brought cheer to Grandfather. If I'm ever sick again, I'll come to you." He turned to the window and breathed deeply. "We *are* friends."

Do it!

The carriage stopped, and a moment later he went out and took my tingle with him.

Trunk came in. "Good morning, Mistress Ogre." He leaned back with his head near the window.

I tingled again, but faintly.

A moment later, he snored, which quieted my tingle even more. He continued snoring all morning and half the afternoon. I devoured many meat sticks so I wouldn't eat him to stop the sound.

When he awoke, he felt it his duty to take back the driving. Squire Jerrold didn't return, however. I remained alone. Both must have preferred napping on the bench to my stink.

I wondered how Wormy would act if he were here. Would he endure my smell for the sake of my company? Would he even like it because it was mine?

No one could.

Did he still love me?

Two afternoons later, I developed a headache and dosed myself with oilybur. The headache receded, but I felt dull and low in spirits. Listlessly, I watched the landscape through the window. The low autumn sun glimmered through clouds. Two dun horses grazed among leafless trees. Nothing bright or cheery.

Forty-two and a half days wasted, nineteen and a half left, the end of possibility approaching.

If I'd had the energy, I would have sat up. Today was my birthday, November 3.

I'd never had a terrible birthday before. Mother and Wormy always made a fuss.

Last year, I'd awakened to discover that a fall snowstorm had left six inches. After Wormy came, bundled and mittened against the cold, and after the three of us shared Mother's raisin pudding, he and I had gone to Rushy Square to make snow people.

Not your customary pile of three precariously balanced balls, though. Ours had to be realistic. And, in honor of my birthday, each had to illustrate a medical condition.

Wormy was the artist and I the scientist. I knew where the bones and muscles were, and he knew how to make the figures pleasing.

We made two, both male, one with a dowager's hump, because men get them, too, and one with a wooden leg. We made the humpback wealthy, with the hump straining the cloth of his (snow) jacket. The ruffles in his cravat were Wormy's crowning achievement. The peg-leg snow-man was a laborer, with a rough coverall shirt and trousers rather than our gentleman's breeches. Both wore spatter-dashes to keep their feet and legs dry, but, naturally, our toiler needed only one. We spent half an hour searching for the perfect branch to be his wooden leg.

After we admired our creations, I inscribed *Healer* in the snow and below it my name and address. Wormy would never have taken credit, but I also wrote *Artist* with Wormy's name below.

When we returned to Mother, she served us steaming cider. It may have been the best birthday I'd ever have.

I wept weakly at the memory and used my melancholy to explain how tired I felt. I should have noticed my chill, but I just sidled close to the coal brazier and spread another blanket over myself before falling into a restless sleep.

In the morning, I tried to reach for a meat stick but my hand was too heavy. And I had no appetite anyway.

This was more than sadness.

I managed to raise my thumb. The fingernail had three pronounced bumps. Ogres could catch barley blight—or *I* could.

"Squire Jerrold!" My voice was so hoarse I could hardly hear it. I had no strength to bang on the wall.

I closed my eyes and wondered how quickly I'd die.

With nineteen days left.

If I weren't a stinking ogre, Squire Jerrold would have been here to dose me.

My chest was so tight I could barely breathe. After a minute, I lost the strength to remain seated and slid to the floor of the coach.

Would my corpse be human?

My mind faded out.

CHAPTER TWENTY-THREE

I WOKE UP. The carriage wasn't moving. My throat stung.

Trunk leaned over me. "Mistress Ogre?"

"Yes?" I opened my eyes. Beyond Trunk's shoulder, I saw Squire Jerrold's worried face. I sensed fear from them both, fear *for* me, I thought, not *of* me. "Did you dose me with purpline?"

Trunk's expression cleared. Satisfaction replaced fright. "We don't have tea, but I dripped four drops right down your throat."

Brave! He'd inserted his fingers beyond my fangs.

He added, "Four because you're so big."

"Thank you." I hoisted myself back on the bench and then breathed hard, but, once established, I ate a meat stick—my appetite proof of returning health. "How did you know something was amiss?"

They hadn't. Trunk's jug of sheep's milk had run out.

"Mistress Ogre, when the squire saw your poor fingernails, we knew."

I checked my hands. The bumps were still prominent. "You could be a healer, Trunk."

"I believe I could be." His pleasure threatened to burst the carriage apart at the seams. "It's like cooking. You have to know your ingredients."

I smiled. That was part of it.

Squire Jerrold said, "We're about an hour from Frell."

My hands chilled from fright, not illness. My throat tightened. Even another meat stick didn't quiet my stomach.

I must have looked bad again, because the two watched me anxiously.

Only hatred would greet me in town. How many arrows would it take to finish me off? Or would I be killed by a sword or a knife?

"If people attack me, take my satchel with the purpline. Don't defend me. If we're all dead, no one will be cured."

Admiration for me engulfed Squire Jerrold.

ZEEn him into proposing now, I thought.

I said, "If the outbreak is bad, you'll run out of purpline." Hurriedly, I described my other remedies.

They nodded and left me. The carriage started again. I looked out the window. Clouds scudded across other clouds in a brisk wind.

After a while, I checked my fingers again and discovered that the bumps had almost flattened. I felt fine.

- Ogres are excellent at recovery.

The road became lined with a decorative wrought-iron fence in a pattern of flowers, frogs, and large leaves. Along the top were spikes. We were approaching Frell, but the way was empty of traffic.

Soon we crossed a bridge. On the other side, on a wooden stake planted in the ground, was the *BB* sign—*barley blight*—lettered in green paint.

Perhaps ten minutes later, the carriage stopped, though we hadn't reached the castle.

Oh! Faces I knew topped the fence spikes, three heads on each side of the road. I swallowed convulsively as I jumped out of the carriage.

SSahlOO, whose last sight was me, wore an eager expression.

AAng had died snarling.

"I pulled that one," I told Squire Jerrold and Trunk, pointing at the gap in the line of fangs.

"You knew them?" Trunk said.

"I killed these two." I pointed. "This one had a toothache. Her name was AAng."

"They have names?" Squire Jerrold said.

"I have a name!" I named the others.

Squire Jerrold said, "Sir Peter lied about killing them. We have to tell King Imbert."

If he lived. "The king won't believe us," I said flatly. "No one will."

I lifted the heads off the pikes and set them on the ground. We had no time to bury them, though that didn't matter. Ogres didn't have rites. I climbed back in the carriage. Squire Jerrold followed me in and opened the window. Unwillingly, I tingled.

And thought about Sir Peter. Lying to the king was serious, especially since King Imbert had knighted him for valor. But lying itself wasn't much of a crime. Sir Peter hadn't killed anyone, and the heads had once been attached to ogres. This was the act of a rogue more than a complete villain—though he might be that, too.

If he still lived, he could be a threat to me for knowing the truth and to Squire Jerrold and Trunk simply for being my companions.

We galloped through the city gates. Squire Jerrold kindly named the streets as we careered along them: Progress to Merit to Larkspur to Eastview. The only other vehicle on the road, a two-horse carriage, trotted toward us and passed by. Few people were out. The attack on me that I'd expected wouldn't occur. The barley blight had progressed too far.

A figure slumped in a doorway. Dead? We zipped by.

A woman, seemingly healthy, leaned into the wind, bent on some purpose. A man pushed a wheelbarrow piled with corpses. My wicked stomach growled.

The carriage entered a roundabout and took the first right-hand street.

"Peaceable Road," Squire Jerrold announced. "The highway to the castle."

I fought my fright. "Where will we find the king?"

"Sir Stephan—my patron—says he's usually in the great hall unless he's dining. Or he could be in the library or in one of his drawing rooms. At night, he's in his apartment." He burst out, "Let him still *be* somewhere, alive!"

Yes.

The drawbridge was down. We clattered across. Trunk reined in the horses before the castle entry arch, which was unguarded. No grooms came running.

I took my satchel and jumped out. We hastened under the arch. Trunk opened carved double doors into a vast receiving room. The doors swung closed behind us. The castle clock chimed three times. Three in the afternoon.

Squire Jerrold and Trunk stopped. Except for a faint glow from a window at the top of a long and grand stairway, we were in darkness. No one had lit the candles in the many-armed chandelier. The fireplaces had all burned down to ashes.

"Ogres see perfectly in the dark. Follow me." They'd be able to make out my shape in the gloom, but castle folk, unless they had a torch, wouldn't see clearly enough to tell what I was. I started up the stairs.

A woman lay on the first landing. I bent over her.

"No time! The king!" Squire Jerrold tugged me away.

I felt his touch in the pit of my belly and all the way down to my toes.

We continued up the stairs. A carved and gilded door opened into the great hall, where light flooded in from a wall of windows.

Perhaps a dozen people sprawled unmoving on sofas and chairs, islands on a sea of carpeting. I didn't smell decay. If some were dead, they'd died recently.

I rushed to the closest person, a man in a high-backed chair, his head flopped back, mouth agape. Not the king, whose face I knew from our coins. This man's chest hardly rose.

Somewhere in here a woman was sobbing.

All healer, the Evie I'd always been, my hands were steady. I pulled out my jug and let three careful drops fall into the back of the man's throat. His next breath was deeper.

I straightened. Squire Jerrold was dashing from figure to figure. The next person I reached, collapsed across a couch, was past saving.

Equidistant from me, an old woman sat stiffly on a straight-backed chair and a woman sobbed into the knees of a man on a yellow sofa. I chose to go to them.

When she looked up, the woman—not much older than I and more beautiful than I'd ever been—reminded me by her terrified face of what I was.

Oh! My knees weakened. The man, in a green silk waistcoat, was Sir Peter, barely alive but still handsome and still able to squeeze my heart.

The young woman draped herself across him. "You can't eat him!" Her voice trembled. "Or me."

He'd made another conquest.

He hadn't been grieving me.

"Please move aside."

"I won't!" Then, "*Please*'? Is that your persuasion?" She stood away.

Had he duped her as he had me? I dripped in the purpline. "He may sleep awhile, but he'll get well, Mistress." I hurried on to the old dame, who died as I reached her.

Squire Jerrold cried, "The king isn't here! Come, Mistress Evie!"

How could I leave everyone?

Plates and teacups rested on several tables. I called

to Trunk, who stood in the middle of the floor, gaping around the hall.

Squire Jerrold shouted, "Mistress Evie!"

When Trunk reached me, I dumped the contents of a teacup on the carpet.

He gasped. "You stained the rug!"

I poured half an inch of purpline into the cup. "Three drops each. Don't waste any. Save what's left."

"Mistress Evie!"

Squire Jerrold and I left the light for a murky corridor.

"Third door on the left."

The chamber was the library, also window-lit. I ran through the stacks on the left, Squire Jerrold through those on the right. No one rummaged for books or sat in the armchairs under the windows.

When Squire Jerrold and I left, we discovered the young woman who'd been with Sir Peter waiting for us.

"Lady Eleanor!" Squire Jerrold said. "Is the king alive?"

A lady? Could she be Sir Peter's *wife*?

In the Fens, had he been married?

She didn't know about King Imbert's health, but she thought he was either in the red drawing room or the dining room. We pelted through endless corridors to get to the closer room, the red drawing room.

As we ran, Lady Eleanor said in a puffing undertone,

"You're . . . you're . . ."

I looked at her to see if she was all right.

Her face was strained. "A fairy—" She tried again. "My uncle—" She gave up and fell silent.

Something had been done to her uncle, probably by Lucinda. She knew what had happened to me.

We reached the red drawing room. While Squire Jerrold and Lady Eleanor went from one figure to another, I dripped purpline into the mouths of two and passed by one who had succumbed.

King Imbert wasn't in either this chamber or the dining room. We entered chamber after chamber. I dosed as many as I could while the two of them searched.

Moments stood out.

A man shouted at a corpse to sit up.

Two people had died folded into each other in an embrace.

A woman sang to a child in her lap, whom I was able to save.

A cat had died with a mouse in its mouth. In death, the cat's jaw still clasped its prey. The mouse's feet scrambled in the air. I pulled out the mouse and swallowed it whole.

In a small parlor, a young man bent over a middle-aged woman, trying to force her to drink broth.

"Sir Stephan!" Squire Jerrold ran to the man.

195

I remembered the name. This was Squire Jerrold's knight.

"When all fails, Jerrold, try broth."

Squire Jerrold stooped down. "I'm sorry, Sir Stephan. She's dead."

The knight broke into sobs. Squire Jerrold stood helplessly for a moment. Then we left for other chambers.

Finally, before climbing to the servants' quarters, we entered the castle kitchen, where the king lay spread-eagled on the floor, surrounded by pottery shards, his cloak and neck wet, doused, by the smell of it, with broth.

We crouched over him. I felt a wisp of breath. "Prop him up!"

They both did, getting in each other's way. I pinched his mouth open and dosed him. His breathing continued, unchanged. Had we come too late?

Finally, after an agonizing minute, his chest rose so high that even Squire Jerrold and Lady Eleanor saw.

"Will he recover?" Lady Eleanor asked.

"I don't know. He's been weakened, and I see he wasn't robust before." He was almost as thin as Trunk had been. "He needs to rest. I have herbs to help him sleep soundly."

As if to prove his wakefulness, King Imbert opened his eyes and smiled weakly at Lady Eleanor. "Did I die?" He saw me. The smile vanished. "I must have."

She said, "Oh, no, Sire. She's a healer ogre. She saved you."

I heard footsteps behind us.

The king's gaze lifted above my shoulder. His smile returned. "Peter! My boy! Are we alive? I'll believe *you*."

CHAPTER TWENTY-FOUR

I HAD BEEN CONCENTRATING too hard on the king to sense Sir Peter's approach. He leaned on the big worktable for support.

How would he greet me?

I hoped no one noticed I was trembling.

And tingling.

He bowed to Lady Eleanor, a half bow because of weakness. When his head came up, he smiled at her—the same loving smile he'd once beamed at me.

She blushed.

I gripped the purpline jug hard enough, seemingly, to soften the metal. I imagined slamming it into his smile.

His eyes moved on. For me and Squire Jerrold, he had an equable nod—as if I were any healer and neither an

198

ogre nor someone he'd romanced.

Did he believe I'd understand he had to behave this way in this circumstance and that he loved not the comely Lady Eleanor, but me, who'd first claimed his heart?

I gripped my common sense. I wasn't an idiot!

He turned to the king, and his smile blazed again. "Majesty! Indeed, all of us are alive. How happy I am to find you awake and yourself again."

"As I am to see you." He waved his hand feebly in front of his nose. "What is that?"

My odor.

After a moment, he added, "Have many died?"

None of us knew. Squire Jerrold volunteered to collect information.

I curtsied. "Sire, I'll make a tea with herbs to help restore you." I crossed the room, stirred up the embers in the stove, added wood, and filled a kettle and placed it on the stove, a newfangled one, such as the master had.

Lady Eleanor told the king that I'd also saved Sir Peter and others. "Mistress Evie is the hero of Frell."

I couldn't hate her.

I found cups in an open cabinet, took one and, on second thought, another. Evidently, I couldn't yet hate Sir Peter, either. Into both mugs, I spooned the same herbs from my carpetbag.

Squire Jerrold coughed. "The hero of Kyrria and Frell."

"How did she save us? What was the remedy?"

Squire Jerrold said, "Purpline."

"That's dragon urine, isn't it?" The king's face reddened alarmingly. *"Urine!"*

Hoping to improve matters, I said, "You've probably had it before, Your Highness. When it's available, healers put it in physics and tonics."

King Imbert was unappeased. "That I've had it unknowingly doesn't comfort me. Sir Titus would have found another way to cure me. Does anyone know if he's all right? I'd like his opinion."

Rather than an ogre's.

The kettle whistled. I poured the tea and let it steep.

Trunk came in. "I used up the purpli—" He saw the king. "Oh! Oh! He's alive. Beg pardon. Long live the king!" He bowed.

Lady Eleanor said, "I don't know where Sir Titus is. Begging your pardon, Your Majesty, I didn't see him dashing from chamber to chamber as Mistress Evie did, restoring people to life."

Sir Peter said smoothly, "If she saved only you, Sire, we'd be in her debt forever."

In that case, he wouldn't be in anyone's debt. He'd be dead.

King Imbert seemed to like flattery (as I had, too). "Thank you, Peter, but a monarch needs subjects. I'm grateful to you"—he took in my dress—"er, Mistress Ogre."

I curtsied. "Evie. Mistress Evie."

King Imbert waved his hands across his nose again.

"Shall I open a window?" Squire Jerrold asked. "Will that be safe, Mistress Evie?"

I knew he wanted the answer to be yes for his own sake. "If we start a fire."

Squire Jerrold cranked open two casements, then added logs and kindling to the fireplace, while Sir Peter did nothing to help. I judged the tea ready and carried mugs to him and the king.

King Imbert hesitated.

Sir Peter drank. He tilted his head appraisingly. "Fenuce, ginger, camphor. You'll taste the camphor first, Sire. Sharp but not impossible. Any more ingredients, Mistress Evie?"

He had discernment, one of the compliments he'd paid me. "Mugwort, which elf healers use. Majesty, the ingredients will strengthen you and increase your appetite."

Trunk recounted how he'd been Twig before I'd intervened. "Mistress Ogre, should the king drink ginger sheep's milk, too? Your Highness, that's what she dosed me with."

King Imbert looked amused.

"When His Majesty is more recovered," I said, "sheep's

milk will benefit him greatly."

The king sipped his tea. "If anyone sees Sir Titus, please send him to me."

I left the kitchen to treat others.

While I was gone, the king was helped to his bed-chamber, as Trunk told me later. When I returned, I commandeered a corner of the enormous kitchen as my infirmary. Trunk kept broth and tea hot for my patients and cooked roasts for me. The castle cook and both her undercooks had died, so he was also preparing food for everyone, assisted by three kitchen maids.

Squire Jerrold and his knight, Sir Stephan, and others brought the afflicted to me. Servants carried in mattresses and blankets. Several stayed to watch me work. People couldn't have failed to notice that I was an ogre, but no one seemed to care—except that the corpses were carried away immediately, before, as my onlookers may have feared, I could eat them.

My supply of purpline ran out in two days, and making patients better became slow and uncertain.

My almost constant companion was Lady Eleanor, the only child of the duke and duchess of Evesby. Lady Eleanor didn't let rank get in the way of being useful. If I needed a hot compress, she had it. If a patient shivered, she fetched another blanket. After a patient died—one I'd thought would live—she saw my distress and, with no disgust that

I could detect, stroked my arm. I never saw her wave her hand in front of her nose.

When she'd gone that first night, I asked Trunk if he could find out whether or not she and Sir Peter were wed.

He left the kitchen and returned a few minutes later. "I asked two chambermaids, and they didn't mind telling me that Sir Peter is a single gentleman." He chuckled. "One said, 'Sir Peter calls my spirit *sweet.*'"

As he'd called mine.

CHAPTER TWENTY-FIVE

"THEY BOTH want to be Mrs. Sir Peter, so they'd know if the position was already filled."

Sir Peter was certainly a rogue who wouldn't want a chambermaid unless she had something else he desired. He'd flattered an ogre to save his life, but he might truly love the beautiful and worthy Lady Eleanor.

Once, she whispered to me, "You're my second favorite being in the castle."

For the first two nights, both Trunk and I bedded down in the kitchen, along with my patients. Somehow I remembered, even in sleep, not to snuggle against anyone.

For the convalescents, I had Trunk brew recovery tea, which contained my secret ingredient: cat saliva tempered by cinnamon and honey. (Luckily, the many castle cats could be induced to contribute.) When I'd been human, I hadn't minded drinking the tea myself. Now I couldn't have choked it down—because of the cinnamon and the honey.

Whenever someone came to help, Trunk asked about Squire Jerrold's doings. Then he'd interrupt the speaker's narration to call, "Did you hear that, Mistress Ogre? Our squire's a fine one, isn't he?"

Yes, a fine one. Squire Jerrold dug graves, attended funerals, watched children who no longer had parents, even fed the pets of the stricken. And, every day, like clockwork, he visited us, though he never stayed long or said much.

Whenever he left, my excitement at the visit would take an hour to quiet.

I could have asked to speak privately with him and zEEned him into a proposal. But I didn't. I reasoned I could wait until the last day and still do it if I had to.

Yes, I honored him. He deserved to be our acknowledged prince. But—tingle aside—he made me sleepy.

During our first week at the castle, while my remaining days diminished to eleven, the tide of new blight patients also dwindled, then ceased, but I still had my recovering people to care for.

On the third night I bedded down with the castle pigs, who were as willing to accommodate me as the master's had been. Here, too, I bathed in the morning before going indoors.

By the end of the week King Imbert, through a servant, invited Trunk to continue as royal chef until a replacement could be found. Though he yearned to return to the master, he considered it his duty to stay.

Since the servant had no message for me, I decided to remain at the castle until I was expelled. I wrote to Mother. *My fingers are awkward with a pen, but I'm well. You are not to worry about me.* I didn't mention Sir Peter or the king's distrust or my lack of marriage prospects. Instead I told her about the blight and using up the purpline. *People realize I cured them, and they're grateful. When I'm established, I hope you'll come. But not yet, if you please.* Though I longed for her.

Not much of a letter, so I added details about my cases, as I would have if we'd been talking at home. *After they'd recovered from the blight, I dosed a boy out of his stutter and cured a woman's catarrh. She said, "I'm throwing away my handkerchiefs, Mistress Ogre."* Mistress Ogre *is what they call me. I'm learning not to mind.*

Trunk, who was as good as a gazette, said he'd be able to post the letter, because the *BB* sign had been taken down. Traffic had begun to enter Frell again. He added in a whisper, "They found those ogre heads on the ground. I'm sorry, Mistress Ogre, but they're back on the pikes."

Whenever SSahlOO had bested EEnth, he'd told me, exulting made his victory tastier. My gorge rose. When humans gloated, we were no better.

He went on. "Folks guess it was you who took them down."

This marked the beginning of the general mistrust of me, now that I wasn't saving people from death every few minutes. Whenever I left the apothecary, castle folk looked away and even flattened themselves against the walls as I passed by.

Twice a day, I braved the corridors to bring recovery tea and fortifying meals (including ginger sheep's milk) to King Imbert. I wanted the king not merely well, but improved—stronger, plumper, more youthful.

I would have sent someone else if not for Lady Eleanor, who urged me to go. "Let the king grow accustomed to you. Let his subjects see you entering and leaving his chamber with no harm to anyone."

I was almost grateful to Lucinda for having changed me, because otherwise I wouldn't have found such a friend.

Not that King Imbert did get used to me. Servants rushed to open windows as soon as I entered, and the king himself wrinkled his nose.

I supposed good manners didn't apply to a king's dealings with ogres.

Whenever I visited him, there at his side was Sir Peter, whose manners were all one would wish for from an honorable person—and exactly what one would expect from a scoundrel. He bowed, he smiled, and he never wrinkled his nose.

My mind would groan, but my heart would warble.

King Imbert hung on his every word, every gesture. When Sir Peter stood up or crossed the room, the king's eyes followed him.

If Lady Eleanor came with me, Sir Peter's smile for her was tender enough to soften stone. He'd leave the king to take her hands in his and murmur something in her ear that would make her laugh or nod emphatically.

His affection seemed sincere, but I'd been the victim of his false sincerity. Still, he had the sense to recognize Lady Eleanor's worth. Might his heart have been captured? Might her goodness reform him?

I found out.

Five days after my arrival at the castle, when I left King Imbert, Sir Peter followed me into the corridor. Lady Eleanor wasn't with me.

"Mistress Evie . . ."

I felt his rich voice from my scalp to my toes.

He smiled his charming smile. I sensed his fear and his attempt at courage.

He went on. "I have you to thank."

"For supplying the heads that won you a title?"

He nodded. "That . . . and for educating me in the ways of ogres. Not in your ways. You're still a mystery."

There was the flattery.

"How did you get out of the Fens and take the heads, too?"

I sensed his pleasure. He was yearning to crow over the escapade.

"Your band was afraid to eat me in case you came back. They debated in Ogrese, but their gestures were eloquent. They let me live and took me with them when they went hunting. I knew it would be the end of me if you didn't return, so when they started on the giant—"

"Did you even try to help her?"

He raised his eyebrows in mock surprise. "A human against six ogres? No. I slipped away and hadn't gone far when I heard you rushing along. I tiptoed back—rash, but I trusted you."

My mad mind whispered, Trust is a sign of love, isn't it?

"When you and the giant had killed the ogres, I hastened away again. That was the most dangerous time. Luckily, the other bands were off hunting."

He'd known I was alive all along.

"I didn't want to waste the heads"—he grinned, proud of his cleverness—"so I returned with a party of gnomes, whom I met on the road."

The only creatures other than dragons that were too tough to eat.

"They helped me in exchange for the dragon fang. With their mining tools, severing heads is quick."

Ugh!

"I may soon be able to be useful to you."

"I need your services?"

"You will. Some still trust you, but many don't, and the favorable memories of those who do will fade."

I'd continue to heal them! They'd have new memories.

"Some healers and physicians must have survived." He had thought this through. "More will come. I hate to cause you pain, but people will prefer them."

I felt him enjoying himself.

"My fortunes seem to be on the rise. You'll do well to ally yourself with me."

"And not well if I don't? I could have let you die of the blight!"

"I'm also grateful you didn't. Lady Eleanor thinks that you would make an excellent court physician. If you were—"

"Do you really care for her?"

"She's beautiful, isn't she?"

"But do you care for her?" Using zEEn, I added, "Of all creatures, you can be frank with me."

He relaxed. "I became a merchant for the sake of beauty—and to become rich. I adore Lady Eleanor's outer perfection, which I'd love even if she were as unintelligent as a worm and as unpleasant as a wasp. I'm fond of her family's position and their money. I don't care about anyone's goodness. I made her love me." He smiled. "As I made you."

I curled my toes to stop myself from springing on him.

He held up a hand. "It's pleasant to speculate like this. I believe your nature, meaning your toughness and loyalty, if they could be inserted into her beauty, might bring me to the brink of love and over the edge. We'll never know."

My jaw hung loose. He couldn't lie while he was zEEned.

"But since she can't be an amalgam of both of you, I'm glad her nature is sweet and her brain excellent—they're likely to be helpful, too."

How far would he go? "Would you kill her or have her killed, if that served you?"

He thought about the question as if it were a puzzle. "I surprise myself. I wouldn't kill a person or cause a person to be killed. I don't even enjoy using my kind of persuasion to deprive people—like the king and Eleanor—of their ability to choose."

Ogres, too, robbed thinking creatures of choice.

"I do so only to advance myself." He laughed. "There

seem to be specks of goodness in my heart. But not enough to extend to an ogre. If you happen to die and I happen to have a hand in it, I won't be troubled."

I abandoned zEEn. "I can dine on you anytime, regardless of how much His Majesty likes you."

"You won't. You're too virtuous."

I raised my eyebrows and my hairy forehead. And made my mistake. "I'm very virtuous, so believe that I'll eat you if you're going to hurt Kyrria."

His fear blew back in. He bowed and returned to the king.

I felt a moment of satisfaction, followed by alarm. I'd made him my enemy.

And he was right that I'd never kill him.

CHAPTER TWENTY-SIX

AT HIS NEXT VISIT—on my fiftieth day as an ogre—I drew Squire Jerrold aside and told him about the conversation.

"I'm sorry for Lady Eleanor," he whispered when I finished. "A friend of mine, who is an intimate acquaintance of hers, will be distressed."

What friend? "You mustn't tell anyone!"

"I won't. I promise." After a pause, he added, "Trying to bribe you was wrong."

I didn't say, *What about threatening my life? Don't you care about that?* "I'm worried about you and Trunk, because you both know me and came to Frell with me."

He said, "You cured King Imbert, and we brought you here to do so. That will keep us all safe."

It wouldn't. However, he was too honorable and, though I hated to think it, not imaginative enough to understand Sir Peter's character.

I wanted to tell Lady Eleanor the truth about her beloved but equally didn't want to be the one to break her heart. She might discover his falseness from some other source, or he might find a wealthier or more noble maiden to bedazzle.

Trunk, who had taken mightily to Lady Eleanor, opined that she'd be the making of Sir Peter. "He won't dare lie again for fear of disappointing her."

If only Wormy were here! He'd advise me. Or, if he had no good ideas, he'd sympathize.

Horrible to be unique and alone.

By the ninth morning after my arrival—nine days left!—a mere two patients remained on their pallets in the kitchen apothecary and four others were recovering in their chambers.

Trunk announced that a third of the castle's two hundred residents—courtiers and servants—had died of the blight, most of the deaths before I came. "Because of you, Mistress Ogre, the castle still has a lot of people." He set two kitchen maids to peeling carrots and a third to sweeping and tending the fire.

I said that most of the credit belonged to the purpline.

"And who brought that?" Lady Eleanor asked, crushing

fenuce leaves in a mortar, as I'd shown her.

Squire Jerrold came in.

My tingling fingers dropped the dried coweye daisies I'd been holding. Gallant as he was, Squire Jerrold picked them up and put them on my worktable. I curtsied as daintily as I could.

Lady Eleanor was watching me. I saw her pity.

Save it for yourself, I thought angrily.

While I stripped the coweye leaves, I said, "Coweyes in a sachet under the pillow bring calming dreams."

Such a timid knock came on the door that I was the only one to hear it. I went to answer it.

Wormy stood in the corridor, holding his hat by the brim. "Evie?"

"Wormy!" I tingled.

He seemed surprised, too. His eyes twitched. He was feeling something strongly, but I couldn't tell what because of the people in the kitchen. "It's just that I didn't expect you, yourself, to open the door."

"Is Mother all right? No one in Jenn caught the blight?" I couldn't help smiling. And with him, I didn't have to hide my fangs.

He smiled back. "No. I mean, yes, she's all right. No one caught it. I'm glad you're safe."

I pulled the door wide. He bowed to everyone, including Trunk, the kitchen maids, and the convalescents.

His bow was smooth, springy. Had I never noticed? When he straightened, his weight rested on his back leg, as if he were about to begin swordplay. And he had taken to heart my frequent refrain—*shoulders back!*—because he stood erect.

"I am Lady Eleanor." She curtsied and looked at me—a hint of a look.

Oh! I introduced him to everyone. "Master Warwick—Wormy—is my friend from Jenn."

Lady Eleanor curtsied. Squire Jerrold bowed. Trunk bobbed and touched his head in a salute.

How comely these people were, especially Squire Jerrold, Lady Eleanor, and Wormy.

Lady Eleanor said, "I'm Mistress Evie's friend in Frell." She touched my arm, and it jumped an inch as a fresh tingle ran through me.

Could I be in love with them all, including Lady Eleanor? Half swooning with hunger and feeling, I imagined a chorus of marriage proposals and my ecstatic cry. *Yes! Yes! Oh, yes! Ah, yes! Come closer, yes!*

To quiet myself, I reached for a leg of the goose Trunk had taken off the spit half an hour before. I'd already eaten the breasts. When my thoughts became civilized again, I was able to listen to the conversation.

Lady Eleanor had been questioning Wormy about his journey.

216

He said, "A farmer was kind enough to shelter me until the *BB* sign was taken down. Now I must find lodgings in town."

The farmer would have been well paid. "Wormy is generous," I said while chewing, glad to boast about my friend. "Lady Eleanor, he keeps his family's ledgers. Squire Jerrold, numbers turn cartwheels for him. If you need his help, he's most obliging. Wormy, dear, what will your parents do without you?" Oh! "But you may be hurrying home before you're missed." He may have come as a favor to Mother—

—and not to propose again.

He bowed to me, acknowledging the compliments and surprising me by the formality. In the gesture, he reminded me of the young man I'd watched through the window at the master's manor.

He said, "I'm not sure how long I'll stay."

What did it depend on?

At least he hadn't become a rock of certainty. He *might* stay. In this one way he was still my Wormy.

"Squire Jerrold," I said, "you're never ill—except for the barley blight—but Wormy has benefitted from all my remedies." Now I seemed to want to boast about myself.

"I'm better for them," Wormy said stoutly.

"What was the last malady before I—" I couldn't finish the sentence.

He coughed.

"You have a cough?" I dropped the gnawed bone on the platter that held what remained of the goose. Then I pumped water into the basin in the sink and scrubbed my hands. "I have elecampane. It will just—"

He coughed again. "I'm fine."

I dried my hands and didn't reach for the elecampane, but if he kept coughing, I'd insist.

Lady Eleanor said, "I hope you'll stay until Friday."

Just five days away. I hoped he'd stay longer!

She produced two creamy envelopes from her apron pocket and gave one to me and one to Squire Jerrold. "Now that health has returned to Frell, my parents are hosting a ball and, afterward, a supper. Mistress Evie, you'll be the guest of honor. . . ."

I didn't hear her next words. An ogre honored at a ball?

Might that protect me from Sir Peter?

Or had he suggested it?

Would he spring a trap?

What could I wear?

CHAPTER TWENTY-SEVEN

WORMY THANKED LADY ELEANOR. "I'll certainly stay and hope Evie and you will spare me a dance."

"Of course." I doubted I'd have to *spare* him one. "Thank you."

As a human, I could dance decently well. Wormy, who'd learned from a dancing master, had taught me. Would I still be able to?

He said, "Thank *you*."

Dutiful Squire Jerrold asked me for a dance, too.

"A slow allemande," I said, remembering our conversation in the carriage.

"Oho!" Trunk said. "The courtship dance!"

It was so called because couples stayed together more than in other dances.

Wormy frowned.

Squire Jerrold waved his hand in front of his nose, though I'd bathed an hour earlier. "An allemande," he said. "Or something else will also do."

"As long as it's with the guest of honor." Lady Eleanor beamed at me.

I wondered if Wormy might learn to admire her. She'd soon notice how much kinder, sweeter, and more genuinely sympathetic he was than Sir Peter. They were both wealthy. Their parents would approve the match.

How strange it would be to see Wormy the doting husband.

Squire Jerrold bowed and left.

Wormy turned to me. "I had a headache for two weeks in Jenn. No one could cure it."

Really? Every healer was equal to a headache.

"I woke up with it again today. If you have a moment . . . If you aren't too pressed by other patients . . ."

Had he come to Frell just for me to cure a headache? A rocking chair idled by the fireplace. I pulled it to the worktable. "Sit."

Lady Eleanor's eyebrows rose.

"Er, if you please." I opened my clay pot of honey balm. When I dabbed the salve on Wormy's temples, a spark leaped from my fingertips to my chest.

Wormy's shoulders trembled. Was he afraid?

"Lady Eleanor, would you rub the balm in for me? I should start my recovery tea. It's delicate."

Lady Eleanor took the pot from my hand, and, when her fingers touched mine, I felt a lesser spark. She didn't seem to notice.

"Evie, I'll wait until you can do it. Lady Eleanor, she knows exactly where to press."

How like Wormy that was. I frightened him, but he cared more that his headache be properly treated.

Lady Eleanor pretended to be affronted, but she was laughing. "Old comforts can't be supplanted by new fingers." Then she suggested lodgings for him, a family with rooms to let. "I'll write a letter of introduction."

How comforting to have him in Frell, he who saw me in the old good way as well as the horrible new. I finished mixing the recovery tea and applied myself, despite the tingling, to his headache.

How would he occupy himself here? He was too delicate to dig graves with Squire Jerrold, but perhaps he could help with the squire's many other acts of kindness.

I wished the two of them could be combined. Both were honorable. One had energy and resolve, the other warmth, humor, and sympathy.

But this perfect blend wouldn't propose, either.

"There, Wormy." I stepped away. "Is it better?"

"It's gone!"

Why was Lady Eleanor smiling?

He opened the purse at his waist and produced a copper KI, my usual headache fee. No one else here had paid me, and I hadn't asked.

I took it. "I'll brew some darkroot tea to keep it from coming back." I shaved four slivers from my knob of root into a mug and poured ginger tea over them. "Let it steep for a few minutes." I gave it to him, careful to keep our fingers from touching.

"Will it taste bad?"

How I'd missed him! "You'll like it."

Lady Eleanor ground pepper and bonny-jump-up leaves in my mortar. While he butchered a side of beef, Trunk warbled a ditty about a cat and a butterfly. I rolled dough for pill casings that would hold a dollop of remedy.

Finally, I nodded at Wormy, and he drank.

How pleasant this was. Healing work. My three friends. The company of the kitchen maids too, who, unlike the castle's other inhabitants, were used to me enough to chat among themselves and rarely glance my way.

When my dough was thin enough, I cut it into circles. Next I dabbed on the medicine and enclosed it in pastry, which I patted onto a greased pan for Trunk to bake. "Half an hour will do. I have patients to visit."

Wormy drained his tea. "May I come?" When he

stood, the rocking chair went over backward.

I was eager, too. Was he planning to propose? What would I say?

At least, if we were alone, I'd know his feelings.

If only I knew my own. If only I could zEEn myself!

Trunk put four cups on a tray and poured recovery tea into each. I sprinkled in a pinch of fenuce and stirred. Wormy surprised me by taking the tray. He started for the door, which I opened. Then, feeling useless, I trailed him out.

The corridors were too busy for me to sense anyone's emotions. In my patients' bedchambers, I discovered that Wormy was happy—but, alas, not why.

When I closed the door on my last patient, Wormy asked if I had to return to the apothecary. I had no emergencies that I knew of, so I led him to the library, where, now that the castle had enough servants again, a fire was always burning in the two fireplaces. From my visits to consult the medical tomes, I expected it to be empty of people, as it was.

We pulled chairs up to a fireplace between a bookcase and a longcase clock, which showed the hour: ten before two in the afternoon. Every day rushed by more swiftly than the one before.

Wormy leaned forward in his chair and squeezed his

hands together. He was roiled by an internal commotion: joy, affection, sadness, worry, elation. "It's November thirteenth."

"Indeed." So? "I hope you brought your muffler."

"I have it. A little snow fell on my way here."

Were we going to keep talking about weather?

"November twenty-second is nine days away."

He remembered. My heart fluttered.

But I couldn't tell what I wanted. Being an ogre muddled love. I appreciated him more than before, but I didn't think love meant weighing this virtue against that fault on a scale. I wanted every scintilla of me to shout *Yes!*

I couldn't wait for certainty. I'd say yes.

He didn't propose. "Are you safe?"

This was new! I'd always been the professional fusspot, protecting him with tonics, physics, and advice. I wanted to tell him about Sir Peter and his threat. Wormy might be at risk, too, for being my friend. And I wanted someone who cared about me to know. But if I worried him, he'd get a stomachache and his other usual complaints. His headache would return. I just said, "Beware of Sir Peter."

His gaze sharpened. "Might he hurt you?"

"Me?" I forced a laugh. "I could eat him, and they're going to honor me."

"Yes, but are you safe?"

How well he knew me. "Yes."

"Then why should I beware?"

"He isn't honorable."

"Many aren't."

Where had this worldliness come from?

"Why should I distrust him in particular?"

What to say? I picked my words carefully. "He doesn't like me. He may try to harm me through my friends."

He didn't press me further.

"Wormy?"

"Yes?" He moved his chair closer to the fire.

"You're different. What happened?"

I sensed surprise. "My feet grew." He laughed and extended his feet. "New shoes."

The buckles were set with tiny quartz stones. "Not your feet!"

"Then I'm the same."

"People want to marry you." I clapped my hand over my mouth, but the words were out. "I saw it at the master's."

He flushed but said nothing.

"I should go back to the apothecary." I didn't move, though.

"If you have to." He didn't move, either.

"I've made a friend," I said into the lengthening silence.

"Lady Eleanor?"

"Yes. I've never met anyone so kind and delightful. And beautiful." The opposite of an ogre.

"She's very pretty."

Naturally, he'd noticed.

"She has many suitors?"

Ah. "Only Sir Peter, and he isn't worthy of her."

"I see."

But I sensed no more than polite interest, so I added, "She deserves someone as good as she is."

He turned his chair to face me. "Squire Jerrold?"

"He's extraordinarily good, but I wasn't thinking of him."

He saddened. "I see." He leaned forward, elbows on his knees. "I've decided never to marry. That could be how I've changed."

Oh. He would never propose.

What had changed his mind?

I sensed he was feeling love, but I'd misjudged that emotion in Sir Peter. In Wormy, it probably wasn't self-love, but it might be love of me as a friend. That was probably it.

He wouldn't be happy alone. "You must marry! I prescribe it for you."

Wormy became both glad and even sadder. "Not marrying isn't an illness, Evie. For you . . ." He didn't finish.

For me, it was a life sentence. "While you're here, I'm your healer. Isn't my advice always good?"

I sensed his pleasure in my words, but he changed the subject. "Is Squire Jerrold your friend?"

"He says he is, and I believe him. He's a good friend to have—brave, loyal, trustworthy, honest."

"Handsome."

"I suppose." Edible.

I described Squire Jerrold's activities since the blight. "You know I like people who work hard and serve other people."

Wormy stood. "You said you should get back. Patients may be waiting."

This was the first time he'd ever ended a chat with me. We returned to the apothecary, where Lady Eleanor had written the promised letter of introduction. She gave him street directions.

"The house is well kept, the rooms suitable for a gentleman."

I said, "Come back if your headache returns." Even though I'd promised it wouldn't.

The rest of the day passed in restocking medicaments, rolling bandages, whittling splints, waiting for patients who didn't come.

Lady Eleanor said, "I like your Master Warwick." She rolled bandages at my side.

"He isn't mine." If anyone could change his mind about marrying, it would be Lady Eleanor. "I believe he's as good a man as Squire Jerrold."

"As good as Sir Peter?"

"Yes." Which was true but an enormous understatement.

"He admires you."

"He can tell a good healer."

She laughed. "He admires *you*."

He used to.

CHAPTER TWENTY-EIGHT

WORMY DIDN'T VISIT the next day—or the next, or the day after that. Three days out of my dwindling store—from nine days to six.

Only two patients sought me out: one with a bunion and one with dizzy spells. Thus far, though the blight was over, the king hadn't tossed me out. Trunk gave me food, and the pigs liked me.

Lady Eleanor said Sir Titus had resumed his practice on Eastview Street. "People of fashion and the king consult him, but I would go to you." She stirred an imaginary spoon in an imaginary beaker. In a cracked voice with a wheeze, she said, "'This decoction cured my grandmother's grandmother and her grandmother's grandmother and her . . .'" She laughed. "You're more modern. But I'm rarely sick. Sorry!"

During Wormy's absence, Squire Jerrold continued his visits. I'd have guessed he came for Lady Eleanor's company, but she seemed not to interest him. He appeared gladdest to see Trunk, who was probably the reason for his calls.

I imagined that he was also drawn to the puzzle I presented: whatever it was that neither I nor his grandfather could tell him. Or I was one of his good deeds—calling on the poor ogre, who had few friends, who was distrusted by almost everyone.

He generally kept half the kitchen between us, even though I stayed tolerably clean, continued to shave every morning, and hadn't ceased dabbing myself with my dreadful perfume. I couldn't afford to pass up an opportunity in case he decided he loved me and I decided I loved him—or in the event that some other charming person happened by.

On the third morning without Wormy, I asked Lady Eleanor what she planned to wear to her ball.

"My green gown." She smiled. "Grass green with a thin stripe of moss green. It's my favorite. The stripes run—Oh! What will you wear, Mistress Evie?"

"Faded brown or faded mulberry. Which will be best?"

"I'm sorry." She considered the choice. "I like the brown better."

I happened to be wearing the mulberry. Perhaps she would have preferred it if I'd been in the brown.

Trunk intoned, "Dame Baita died."

I hadn't heard of her, so she might have succumbed before I came. Trunk hadn't been here, either, but he knew everything.

Lady Eleanor's face lit up. "She had excellent taste."

And a large body, I deduced.

People thought it bad luck to wear a dead person's apparel. I shared the superstition, but I doubted my fortunes could worsen.

"I'll go," Lady Eleanor said. "The family knows me."

How kind she was.

She left the castle and returned in an hour with a gown. "This one isn't right. I know it isn't. I just brought it to see if it fits."

Why hadn't she come with one that might be right? Oh. Because hours had passed since I'd bathed.

The gown was big in the chest, tight in the waist, and perfect in length. One of Dame Baita's frocks would do.

Lady Eleanor clapped her hands. "Come to my house early. Come at noon. We'll have hours to choose your gown and primp. Our cook, Mandy, is a wonder with the toilette."

Trunk said, "Cooks have many talents."

* * *

Wormy didn't come the next day, either. I had five days left. Why wasn't he with me, giving me the comfort of his company and the assurance that his friendship would continue? Unless it had already ended. Unless, when we were in the library, I'd said something to wound him. I went over our conversation again and again without guessing what it might have been.

In the morning, Trunk returned from the market and slammed his purchases down on his worktable.

"What's amiss?" I put aside the bandage I'd been rolling. I had enough bandage to swath the entire castle.

"Nothing, Mistress Ogre."

Lady Eleanor came in a few minutes later and seemed troubled, too.

"Will someone tell me what's wrong?"

"There are wolves." Lady Eleanor warmed her hands at the fire. "There have always been wolves."

"Are wolves attacking Frell?" I asked. That would be unheard of.

"No attack, Mistress Ogre," Trunk said.

What then?

Wolves . . . livestock. "Wolves have gotten some live-stock?"

"Yes," Trunk said. "That's what I think."

232

But not everybody agreed? Other people thought . . . what?

The answer arrived. "People think it was ogres?"

"Not everyone thinks that." Lady Eleanor perched on a stool by my table. "Just some do."

Trunk untied the knot on one of his bundles and didn't look up. "They don't think it was ogres." He emphasized the *s*. "They think it was one ogre."

Me.

They explained that yesterday a delegation of farmers from the outskirts of Frell had had an audience with King Imbert. The farmers had recently lost sheep, lambs, and goats but not their dogs. The farmers blamed me.

This was Sir Peter's doing. I was sure of it.

"Everyone knows that dogs like you," Trunk said unhappily. "They don't think you'd eat one. That's why they believe it was you and not wolves or other ogres."

"Sheep like me, too. So do goats. I sleep with the pigs, and they're fine." My voice sounded raspy, even for me. "I have plenty to eat right here!"

Trunk added, "The farmers knew about the meat sticks."

Only Sir Peter could have been the source of this intelligence, probably through others.

Lady Eleanor looked confused.

"I used to steal them."

"She wasn't an evil thief," Trunk said. "The meat sticks were how we knew she wasn't evil. And after she kidnapped the master, we knew, too."

Lady Eleanor laughed. "But if she hadn't stolen anything or kidnapped anyone, you would have known she *was* evil!"

"It wasn't that way," Trunk said earnestly. "The master has sheep and goats. She didn't bother them. She just took dried meat. She didn't hurt the master, either. She told him to feed me sheep's milk."

"Ah. Now I see." Lady Eleanor's face was merry.

Squire Jerrold came in and went to the table where Trunk was unknotting another bundle of provisions. As usual, the squire didn't remove his cloak—he never stayed long. He said nothing, which wasn't unusual, either, but ordinarily he helped Trunk with whatever was going forward.

"The livestock?" I said. "Squire Jerrold, you've heard?"

He hadn't. Trunk and Lady Eleanor retold the tale.

"I see," he said at the end. After a pause, he added, "I heard worse yesterday."

What? We all waited.

He addressed the floor. "I don't know whether to tell you or not."

"Now you must!" Lady Eleanor said.

"They're saying that the blight dead were bothered—were partly eaten."

Lady Eleanor made a strangled moan.

Absently, to give my hands a task, I began to roll bandages again. My anger rose. How many of those who believed the rumors were alive because of me?

The squire's eyes finally met mine. "I went to the pits."

Because so many had succumbed, most of the dead had been buried together in two pits, one outside the castle on the far side of the moat, and the other outside the town walls.

"I don't think the pits were disturbed at all," he said. "I keep asking, but I can't find anyone who's seen a half-eaten corpse."

"People believe it anyway?" I asked, keeping my voice neutral.

He nodded. He glanced at Lady Eleanor and held back what was certainly true, that Sir Peter was the source of this rumor. And the other one.

My voice rose. "Why would I stop at half a body? I could eat dead humans. I'm always hungry enough." I went to the cutting board and carved a shank off the boar Trunk had roasted overnight. "I'd pick the youngest and plumpest ones, and I'd eat them down to the bone." I bit into the boar.

Lady Eleanor embraced me, undeterred by my odor.

"The ball will reassure everyone." She choked out a laugh. "They'll dance with you or see you dance. They'll know you're civilized."

But should I leave Frell tonight? That was probably what Sir Peter wanted. Returning to the actual accusation, I said, "Trunk, what did the king tell the farmers?"

He didn't know, but he winked. "I'll visit the laundress."

Half an hour later he was back, his expression no less worried than before. "King Imbert sent soldiers to guard the flocks."

"Did he believe the accusations against me?"

"He said he'd wait for proof to decide."

Proof wouldn't come. Sir Peter's accomplices wouldn't attack livestock with soldiers on patrol. Small comfort.

The corpse rumors were the stuff of nightmare. Fear would grow.

And I doubted Sir Peter had just two arrows in his quiver. What would he do next?

CHAPTER TWENTY-NINE

SQUIRE JERROLD ASKED to speak privately with me. Lady Eleanor raised her eyebrows.

Heart fluttering, I followed the squire out of the kitchen. Was this about the rumors, or something else? Had his noble heart been touched by my plight? Did he want to offer me the protection of marriage to a human? Had that occurred to him? Might his goodness go that far?

When we entered the corridor, a manservant coming toward us turned and ran the other way.

Sensibly for anyone who didn't enjoy ogre odor, he led me through the castle entrance into the outer ward. Sleet slanted down. Except for guards at either side of the doors, no one was out. Squire Jerrold had a hooded cloak, but I had nothing. Kind as he was, the squire seemed not to know that an ogre could shiver and be cold. I didn't complain.

Wormy would have realized. Wherever he was, he was certainly indoors, likely near a roaring fire.

Might he have returned to Jenn without saying good-bye?

Squire Jerrold began to circle the castle, taking long steps. "You were right about Sir Peter's threat."

"I made him afraid of me."

"I'm ashamed to be a human when an ogre behaves better than we do."

I sighed. He had enough information to work out the truth.

He stopped between the granary and the stables, faced me—and half stepped back. "I'm going to follow your example. I have an audience with King Imbert on the hour. I'm resolved to tell him how the ogres really died."

No!

He went on. "They say he hardly cares for anyone but Sir Peter. The scoundrel's influence must be stopped."

"You won't be believed." My teeth chattered. Wet plastered my hair, my gown. "Don't do it. You weren't there. You have no proof, and you won't be believed."

"I may not be believed, but I still have to speak."

The king's true son, noble from skin to heart. And as headstrong as both his parents.

I argued. King Imbert had done nothing to me yet. Squire Jerrold could wait and speak up later. "A better opportunity may present itself. Your grandfather would urge caution."

"He'd be proud." Squire Jerrold resumed walking.

If only zEEn lasted, I'd make him stay silent.

He added, "For king and Kyrria."

"Sir Peter will find out. He may even be there. If he's there, you mustn't! He's ruthless."

Squire Jerrold's face might have been stone for all I was convincing him.

My voice rose. "Did I cure you of the blight just to have you risk yourself now?"

"I understand why Grandfather admires you." He bowed and, unpersuaded, turned back toward the castle.

A fresh terror struck me. "Stop!" I cried.

He did.

"Say I killed all the ogres. Don't mention Udaak, I beg of you." She'd be in danger, too.

Had Sir Peter already harmed her? I doubted his specks of goodness would extend to a giant.

Squire Jerrold objected. "But she's the only one who was there."

"That won't matter. If she lives to testify, Sir Peter will say she was persuaded by an ogre's spell to think I saved her. The king will believe him."

He looked dubious. "Mistress Evie—"

I cut him off. "If you mention her, I'll say I lied to you about killing any ogres myself. It will mean the end of me, but Udaak will be safe, and you will be, too. The king will think you my dupe, rather than a slanderer."

That threat succeeded. Squire Jerrold agreed, though resentfully. He went in to his audience.

I returned to the kitchen and steamed dry in front of the fire—dry, but not warm. A chill had entered my bones.

That evening, after Lady Eleanor left, a horrified Trunk had unsurprising news: Squire Jerrold hadn't been believed.

"What's wrong with the king? Why couldn't he tell that Squire Jerrold would never lie?"

"Was Sir Peter there at the audience?"

Trunk nodded. "And other courtiers and Squire Jerrold's knight. The laundress says Sir Peter just smiled. She says he's above such accusations, but I say he's below them."

"Was King Imbert angry at Squire Jerrold?"

"The laundress didn't mention him being angry. She did say Squire Jerrold"—Trunk switched to what he or the laundress considered proper speech to a king—"bespoke himself thusly: 'The coward shall reveal his poltroonery. I shall not rest until the lie manifest is made.'"

I would have laughed if I hadn't been horrified, too. Squire Jerrold wouldn't express himself so ornately, but he probably did swear to expose Sir Peter.

Trunk pounded down his mound of risen dough. "When Jerro says a thing, he does it."

How? Might he have a plan?

There could be no plan. Heads on pikes can't talk.

"Was he imprisoned?"

"No." Trunk explained that Sir Stephan had saved him from punishment for defaming Sir Peter by arguing that the ogre was the real source of the lie.

I didn't flee Frell, because flight would be taken as an admission of guilt. I'd be pursued.

The next morning—the morning of Lady Eleanor's ball to honor me—four guards entered the kitchen and stationed themselves in pairs on either side of the door.

Half an hour later, the guards and Trunk accompanied me, clutching a blanket against a biting wind, to Lady Eleanor's mansion on Larkspur Street, where the ball would be held. I was to spend the day there, trying on gowns and getting ready. On the way, several people crossed the road to avoid me. A man yowled in fear, then recovered enough to beg me to spare him. "Not for me," he cried, "for my family."

I kept walking.

A few yards later, a woman curtsied to me. "You saved my happiness when you saved my daughter."

I told myself that she made up for everyone else. I curtsied back and we continued on.

Trunk said, "I've heard news of your Master Warwick."

"He isn't *mine.*"

"Your friend is giving people money."

"Lending." That was what his family did.

"Giving, as I've heard it. He goes from house to house where the blight struck. If someone is too ill to work, or if someone who used to work"—Trunk whispered, "*died,*" then spoke normally again—"Master Warwick counts out KIs, as many as are needed."

Oh, Wormy! How generous! As kind in his way as Squire Jerrold was in his.

But the squire had found time to visit the castle.

Trunk added, "Master Warwick is often accompanied by a young lady. Pretty, I hear. Very dainty Mistress Chloris is, the laundress says."

Well, good. He was taking his healer's advice to marry.

But why couldn't he court her and still visit me?

And why wasn't I happier for him?

How could I be happy for anyone, with the end of possibility for me looming in four days?

Lady Eleanor's house took pride of place in the center of a row of limestone homes. The ogre didn't care, but the girl in me noticed that the building rose three stories, with a frieze of dancing gnomes and elves separating the first from the ones above. The polished oak door was topped by a fanlight.

Trunk said, "There's the knocker, Mistress Ogre. You lift it and let go. That's how a knocker works."

"Thank you."

He bobbed his head and left me. The guards stayed.

Though a manservant hovered behind her, Lady Eleanor herself opened the door, her face a hurricane. But when she saw the guards, she wiped the clouds away and smiled. "Come in! This will be such fun."

Was something wrong that she didn't want the guards to know?

She addressed them. "I hope you like meat pies just out of the oven. Lamb and beef, I believe." She turned to the manservant. "Vale, please conduct these gentlemen to the kitchen."

A guard began, "Lady—"

"Mistress Evie is here for the ball. Tonight, Vale will let you know when she's ready to leave." Lady Eleanor swept away.

The guards followed Vale.

I trailed Lady Eleanor through two elegant drawing rooms. Then she wheeled on me. "You coward! If you had to slander him, why didn't you slander him to me?"

Sir Peter must have related Squire Jerrold's accusation to her.

She set off again.

Why hadn't I realized?

I was surprised she hadn't rescinded the invitation. How would I bear the loss of her friendship?

When we entered her bedchamber, she sat on her bed with a thump and tilted her head up at the ceiling, deliberately not looking at me. "Mandy has persuaded me to remain your friend, but know that my friendship is grudging."

Was grudging friendship friendship at all?

Mandy? Oh, the family cook. Next to a mahogany fretwork screen stood a middle-aged woman with tight gray curls and a shape that reminded me of a stuffed chair.

The woman addressed me. "I do *not* approve of what was done to you, Mistress Evie." She shook her head, making her double chin wag. "To change a maiden into an ogre!"

How could she say the words when no one else could, when even I couldn't? How had Lady Eleanor been able to tell her about me?

"May I introduce Mandy, my fairy godmother?" Lady Eleanor asked the ceiling.

Really? Might she help me, despite what Lucinda said about other fairies?

Lady Eleanor lowered her chin but still didn't meet my eyes. "She said you could know she's a fairy, though no one

244

else outside my family does. She also said I mustn't blame you for anything. I'm finding that difficult."

This cook looked ordinary, nothing like Lucinda, who was every inch the fairy. And Mandy's inner state was calm.

"Would you—" *Turn me back?* But I still couldn't say it.

Mandy understood. "I never know what could result if I step in. Lucinda is the foolhardy one."

She could but she wouldn't? My rage surged. How might fairy taste?

Could I zEEn her? I sensed no fear for me to diminish, but I had to persuade her for only a moment. I sweetened my voice. "You want the best for me. No harm can come from such a merciful act. I'll heal more people if you help me."

Lady Eleanor was persuaded. "Mandy, won't you? She deserves big magic if anyone does."

ZEEning had no effect on the fairy, but I felt her relent—and then unrelent. "Sweet, I mustn't. Mistress Evie, would you give your patients medicine that would cure them today and might sicken them tomorrow?"

"If the patient would die today, I would." But I probably wouldn't die today.

Mandy went on. "Being an ogre may save more than you."

It already had. My band would have killed Grellon and others, if I hadn't stolen meat sticks—and then murdered two of them. As an ogre forever, I might save more creatures.

I asked a question I'd wondered about. "How did Lady Eleanor guess the truth?"

Mandy said, "Lucinda turned her uncle into a squirrel years ago. Squirrel transformations are her particular favorite."

"As soon as I mentioned an ogre healer, Mandy realized what had been done to you, just as I had." She turned to the fairy. "Why does Lucinda do it?"

Mandy smoothed her apron. "She loves occasions—births, proposals, weddings, even funerals—and believes she can improve them with her dreadful gifts. Luckily, even a fairy can't be in more than one place at a time, so she misses many. Mistress Evie, you were unfortunate."

"What if I never—" Never become myself again. Please say that won't happen. Please say Lucinda sometimes takes pity on her victims. Please say I'll find someone I can love in time.

She said nothing. I felt her sadness.

I had an idea. "Do I have a fairy godmother, too?"

"Certainly. But many fairies—not I—aren't interested in humans. They keep to the company of other fairies."

"Can I find her?" Appeal to her.

"No one but Lucinda does big magic. None of us would lift your spell, and your particular fairy tends to be acerbic.

She'd say there are worse things than being an ogre."

Being a helpless squirrel, I supposed. I pulled back my shoulders and remembered that I was still a healer. "Can you spare a unicorn hair?"

"My only one vanished six months ago. I think someone took it." Mandy looked pointedly at Lady Eleanor. "I hope to have another soon. You can borrow it when I do."

"Please take it entirely," Lady Eleanor said. "It's foul—how pale it is, the way it drifts along in soup"—she shuddered—"like the tail of a dead mouse. I'd rather be sick."

My anger surfaced. "Healers hate your sort."

She glared at me. "Loyal people hate defamers."

We were back to that.

I should have told her as soon as I knew about Squire Jerrold's audience with King Imbert, but I'd been too worried about the squire, Trunk, Wormy, and me to think of it. I apologized profusely. "I didn't defame Sir Peter. I killed the ogres." (Just two, really.)

She twisted her hands in her lap. "I wondered. I could hardly sleep." She finally met my eyes. "I accept your apology. Not grudgingly. Last night, after hours of thinking, I decided you did lie, because I know your character and his. Sir Peter is a brave, honest, and kindly ordinary human. Ordinary humans kill ogres if we can. *You* are extraordinary. You'd never kill anyone, not even an ogre."

CHAPTER THIRTY

OH.

How wonderful she was.

How lucky-unlucky I was.

I exhaled the breath I hadn't noticed I was holding.

Mandy said, "Time reveals truth, Lady."

Lady Eleanor sprang up. "Mistress Evie, we chose gowns for you to decide among." She disappeared behind the screen. "Mandy, help me!"

I hoped the fairy would do magic—make the gowns sail to me on their own, for example—but she just followed Lady Eleanor. A moment later, the two of them staggered out with stacks of finery. Lady Eleanor kept her pile from cascading by pressing down on it with her chin, which made her entirely adorable.

They deposited their burdens on the bed.

Lady Eleanor went to the cheval mirror that stood between two windows and dragged it close. "Dame Baita kept her seamstress busy. I like all of these." She waved me to approach.

I didn't want to look in the mirror. "You decide. Please."

They took turns. One held a gown almost against me while the other stood back. The fabrics never touched me, so only the one I wore would be ruined by my stink.

Nerves took me over. I couldn't stop chattering. "Something busy, please—something people will look at." Other than me. "That one." I pointed at a brocade gown in a large diamond pattern.

"We'll see," Lady Eleanor said. "What color complements your complexion?"

"None?" What color did Squire Jerrold like? Which did Wormy?

"Everyone has a best color," Lady Eleanor said. "Yours may be this light blue."

"A cloak of invisibility would suit me best." I wished something in the room other than Lady Eleanor and Mandy were edible—if fairies were. I scanned the floor for mice.

Mandy said, sounding prim, "Only Lucinda dispenses such trifles."

"Lady Eleanor," I said, "I suppose everyone accepted your family's invitation."

She said almost everyone had.

"I imagine that would be many people."

"Not many for a ball, but some are still convalescing. A hundred and fifty-three. A smaller number will stay for supper."

"I imagine they all know I'll be here."

She said she hadn't kept my attendance a secret.

What had I expected? Balls were always big affairs.

"King Imbert isn't coming for the dancing, so you needn't worry about that."

I hadn't thought of the king!

"He plans to honor us for the supper."

For a meal, when I was at my worst. I shook my head. "I'm sorry. I can't . . ." I trailed off. The house would have a back door. I'd find the guards. Then I'd go straight to the castle kitchen and gorge.

Lady Eleanor and Mandy didn't try to persuade me or console me, for which I was grateful. Lady Eleanor busied herself, sifting through gowns.

She'd taken all this trouble for me. The entire ball was for me. It was meant, as much as possible, to make me acceptable to Frell society.

I had to stay. I began to babble again. "I never paid attention to fashion, not even when—" I gave up. "I'd just look for bright eyes, clear skin. I always noticed posture."

"I've told Mandy what a consummate healer you are."

She must have failed to mention how hungry I always was. "When she gets the unicorn hair, Mandy will be a better healer than I am." And she could cure anything by magic if she chose. I went on talking, commenting on each gown, wondering what a seamstress's life might be, hoping the cold would keep everyone away, and then apologizing for the wish.

Lady Eleanor begged Mandy to do something to make me stop worrying.

Mandy refused.

With an attempt at dignity, I said, "I prefer to antici-pate every possible catastrophe."

At last, they settled on a gown—and then repeated the process with fichus and headdresses. I begged for a turban and a mask.

Half the starving afternoon passed before all my gar-ments were chosen. I went from enumerating disasters to praising Wormy.

Fall in love with him, Lady Eleanor, I thought. He no longer wants me, but he won't be able to resist you when he knows you better. Mistress Chloris, the *dainty* young lady mentioned by Trunk, whoever she is, can't compare with you.

"Wormy's family is good, too," I said. "Not as elevated as yours, but good."

Lady Eleanor grinned. "His extreme fondness for you speaks in his favor."

Extreme? "He knew me bef—" I couldn't continue. "I've cured him of everything."

"Mandy, isn't this perfect?"

She arranged on the bed a gown, a fichu, and a cap. If a passable-looking person filled them out, the effect would be charming. The gown had a midnight-blue bodice that tapered to a point below the waist and pale blue flowing skirts. The fichu was creamy lace, the bonnet creamy, too, and small.

I was too hungry to think.

"Bath next." Lady Eleanor laughed at my expression. "The tub is in the kitchen, where the food also is."

The guards were shooed into a parlor. Before bathing, I was served a dozen mutton chops. Lady Eleanor ate the remaining chop, which I begrudged her.

On to the bath.

Mandy thought keeping the water hot and clean wasn't too much magic, an improvement that mattered little to me, and shaving was no more pleasurable than usual, though the suds on my face remained hot, too. She did more, however, and better. I felt nothing when she cast the spell, but she promised the hair on my face would cease growing until the ball was over. "And you will smell sweet."

I thanked her, then frowned. "I still smell pig, sweat, and earth." As I preferred.

"Not to me." Lady Eleanor came close and breathed deeply. "Peonies."

I sensed Mandy's satisfaction. "Pigs and dirt to one. Peonies to another."

Back in Lady Eleanor's bedchamber, I donned the gown. Mandy laced it loosely so I could breathe. The fichu was draped over my shoulders and anxiously tied and retied. I squeezed my feet into Dame Baita's satin slippers. Pinched toes would remind me to take small steps.

Lady Eleanor seated me at her vanity. I closed my eyes.

"You needn't look at yourself now, but when we're finished and your bonnet is on, you must."

She related every step as she performed it. "Rice powder, just a dusting. Rouge, not much, either. Lip rouge."

"Ouch!"

"Luxuriant eyebrows are no longer the thing."

Might the result of their labor resemble the old me? I imagined, when they finished, that I'd see in the mirror my true self merely made large and stately.

If I didn't smile, no one would see the fangs.

If I danced well—

If I didn't get angry—

If I minded my table manners—

If I thought of interesting conversation and didn't go on about herbs—

Then, perhaps, before the evening ended, people would look at me and not see gnawed corpses and dead sheep. Perhaps someone would fall headlong, instantly in love with me. And I would love the person back.

I'd never have another chance like this one.

I didn't cry out when Lady Eleanor and Mandy each took a side of my head and attacked my hair with a brush and comb, but I ground my fangs so hard I probably loosened them.

Lady Eleanor, on tiptoe, placed my cap, tilted it, straightened it, and tilted it again to an angle that she declared *fetching*. I tugged on pale yellow gloves.

The day had grayed to dusk. They pronounced me ready.

I had hopes.

"You may—you must!—admire yourself now." She took my hand and led me to the mirror.

I was a monster in the latest fashion, as much performing bear as ogre.

My rouged lips became redder as I bit them to keep from weeping.

Lady Eleanor saw my reaction and put her fist to her mouth in distress.

"I'm sorry." I asked to return to the kitchen, where I

pumped water and scrubbed off the cosmetics. Back in Lady Eleanor's room, I looked at my reflection again, which now revealed the ogre clearly. Better to frighten than be laughed at.

The finery did improve me a little. The waist of the gown made my own waist slimmer. And my hair had been softened in the vigorous brushing. By my hair alone, I could have been human. If I kept my back to everyone for the entire ball and supper, I might not be recognized.

"Thank you," I said. They had spent hours on me. "I don't mean to be ungrateful. I'm not." I thought about it. "This afternoon was wonderful."

Lady Eleanor stepped back from me, considered, nodded. "I should have realized the cosmetics were wrong." She started. "It's late!" She escorted us out of the room. "Mandy, I want to make my toilette myself and surprise you both. Prepare to be amazed."

We stood outside her door. I whispered, "Have you met Sir Peter?"

Mandy's whisper was so explosive I felt the wind of it on my face. "The upstart? The cad? The charlatan?"

She'd met him. I let out a long breath, relieved she agreed with me.

"There's never been a more loyal heart than Lady's— which the scoundrel carries in his waistcoat pocket."

"Can we do anything?" But I meant *you*, not *we*. Sir

Peter would make a handsome squirrel.

She shook her head. "I don't dare. It would be big magic."

After that, we waited in silence. I was grateful for her small magic, but most fairies, in my estimation, were worse than people. At least people tried.

CHAPTER THIRTY-ONE

FINALLY, LADY ELEANOR cried gaily from the other side of the door, "Come and see me!"

I followed Mandy in. Lady Eleanor twirled between the vanity with its small mirror and the cheval mirror, yielding three beauties. "The stripes are the best part."

She was lovely enough to bring hope to the despairing, a breathing, human tonic. If only I could look a tenth so comely. The stripes—vertical in the bodice and halfway down the skirts, where a hem introduced the horizontal—showed off her slender form. A tiny pale green slipper peeped out from her skirts.

"Do you approve, Mandy?"

"Yes, Lady. You're splendid."

For a moment I thought they were flaunting her beauty

at my expense. Then I realized how much worse it would have been if she'd apologized for looking pretty or pretended she was ugly, too.

"Mistress Evie, Mandy is bossy. If you weren't here, I would never have had the pleasure of surprising her."

Voices came from the front of the house.

"Come, guest of honor. Meet the grateful of Frell."

Mandy returned to the kitchen. Lady Eleanor and I crossed the dining room, where a long table had already been set for the supper after the ball. Beyond the dining room, in the library, small tables had been put out for refreshments and card games. Those who preferred not to dance or had exhausted themselves would come here.

At the door to the drawing room, Lady Eleanor held out her arm. We made an awkward couple—the fairy tale come to life, Beauty with the Beast.

A knot of people stood near the distant vestibule door. I didn't see Wormy or Squire Jerrold.

My stomach rumbled.

A man and woman whose backs were to us turned. The woman held out her arms.

"My good mother," Lady Eleanor whispered. She tugged me toward them: two of the highest peers in Kyrria.

After her parents hugged Lady Eleanor, they turned to me. Their faces were calm, the guests' agog.

Let everyone see how civilized I am.

Benches lined the walls for those who preferred to watch the dance, or who lacked partners.

Lady Eleanor had stayed with her parents to greet new arrivals. In the middle of the room, I became an island, everyone aware of me but afraid to approach. I distracted myself in the old way, by looking for signs of illness. I saw only health, but I wanted to deliver a lecture on slouching.

I checked the entry again.

Sir Peter stood close enough to Lady Eleanor to make my skin crawl. She whispered something in his ear. Then she pushed his shoulder playfully. He bowed, turned, and headed for me.

When he came close, I curtsied—and tingled.

And felt both furious and frightened. Did he have a plan to finish me off here?

He bowed. "Lady Eleanor has commissioned me to beg you for the first dance, and I'm happy to oblige."

I accepted and thanked him. "I'm as happy as you are."

A Kyrrian fredasta began. The room organized itself into dancers and observers. Two lines formed, women facing men.

There was Wormy, next to Sir Peter!

He nodded and smiled at me, his smile warm, but I grew even angrier. Why hadn't he said hello as soon as he arrived?

I turned to see who his partner was: excellent posture,

pleasant expression. Small, if not truly dainty, but this must be Mistress Chloris.

We began. Sir Peter had grace, command, and lightness. My body, though I'd been in it for fifty-eight days, felt too large. My heart raced, and my stomach growled.

The nearness of all these people—all this meat—made me light-headed. I took in great gulps of air, thought of the sight I'd be, laid out on the floor, and didn't faint.

The moment came when Sir Peter and I had to clasp arms at the elbow, my right with his right, swing around, let go, and dance off to the next in our line. Unbalanced as I already was, I thrust my arm out too high. He could have adjusted, and the mistake would have had no consequences, but he placed his arm properly and let me sail by.

I glimpsed astonished faces and the beginning of laughter. Unable to catch myself, I stumbled into Wormy, who took my arm in a natural way. He smiled.

Wormy and I spun once. I was stiff with rage—at Wormy for not seeking me out, at Lady Eleanor for inviting me. At Sir Peter for half my misery and most of the danger I was in.

Gentlemen and maidens returned to their separate lines. How stylish Wormy looked, in an ivory waistcoat, brown breeches, and a narrow-brimmed hat set at a rakish angle. I'd never thought I'd call anything about him rakish. How at home he looked in the line of courtiers.

The dance returned me to Sir Peter, who said, "My apologies. I should have anticipated how you'd go. My partners aren't often so tall as you."

I considered scratching his face and passing it off as more awkwardness. "Mine aren't often so ungallant."

The dance ended.

Lady Eleanor appeared at his elbow. "Peter!"

Not *Sir* Peter?

"I hope you apologized for your heedlessness."

"I did. I am covered in remorse. You promised me the next, love."

Love?

She blushed. "Mistress Evie, I hope you can forgive him—and me. I'm a failure at staying angry at anyone."

Anyone included me earlier. I nodded.

The musicians started a gavotte. Sir Peter and Lady Eleanor took their places. I was blundering toward the benches when a young man begged a dance. I was sure he wanted to dance with the ogre so he could forever boast that he had.

I begged off, saying I had tired myself.

But from the bench, I felt guilty. Lady Eleanor would be disappointed if I didn't seem to be enjoying myself, so I accepted a request to dance a saraband from a young man with a hairy mole on his cheek.

I pitied him for the mole until he asked me, during a

moment in the dance when conversation was possible, to describe the flavor of human. Through clenched fangs, I said that it depended on the human. "I'm sure you would be delicious."

He said no more. I regretted my words but was too angry to apologize or explain. We danced on.

In one sequence, we passed, hand to hand, from one dancer to the next. Even through gloves, I tingled at every touch. More at some, less at others, but no hand entirely failed to thrill me.

I watched for Wormy and discovered him with the same partner as before. Would he dance eternally with her? Had he forgotten about asking me?

His partner was a gentle dancer. Insipid, I thought. Wormy, whose dancing I knew to be more energetic, softened his steps to match hers.

The dance moved us away from them.

When it ended, Squire Jerrold, resplendent in a blue satin redingote and tan velvet breeches, arrived to claim his dance. I'd never seen him look so happy.

He bowed. "Before we begin, I've been eager to introduce you to my close acquaintance, my dear friend." He gestured.

A young woman squeezed between two other guests and curtsied to me.

He smiled. His voice smiled. "Mistress Daria. She . . ."

I didn't hear what he said, but I curtsied, too. Mistress Daria was the reason for his happiness. She answered the question I'd failed to think of in the carriage: Had he already given his heart to someone?

She had a wide face and tawny skin. I swallowed repeatedly. I hadn't really expected to marry him.

Squire Jerrold and Mistress Daria.

Wormy and the dainty young lady.

Of course they were pairing up, as healthy young people do.

Mistress Daria said something polite. I answered with words that must not have been strange, because she replied in turn.

I excused myself from dancing, saying I wanted air and refreshment. Preservation of myself and others took me to the kitchen, where Mandy, without a word, sat me at her worktable. She put a thick steak before me. Each swallow sank like iron.

The fairy bustled, chopping, slicing, stirring, and issuing orders to three dismayed kitchen wenches, who certainly preferred to be where the ogre was not.

Why return to the ball? I'd find only misery there.

CHAPTER THIRTY-TWO

I DON'T KNOW how many minutes passed before Lady Eleanor and Sir Peter came in. I turned but didn't stand and didn't look up.

She ran to me, then stopped. "Did someone insult you?"

"No one insulted me." My gaze stayed at the height of her waist.

Lady Eleanor crouched so we were at eye level. "Many people don't have even two loyal friends, and you have Master Warwick, Squire Jerrold, Peter, and me, who won't desert you, come what may."

My fangs ran with rage whenever she said *Peter* without his title. I knew Mandy was bristling, too. If she turned him into a toad, we'd both rejoice.

Out of the corner of my eye I saw him bow.

Lady Eleanor began, "Won't you—"

"Mistress Evie?" Squire Jerrold and Mistress Daria came in.

I raised my head to see how Sir Peter and the squire would behave in each other's company after yesterday's accusation.

Squire Jerrold's jawline tightened. His cheeks reddened, but he bowed to Sir Peter and Lady Eleanor. "Good evening."

Sir Peter smiled and bowed. "How delightful to see you in pleasanter circumstances than yesterday's. I'm relieved His Majesty was clement."

He was a snake. No—unjust to snakes.

Lady Eleanor frowned at Squire Jerrold—the defamer, she believed—but she embraced Mistress Daria. "How sweet you look."

Mistress Daria hugged Lady Eleanor back and then addressed me. "Mistress Evie, I must tell you . . ." Her voice moistened. "I'll be in your debt forever." Tears rolled down her broad cheeks. "My good father and mother owe their lives to you. Owe them entirely. They were near . . . both were near . . . when you came."

My throat tightened—and I became angry again. I liked her when I wanted to hate her.

"I'm so happy"—she curtsied to Lady Eleanor—"this

267

ball is in Mistress Evie's honor." She turned back to me. "And so happy to be able to thank you."

"I'm glad your parents are well. I hope they and you will come back to me if anything else troubles them."

Squire Jerrold volunteered, "Mistress Daria tells me she's ill as rarely as I am."

If a shoe grew out of Squire Jerrold's rib cage, it would be as useful to him as I was, and as he was to me. I found myself laughing. An orange shoe? A lady's slipper? Round toe? Pointed? I laughed harder.

Except for Mandy, they all stared.

If Lucinda somehow changed me back, would my mind and heart ever return to their old state?

Squire Jerrold and Mistress Daria exchanged a look. She curtsied and left.

As I went on laughing, Sir Peter said, "Mistress Mandy, can you give Mistress Evie a chop or other edible? I believe she's in need."

Lady Eleanor sent him a grateful look for what she imagined to be his thoughtfulness.

I was certain he meant to embarrass me. I gasped out, "I don't need a chop." Of course I did. I always did.

Mandy said, "I wasn't about to bring one unless you asked for it."

Sir Peter said, "Love—"

Ugh! My laughing diminished.

"—your guests may be wondering where you've gone, and I need another dance with you."

"In a moment." Lady Eleanor knelt by me.

"You'll dirty your skirts!" I said.

"Never mind that. You are the guest of—"

"Evie . . ."

Was Wormy bringing his new sweetheart to make me laugh again?

But he was alone. He stood just inside the room, as tentative as he used to be.

Oddly, that cheered me a little. "Yes, Wormy?"

"Evie, I feel faint."

I jumped up. "Sit."

I didn't have my medicaments. What would a cook have on hand? I thought of an easy remedy, one of the first I'd ever learned. Wormy wouldn't enjoy it. No one did.

"Mandy, can you pour two fingers of vinegar in a cup?"

In a trice she had. She knew what I had in mind, because she also gave me the pepper grinder. I turned a generous helping of black pepper into the vinegar. "Wormy . . ."

"Not snail and hedgehog!" he said.

I smiled and extended the cup.

He leaned away at the caustic scent. "I'm better."

I didn't need ogre ability to sense everyone's amusement. "It's a general tonic," I said. "Squire Jerrold, even though you're never sick, you'll feel invigorated." I held it out to him.

His courage had limits. He declined. I extended the cup to Sir Peter, who bowed and also said no.

Lady Eleanor laughed. "I'm not keen for it, either. We're all cowards."

"Wormy?"

He drank it down. The others applauded.

His eyes ran. He sneezed. "I'm better now." He laughed, too. "Don't dose me again." His eyebrows went up. "I *am* better!" He stood. "Evie always cures me."

"You may not know I was the first she cured of the blight," Squire Jerrold said.

Was he boasting about me? "First in this outbreak." I'd treated it before.

"Yes, of course." He added, "If you return to dancing, please remember your promise to save one for me." He bowed and left.

Sir Peter lounged against a cabinet and covered a yawn with his hand.

Lady Eleanor gave him a sharp look. "Mistress Evie, won't you return, please?"

"I will. In a while."

"I'll look for you." She left with Sir Peter.

Wormy stood. "I should go, too."

Why *should* he? "All right."

But he didn't. He just stood there.

"If we were home, you could help me work."

He said nothing. He used to be more eager and more friendly.

"I would have made us ginger tea." Why had he ruined it all by proposing? "Mandy, can I have a few chops now?"

She placed a platter piled with pork chops on the worktable, where we stood.

I sat in the chair Wormy had vacated, took off my gloves, and ate with my hands. "Would you like one?" I spoke with my mouth full. Let him see. At the supper, let them all see.

"I'll have one." He reached.

I moved my platter away. "Mandy will serve you."

Mandy pulled another chair to the worktable, then brought him two chops. He sat and picked one up with his hands.

I wished the kitchen wenches would leave so I could read his feelings.

"I approve of your partner," I said.

"Who?" He spoke with his mouth full, too.

Had he danced with so many? "Dark, petite. Mistress Chloris? I approve of her posture."

"I wouldn't dare dance with anyone who slouched."

I smiled with meat stuck between my fangs. "Or dare court such a person."

He didn't deny it.

I went on. "Why didn't you tell me you were giving people funds?" Why did you desert me and not visit?

He put down his chop half eaten and pushed his plate away. I took it to be a rebuke.

"After a disaster, people need money. That was one of my reasons for coming to Frell. And to report your well-being to your mother."

Not to see me. "I wrote to Mother!"

"She doesn't trust you to tell her the worst."

He didn't know the latest worst, since he hadn't visited. "I've heard the rumors." He did know.

"You didn't tell Mother?" Fear would make her ill!

"I didn't. She'd get sick."

"Thank you."

When I'd devoured everything, including his leavings, I felt as near full as I ever did. I wiped my mouth with the back of my hand.

Wormy said, "You promised me a dance."

"Can we dance in here?" We used to dance in my apothecary in Jenn.

He hummed a minuet. We faced each other, stepped close.

"You don't smell like yourself."

I didn't want to give Mandy away. "It's a remedy, but just for tonight."

He frowned. "But you don't smell like yourself at all. You used to, even after—" He couldn't go on. "Despite the other odor."

Really?

He resumed humming. I joined in, curtsied, and stepped back. He bowed.

The next step involved clasping hands. Our greasy hands met.

I tingled, which meant nothing. But, since the touch was prolonged, the feeling strengthened, became almost painful. Was Wormy enduring anything like what I was going through?

His eyes twitched. His hands were cold.

Mandy picked up the beat of my heart with a wooden spoon against an iron pot.

To my relief, the dance had us drop hands to bow and curtsy again. But more contact was coming. Why hadn't I asked for a saraband?

He took my hand to lead me to his left side. Now both hands for me to cross to his right. We let go again to face each other for a third bow and curtsy—not much exertion, but we both were breathing hard. I took my place next to him. He grasped my right hand. Three steps to the side.

Holding hands without respite, forward and back, side to side—intolerable. I rescued my hand and stumbled into a chair.

I saw his chest rise and fall, too. "Are you faint again?"

He sank into his chair. "I'm fine."

"No more vinegar and pepper?"

He smiled.

I breathed slowly, trying to calm myself. "Warmth would make you feel better." I wished he'd move his chair to the fireplace. He was still too close.

He remained.

I went to the window that overlooked the back garden. My heart and my breath finally settled.

"Evie-ee . . ."

I turned. "Yes, Wormy?"

"Before I met you at that farm, the road passed through a field where a unicorn was grazing. I—"

My breath quickened again. "You got a tail hair?"

"No."

Oh.

"I tried. I thought how happy you'd be if I could give you one." He looked down at his hands. "I didn't know then if you'd be alive to get it."

My good friend.

"I chased. It ran. Whenever I came close, it sped up.

Whenever I fell back, it slowed. It was playing with my horse. They whickered at each other. Finally, after an hour, it galloped away and left me with just wishes."

"More than one wish?"

He met my eyes. "A hair for you was one. But also . . . it was beautiful. Smaller than you'd think, smaller than Biddable. Evie . . ." He seemed to be searching for words. "If . . . You should have seen it. If unicorns did a minuet or a gavotte or any of our dances, onlookers would see music brought to life. I didn't want it to leave. I wanted you to be there, too. Those were my wishes."

"I might have tried to eat it."

He chuckled, although I hadn't meant to be funny. "Bef—" He tried to get the word out, then gave up. "You'd have admired it, but you also would have said, 'Wormy, dear, that unicorn is health itself—its brightness, its energy. But if it got sick'"—he shook his head, conjuring me up—"'what diseases might it be subject to? What would I dose it with?'" He laughed outright. "Then you would have listed possible herbs."

"I would have wondered if its own hair would cure it." I laughed too. "By then, the unicorn would have been miles away."

No one understood me or approved of me as Wormy did. How I loved him.

My head spun. I really loved him. Not as before. As

now. With the chops in my belly, I was less starving than usual. My mind was clear. I loved him.

And I thought he still loved me. Otherwise, why would our minuet have thrilled him, too? Why would he have wished for me when he saw the unicorn?

Why hadn't he proposed again?

Why was he courting someone else?

CHAPTER THIRTY-THREE

LADY ELEANOR RETURNED alone to beg me to rejoin the ball. "The success of the evening depends on you. People are clamoring to dance with the guest of honor."

I went and danced for hours with a succession of partners, including Squire Jerrold, but now he was almost indistinguishable from the others. My fickle hands (washed and gloved again) tingled at every touch. My appetite reawakened.

At the end of each dance, I started for the library, where there would be food, but each time, a new partner appeared. I could have said I had to eat. Everyone would have liked that. Some would have followed me to watch.

Shame and rage kept me dancing.

Finally, most of the guests left. Supper was announced for the elect who had been asked to stay.

Meaning to be kind, I was sure, Lady Eleanor had seated me with Wormy on my left and Squire Jerrold on my right. I edged my chair closer to the squire and wished Wormy were across the table—or miles away. His nearness almost rocketed me to the ceiling.

Wormy's dainty young lady sat across the table from us and a little farther from Lady Eleanor than we were.

Squire Jerrold, after inquiring about my pleasure in the evening and receiving a polite answer, addressed himself to Mistress Daria on his right. I noticed the measured pace of her speech, careful and deliberate as he was. I'd been mad to think he might ever love me.

The king, seated in a high-backed armchair, headed the table. He had regained the health he'd probably had before the blight, but I wished he'd grown stouter. He couldn't have been much older than Mother, whose face was barely lined. Though King Imbert's hair had just a few strands of gray, his forehead was deeply furrowed, which, I allowed, might be inevitable in a caring king. But he didn't have to have puffs under his eyes. Was he sleeping badly? And he didn't have to slump in his chair. Nothing ages a person as much as slumping.

Lord and Lady Evesby, Lady Eleanor's parents, flanked the king. Lady Eleanor sat between her father and Sir Peter. She smiled happily at the scoundrel. He smiled fondly at her, but his eyes flicked to King Imbert, who seemed to have eyes only for him, too. Each leaned forward so they might see the other.

Wormy was conversing with the ancient man on his left. I stared down at my empty plate. When would food arrive?

The humans seemed not to care. Their voices were untroubled. People glanced at me, looked away, glanced again, politely not staring.

Servants filed in, bearing plates. I tried to ignore the stink of vegetables, bread, spices, cider. A trembling arm rounded my head. If I hadn't steadied it, the plate would have dumped its contents.

Surrounding my modest slice of roast beef were poached carrots! Creamed asparagus! Beetroot pancakes!

How could Mandy have? I began to push back my chair. I'd find out if an enchanted ogre could punch a fairy—

—when the scents reached me. The carrots smelled like lamb, the asparagus like rabbit, the pancakes like goat. Small magic at its best.

King Imbert picked up his fork. All eyes snapped to me.

See the ogre eat. With closed lips, I smiled around the

table, cut a dainty morsel, and inserted it, barely opening my mouth. Without a doubt disappointed, the other guests addressed their own meals.

The false vegetables were more delicious than the undisguised beef, more intensely flavored, the distilled essence of meat. My server set an individual carafe in front of me. Before she could attempt to pour into my goblet, I did the job myself. I closed my eyes as beef broth sang an aria in my mouth.

Polite conversation swirled around me. Lady Eleanor was raising a bite of food to Sir Peter's lips. His hand guided hers.

Wormy continued to chat with the guest on his left, whose rasp suggested a sore throat. The woman directly across the table from me chewed only on the right side of her mouth. Toothache. I remembered AAng. And her head, back on a pike.

Lady Evesby coughed genteelly. People put down their forks. Annoyed, I did, too. She thanked everyone for coming and said her daughter wished to speak.

Lady Eleanor stood. "How many here were saved by Mistress Evora?"

Six raised their hands, including King Imbert, Sir Peter, and Squire Jerrold. If more of the guests lived at the king's castle, there would have been additional hands.

"How many of you have family members saved by her?"

Three others, including Mistress Daria, plus four of the first six. Over a quarter of the guests. In my mind I begged Lady Eleanor, Tell them to consult me even when they're not dying!

"How many of you danced as her partner or in a quadrille with her?"

More than half had. Everyone smiled approvingly at me, or because they approved of themselves for courage and open-mindedness.

Lady Eleanor went on. "I'm honored to call her my friend. I hope her stay in Frell will be long. I hope she prospers among us." She paused. "I am relying on you to contradict any gossip about her that you may hear."

The listening silence was broken by a cough and by people shifting in their chairs. My kind friend had discomfited her guests.

"May I speak?" Mistress Daria said.

Lady Eleanor nodded. "Of course, dear."

Mistress Daria told everyone I'd saved her parents. "I myself am rarely ill, but if I have so much as an uneasy stomach, I'll hasten to Mistress Evie."

Squire Jerrold said he would, too, then had to add, "I, too, am lucky enough to have almost constant good health."

People would conclude that only the hale would want to see me.

But Wormy spoke up, too. "In Jenn, where my good parents live, Mistress Evie has treated my afflictions for years. My health"—he took a deep breath—"has been uncertain." Another breath. "Or my imaginings have been dire."

His sweetheart smiled at him for the confession. I wondered if I'd heard right. When had he realized he wasn't always sick when he thought he was?

Servers took plates away, though mine wasn't empty. My fork vibrated as my server lifted it. Was the meal over? Could I leave?

But no one stood, except Sir Peter. "Sire, Lord Evesby, Lady Evesby, Mistress Evie, ladies and gentlemen, tonight I am at a crossroad, as I was when I chose to start toward the Fens. Then—"

I stiffened and so did Squire Jerrold next to me.

"—my choice was between safety and risk." He managed to blush. "As you know, I chose risk." His eyes circled the table and slid past me. "This time the road leads to joy or despair, but I'm hopeful." He smiled down at Lady Eleanor, who smiled up at him and seemed to glow.

No!

Would Lucinda come?

My ogre ears heard someone enter. Mandy stood in the doorway, her face intent.

Sir Peter took Lady Eleanor's hands in his. "My darling—"

Faugh! The stink of lilacs. A beaming Lucinda stood behind Lady Eleanor and Sir Peter.

I jumped up. "Lucinda! Please—"

For an instant, her expression became solemn. I found myself sitting again.

Lucinda! No sound came out.

The fairy jumped in place, as might an excited child. "Continue, young sir."

"Who are you?" King Imbert said, twisting to see her.

She gave him a dazzling smile. "I am the fairy Lucinda. I regret missing your proposal and wedding many years ago. You'd be happier now if I'd been there."

Lady Eleanor paled. Her eyes found Mandy, who also looked frightened.

The king's eyes bulged. "How dare—"

"Continue, young sir."

"How dare—"

"Hush."

King Imbert said nothing further.

Sir Peter bowed to the fairy. "You honor us with your presence."

"Continue."

He took Lady Eleanor's hand again. "Sweet, please ensure my happiness. I admire you beyond what I can express. Your goodness, your excellent mind, your kind heart, your beauty beyond"—he glanced at the fairy—"human compare. I will always love you as much as I do today. Will you make me happy forever and marry me?"

"Er . . ." Lady Eleanor turned to Mandy.

Mandy nodded. Her hands clutched each other, knuckles white.

"Er . . ." Lady Eleanor said. "Will you grant a wish, Lucinda?"

She smiled. "I *may*. What wish?"

"Er . . . Will you . . . er . . . give Sir Peter and me this moment in private, just the two of us?"

Ah. She and Mandy had prepared for such a crisis.

"Without me?" Lucinda frowned. "I mean the best for you. Lovers"—she touched her chest—"have their most ardent friend in me. Your wish is foolish, and I won't grant it."

Why didn't Mandy send her away? How could it be big magic to keep a fellow fairy from doing big magic?

Lucinda went on. "And this young man has waited long enough for his answer."

Say yes, I thought. Now you mustn't say no.

"Say yes, Lady," Mandy said.

Sir Peter looked charmingly confused.

Lady Eleanor drew her shoulders back. "I would have said yes anyway. Yes, my love. I will marry you."

"Hurrah!" Lucinda applauded.

The guests joined in. I didn't move.

"What shall I give you to guarantee your happiness?" A hint of a frown returned. "Young lady, you did promise to marry him, didn't you?"

"Certainly, I did."

"Excellent! Then my gift is that neither of you will ever break your promises to each other, beginning with your consent. He has sworn to love you as much as he does right now, and you pledged to marry him."

Lady Eleanor laughed. "I'll take care with my promises from now on."

Lucinda smiled uncertainly. "I suppose that's wise." She disappeared.

Now Lady Eleanor had to marry Sir Peter, no matter what she discovered about him.

"Congratulations, my dears," King Imbert said. "Lady Eleanor, you are a lucky young woman."

Sir Peter protested that the good fortune was his.

Lord and Lady Evesby embraced their daughter. Toasts were made. Only we four—Mandy, Squire Jerrold, Wormy, and I—didn't share in the delight.

After the toasts, the king spoke, his tone dry. "How fortunate we are tonight"—his eyes flicked to me and away—"to have an ogre and to have had a fairy with us." He stood. "This is a joyous moment, and I intend to make it more so. A month from now, while Lady Eleanor and Lord and Lady Evesby prepare for the wedding, my dear

Sir Peter will lead an expedition against the ogres."

I'd be an ogre forever by then.

From the dismay that flashed across his face and disappeared, Sir Peter hadn't expected this.

If King Imbert had proposed the knave go alone, I would have thought, Good riddance and good luck for Lady Eleanor. But an expedition meant more than one.

The king continued. "How fortunate Kyrria is to have an accomplished ogre killer."

"Sire, I hope you know I'm no warrior. I killed by guile."

"Which we need. You'll have plenty of warriors with you."

"Majesty?"

"Yes, Eleanor?"

"Fighting ogres is perilous. Might Peter and I have a while to marry and be happy before he leaves?"

King Imbert frowned.

Lady Eleanor continued. "Can't you delay this dangerous quest for"—she took a deep breath—"a year or even more?" She laughed shakily. "We'll still have ogres then."

"The *point*," King Imbert said, "is to have fewer of them."

Lady Eleanor reddened and didn't speak again.

Sir Peter leaned farther across the table. "Sire? I don't want to go only as the mastermind. I want to fight, too.

Might I be trained first?" He looked innocent and eager. "I will apply myself."

The king thought about it. "Your preference does you credit. I believe you have the makings of a champion. We'll wait."

How wily Sir Peter was. There would be no expedition. While seeming to bend to the king's will, he would cause delay after delay.

"But," King Imbert added, "we'll begin your training at once." He paused. "I know! With exercises in all the arts of war. My boy, you'll watch and learn, and you'll participate. The ogre will join in, too. She won't be allowed weapons, however. My heart wouldn't survive the sight."

Why didn't he address me directly?

Then he did. "You'll wrestle. That is the ogre's principal form of combat, is it not?"

"Not exactly, Sire, beg pardon."

"No? I thought that's what you creatures do."

Creatures. "There are no rules, and it's as much fisticuffs as wrestling. We scratch and bite, too." I had to say the rest, although everyone probably knew. "Our scratches and bites are poisonous."

"Mmm. Then you must wrestle without hurting anyone."

"Yes, Your Majesty." But could I? Or would my rage take me over?

The servers returned with plates of sweets for each of us. Mine, again, were disguised meat. Soon after, the party ended. I was glad to return to the pigs. My unfortunate guards spent the night on patrol outside the sty.

The fourth of my remaining days had ended.

I had to plan. I had left it too long. Soon Frell would cease to tolerate me.

Only one place would take me in. I came to a decision. When hope was gone, I would concede defeat and leave. I'd already failed to help Lady Eleanor or to weaken Sir Peter. Further efforts would be in vain, too.

If the king gave his permission, as I thought he would to be rid of me, I'd return to the master, where I was trusted, where I'd be able to heal people. I'd take comfort in that and in Mother's company and beloved Wormy's visits, if he came, with or without his wife. I'd appear cheerful and would hide my despair.

CHAPTER THIRTY-FOUR

THE NEXT DAY, Wormy came to Trunk's kitchen. In his tentative way, he hovered just past the guards at the door. From there, he set off my tingle.

"Master Wormy!" Trunk led him to the worktable. "Sit! My porridge is just cooked. I make it with ginger sheep's milk. Best thing for you."

Wormy sat but refused the food. "Evie, last night's supper isn't sitting well."

In silence, I mixed a draft of mugwort, culpepper, and ginger tea. When it had steeped, I pushed the mug across the table to him, keeping my distance for fear of steam shooting out my ears.

He drank it down. "Evie, I volunteered to be in the exercises, and the king said yes."

"You could get hurt! *I* could hurt you!"

He shrugged.

Sir Peter could injure him, too. "Why participate?" He didn't go in for that sort of thing.

"You'll be in it. You may need . . . I don't know what. Something. Trunk agrees that Sir Peter is bad. He may try to harm you."

Trunk said, "I told him he's rotten at the root, Mistress Ogre."

"Evie, if I'm in the exercises, I'll be right there."

Injured or killed. "You mustn't!"

"I must." He stood. "I feel better." He paid my fee, bowed, and departed, probably off to assist Frell's needy again and woo his sweetheart.

The kitchen felt empty without him.

By the next morning, November 20, only today and tomorrow and the day after until four o'clock remained until I'd be an ogre forever. Soon after I reached the apothecary, a red-eyed Lady Eleanor entered and immediately set herself to pounding herbs in my mortar . . . without choosing which herbs.

I said, "That will treat a cold and grow a mustache."

She didn't even smile, just shook her head and glanced at Trunk, his two cook's helpers, the manservant scrubbing the tiles, and the guards. I suggested a walk and took the blanket I kept on hand in case I ever got another patient who needed it. When we left the kitchen, the guards fell in behind us.

In the corridor, Lady Eleanor addressed them with a wheedle in her voice. "Gentlemen, I hope you don't intend to eavesdrop on our confidences." She set off.

They followed, but at a distance.

The day was beautiful, a contradiction of a day, the air chilly but the sun shining with enough warmth to suggest winter would never come. We passed a grove of small trees pruned to the form of candelabra. She led me to the low wall that bordered the moat, far enough from the draw-bridge to give us privacy—as if anyone would approach the reputed corpse eater.

Together, we watched the glassy, half-frozen water. The guards were far enough away that I could sense Lady Eleanor's emotions, which were mostly shame.

"You need a proper cloak," she said.

I supposed.

"I'm finding my courage. I have a request." Her chest rose. "I want a love potion. I beg of you, give—"

She'd discovered he didn't love her? "For Sir Peter?"

"For me. I was happier when I loved him. And if there's a potion to make me admire him again, too, I'd like that as well."

"A love potion will dull your wits while it lasts, but you need your wits. And you'll have to drink it again and again."

She addressed the moat water. "I was witless ever to love him. How much more foolish could I become?"

"What happened?"

The story tumbled out. She didn't look my way. "After the supper, Peter stayed, I think because my dear parents expected him to. Mistress Evie, I'd never been happier. Lucinda's gift didn't matter. Why would I want to break the promise that would extend my happiness forever?"

That fairy!

"Father and Mother left us in the blue parlor. When the door closed, I ran to Peter and threw my arms around his neck."

Which I wanted to wring.

"He removed them and walked to the window. These were his exact words: 'Affection, darling, is for display. When we're alone, I prefer to be unencumbered.'"

"What did you say?"

"I was confused. I sat down. In my mind I ran through how I might have angered or disappointed him. I told him I was sorry. He asked me how long my parents would expect us to remain alone together. I begged him to tell me what I'd done."

I clenched my fists.

"He merely stared out the window. After a minute, he hummed the gavotte we'd danced earlier. That's when I started weeping. I was sure he despised me, that for some reason his love had turned to hate, that I had done some-thing dreadful. If only I could recall it, I could set it right. Finally, I gasped out, 'Do you still love me?'

"He said in a dry voice, 'As much as ever, darling.' For an instant I felt better, and then I understood. That was his promise, which he couldn't change because of the fairy, to love me as much as he ever had. I croaked out, sounding like a frog, 'You never did.' The villain said, 'It's not in my nature, love.'"

She waited for me to speak.

What to say? "He's very bad." It sounded inadequate.

Below us, a child's boat glided by on a slow current.

"Yes. He wanted my money and now—"

"And your rank and beauty." I felt for her, but the moat was stocked with trout. I hadn't eaten fish since I'd changed. I thought I'd like a dozen.

"Squire Jerrold wasn't slandering him. I know that now. Peter didn't kill the ogres. I didn't ask, but I'm sure. How could I have been so easily duped?"

I swallowed my hunger. "How could I have been? He charmed me, too. In the Fens. I believed he loved me." Gently, I turned her shoulders. "Look at me. Imagine the self-deception I indulged in. Sir Peter would as soon love a warty toad as me."

She threw her arms around me and hugged me.

When she released me, I said, "I miss my mother."

Her face melted, which made me weep, too. I wondered what the watching guards thought.

I recovered first, because my grief was old by now.

Finally, her sobs quieted. She set her feet, drew her shoulders back. "We're both the fairy's victims. I won't weep over Peter again."

"Good!"

"You're my model of fortitude. Courage." She smiled. "Humor."

Oh my. In the years to come, I'd repeat her words until they became my motto.

Her eyes widened. "Peter started the rumors about you."

"Yes." I whispered, in case a guard had ogre-sharp ears. "We aren't the only fools. He's also entranced the king." I wished I hadn't promised the master not to tell anyone the truth about Squire Jerrold. Lady Eleanor, raised in the ways of the court, might have had an idea about how to get the squire recognized as crown prince even without the master's help.

"Oh! I've been too caught up by my trouble to think of His Majesty's." She started back to the castle. "King Imbert will be wiser than I was. He'll realize, or Peter will give himself away."

The guards followed us.

I feared she was underestimating Sir Peter and, alas, overestimating the king.

When we reached the castle courtyard, she stopped, and the guards kept a polite distance.

"I have a declaration to make." She took a deep breath. "Before I met him, I didn't love anyone, I mean, other than my family and my friends. I swear to go back to that. I wasn't unhappy then. My mother says I have a strong spirit. My spirit will be my fortress."

"Bravo! You don't need a potion." What she needed was an amulet to protect her, and I didn't deal in those. "Does he realize you no longer care for him?"

She considered. "I don't think so. He came by yesterday, but we weren't alone for a moment. It was all a charade. He must have noticed I'd been weeping, but he'd expect that if I did still love him."

"Try not to let him know. Don't trust him. Even when you think you're not trusting him, make sure you aren't." I hardly understood myself, but I meant every garbled word. "Remember how wily he is."

She nodded. "How fortunate I am you're my friend." She laughed. "When I came to the castle, I thought myself the unluckiest maiden in Kyrria."

Back in the kitchen, the scullery maids scraped carrots,

peeled potatoes, and turned the roasts without their usual chat and giggles. Trunk pounded a steak with a meat hammer as if he hoped to kill the animal all over again. As soon as he looked up, he shooed his helpers from the room. "Do something else awhile. Pick herbs for tomorrow's stew and for the day after that."

They hastened out.

He said, "Mistress Ogre, now I know why the master never called him *King* Imbert. A real king can tell a good man from a rotten cucumber."

"What happened?" I asked.

"*Imbert* has proclaimed the impostor his heir!"

CHAPTER THIRTY-FIVE

"WHAT IMPOSTOR?" I wanted to be certain.

He seemed to notice Lady Eleanor for the first time. "Beg pardon, Lady. I know you love him." Then he couldn't hold back. "That Sir Not-Ogre-Killing Peter is crown prince. The investiture is tomorrow."

Lady Eleanor asked, "Mistress Evie, will he harm the king?"

Would he murder King Imbert, to speed his coronation? I remembered our conversation when I'd zEEned him. "He told me at a moment when he couldn't lie that he wouldn't kill a person or cause a person to be killed." But would that always be true? Was it no longer true in the face of this temptation? "He might change his mind, though. And he said then that he wouldn't scruple at doing me in—"

Trunk gasped. Lady Eleanor paled.

"—if he had the opportunity, since I'm an ogre."

Lady Eleanor said, "We mustn't give him a chance at you."

I shrugged and had only this comfort to offer: "I doubt he's in haste to become king, when he'll have to toil for other people. The wealth and position of a crown prince will please him more."

That evening, I wrote to the master. The time for secrecy was over, and the king wouldn't believe me. I wasn't even sure he'd believe his father-in-law, from whom he'd been so long estranged.

The post left the castle daily but would take a week or more to reach the farm, and the master would need time to come to Frell. By then, Sir Peter might be so firmly established that no one could unseat him.

And I would be an ogre forever.

With just today and tomorrow until four in the afternoon remaining, I felt only weary resignation.

Lady Eleanor had successfully petitioned the king to allow me to attend the investiture. In late morning, the guards and I arrived in the castle receiving room to find the chamber deserted and empty of furniture, which had been removed to accommodate as many as might fit.

I wore my ball finery and was installed along a wall. Shortly, people filed in. Everyone headed first for the opposite side of the room. Sir Stephan did so, too, and the squire had to stay with him, though he nodded and smiled his serious smile at me.

The unlucky and frightened latecomers gave me as wide a berth as could be managed. However, three people elected to stand near me: Wormy, Trunk, and Squire Jerrold's Mistress Daria. I was grateful, though Wormy's closeness kept me agitated.

Trunk glared at my guards. He was also fuming at the king and Sir Peter, but I'd warned him so many times against snorting or *humph*ing or—perish the thought!— calling out that he'd sworn not to release anything more than mild puffs of breath.

Lady Eleanor stood on the dais with King Imbert and Sir Peter, although three paces behind them. King Imbert had decided that she should become a princess when Sir Peter became crown prince, although the wedding wouldn't take place for a month.

How comely the soon-to-be-royal couple were. My stomach bellowed.

The proceedings began with a flute and viola playing a mellow tune. Body heat warmed the chamber. I began to sweat. My guards pinched their noses. My friends did not.

As the ceremony progressed, Sir Peter couldn't have portrayed the humble, valorous knight better. He stood pillar straight, chin up, eyes bright. During the many courtiers' and dignitaries' speeches, he smiled and blushed at each mention of his courage, gallantry, and sacrifice for the good of Kyrria.

Lady Eleanor's smile was pasted in place and her mind was elsewhere—because she applauded only after she heard others do so. Occasionally, her eyes met mine, and her smile sweetened. I believed she meant to communicate, *See? I can survive whatever may come.*

The reason King Imbert had been willing for me to attend the ceremony revealed itself when he announced that the training exercises were to take place the next day. "Mistress Evie, our resident ogre—"

Healer ogre!

"—will take part and will teach us how to defeat her kind. We thank her."

I curtsied.

King Imbert gestured to Lady Eleanor, who stepped forward and knelt. "My dear," he said, "you'll get your crown when you and Peter marry, but I have this promissory jewelry."

She must have known, because she bent her head, and he clasped a silver necklace around her neck. She rose and returned to her place.

The king smiled. "And now, the moment you have been awaiting, the one I have certainly spent many years hoping for, when I ordain my successor. Peter, my boy—"

Sir Peter knelt.

A servant stepped to the king's elbow, bearing a thin gold crown on a velvet cushion.

King Imbert placed the crown on Sir—*Prince*—Peter's head.

I reconsidered my oath not to eat humans. Prince Peter would be a disastrous king. I'd be executed if I killed him. Of little consequence.

At dawn on November 22—ten hours remaining—I skipped my bath. Ordinary ogres didn't lather and scrub for a fight with their food. My guards hung back when they caught a whiff. I clutched my blanket around me, though the mild weather continued. The doomsayers warned of a blizzard tomorrow. Fitting, if it came.

In the outer ward, on the other side of the castle from my bedroom with the pigs, several contenders who'd arrived early were breakfasting at a long trestle table. The stands and the royal balcony were unoccupied.

Frell's master of occasions announced my approach:

"All ye, take note! Now comes the ogre. And see, the higher end of this groaning board holds civilized fare, which ogres despise: a salad, pickled beets, carrot pudding, sweet onions, dried figs and dates, walnuts, and bread so light it may float away. On the end that threatens collapse, we see the dishes humans eat in moderation and ogres devour in excess: three hams, an entire roast boar, a gaggle of roasted geese . . ."

Many short of a gaggle. Just four geese.

"A side of beef, potted mutton, and braised goat."

I ate at a distance from everyone else while the nobles and gentry of Frell filled the benches. The lower classes came, too, and sat on the ground, circling the arena in a ring that grew to five deep. Mandy, with a basket in her lap, sat in the first row, near the bleachers, and chatted with Mistress Daria, who sat on her right.

Wormy came from the direction of the castle entry arch. After helping himself to food, he stood near me, though not so close that my tingle became unbearable. We ate in silence, but I was glad for his company.

The other contestants finished their meal, and I stopped eating. Wormy joined them on a bench while I continued to stand apart. King Imbert, Prince Peter, Princess Eleanor, and three dignitaries emerged from the castle. I scowled when Prince Peter kissed my friend's cheek, but she smiled brightly before following the king and the other eminences up the stairs to the royal balcony. Prince Peter went to the bench, where he brought the number of us contestants to thirty. In light of the exertion to come, he didn't wear his crown.

Because of his late arrival, Prince Peter occupied one end of the bench and, by happenstance, Squire Jerrold held down the other. Prince Peter perched with easy grace, while Squire Jerrold sat solidly. If a viewer who knew neither one were to judge by just the bearing and demeanor of each, the viewer would call the squire prince and Prince Peter a charming impostor.

It was the power of presumption, which hadn't struck me before. Master Peter arrived with six ogre heads, and all virtues accrued to him. Squire Jerrold came empty-handed and was branded a liar. I cured dozens of people and was soon despised.

Wormy came to me with his many symptoms. I recognized some as imagined and never credited him with self-knowledge.

"Mistress Evie!" Princess Eleanor ran down the balcony stairs and rushed to me. "Here." She untied the scarf from her neck and tied it around mine.

It smelled dizzyingly of her skin. I swayed.

"I want you to carry my favor."

"Does Prince Peter mind?"

"I didn't ask him." She whispered, although we were far from the others. "I think he's planning something. Take extra care."

"Why do you think so?"

"Last evening, when we had to be alone together, he compared people to a clock. Mistress Evie, he's stopped being wary with me. I think he likes having an audience for his intrigue."

"In what way like a clock?"

"Because the parts always behave as expected. You wind a clock, like the castle's, and the figures emerge, perform their circuits, reenter the mechanism. 'No surprises,' he said."

Yes, he knew all our levers and pulleys: mine in the Fens, the infatuated maidservants' here, Princess Eleanor's, King Imbert's. Charming smiles, longing looks, calculated phrases. Inevitably, we followed the course he set.

"Be on your guard. I'm frightened." She kissed my unshaven cheek, which almost bowled me over, and hastened back to the balcony stairs.

The castle clock chimed nine in the morning. I had seven more hours. The master of occasions announced the first event, a race three times round the castle.

Of course I won. The human winner was Prince Peter, with Squire Jerrold a close second. I remembered how nimbly Sir Peter had jumped up the first time he'd seen me and his speed when he'd fled.

Wormy finished last. If the contest had been for kindness and goodness, he would have won.

The master of occasions called that the archery trials were about to start.

Squire Jerrold won this. Wormy, to my surprise, came in second. I clapped for him with all my might.

He bowed and waved at me as if I were any human maiden.

Prince Peter was the loser, with his arrows farthest from their mark and often missing the target entirely. He took his loss with a self-deprecating grin.

Quoits followed, then pole vaulting, a tug of war, and swordplay.

• Ogres are superb at both quoits and pole vaulting.

I won both competitions. Squire Jerrold, a close second, surpassed me in grace and almost equaled my strength. His fellows took to applauding him, including Prince Peter, although he hesitated the first time.

King Imbert remarked on Squire Jerrold's performance to Princess Eleanor, and my ogre ears heard. "The liar is almost princely. He'll go far if he stops his foolish accusations."

Prince Peter couldn't have heard, but he may have seen the king's lips move and guessed, and he couldn't have been

305

pleased to have a rival. Nonetheless, he went to Squire Jer-rold. "How happy I am you're on our side. Kyrria thanks you."

Kind words. I'd have felt more at ease if they'd been *un*kind. What was he going to do?

Squire Jerrold merely bowed acknowledgment.

Finally came hand-to-hand combat in turn against me. I was unarmed, but the humans were permitted to keep their rapiers, though King Imbert said not to use them unless their lives were at risk. I supposed forgiveness would be granted if I happened to be slain.

My first adversary was to be Sir Stephan.

We faced each other a dozen paces apart. Neither of us wore armor, because ogres don't, and mail hinders people in a fight.

I recited in an undertone, "Do not scratch. Do not bite."

Sir Stephan was no more than twenty-five years old, tall, sturdy, in excellent health.

My ogre mind said, They are prey. Your competitor is your quarry.

I thought, Do not scratch. Do not bite.

He ran at me. I sprang aside at the last moment—how easy! How slow he was! I lunged at his legs from behind, felled him. He landed hard on his stomach and started to roll over. But before he could, I sprang on top of him and found myself closer to him than I'd been even to my partners at the ball. His back pressed into my chest. His neck was an inch from my lips. His scent filled my lungs. My appetite roared.

So close, so available. My mouth filled with saliva. My human side shrank to near nothing. The knight and I were fighting, and I would win and eat it.

I would *not* eat *him*!

Blood drummed in my ears. I would!

Without thought, automatically taking the only way out, I fainted.

CHAPTER THIRTY-SIX

AND WOKE to the master of occasions declaring Sir Stephan the winner. The crowd cheered. The knight straddled my chest, laughing, pouring water into my nose, my mouth, my eyes. I was glad he was still alive.

He stood and I scrambled up. He hadn't really won.

From her balcony seat, Princess Eleanor cried, "Are you all right?"

I called up, "Yes."

The next contestant, a young woman, was unknown to me. I pulled her down, too, and her meaty scent set me off again. The cycle repeated. I fainted again and woke up wondering if unconsciousness would continue to save both me and my opponent. I remembered my uncontrollable response to the dragons.

Wormy's turn. This was different. His scent, his closeness, overwhelmed me with love as well as hunger. We both fainted.

King Imbert himself came onto the field and stood over us. I got to my feet and curtsied. Wormy tried to stand but slumped back.

I crouched. "I can treat—"

"Mistress Evie, rise."

I stood. "Yes, Sire."

"Would you be this useless if you joined us in a fight against other ogres?"

"No, Your Majesty. Ogres don't make me . . ." I trailed off. I didn't want to say the next word, *hungry.* Or even *tingle.*

"Make you what?"

"Er . . . faint, Sire. I never fainted when I lived among them."

"If you can't stop fainting here, you're useless. I'd command you, but it might do no good. Can you stop?"

I didn't think so. "Maybe if I eat something." Breakfast seemed long ago. Their scents might not affect me as much if there were food in my stomach.

"Then eat. We'll wait."

And watch. I walked to the table and, on the way, had an idea. I returned to the king, who still stood in the arena. "Your Highness, may I have a word with Princess Eleanor's cook?"

"She can hardly cook a delicacy for you here." But he gave his leave, and the fairy joined me at the table.

"It's their scent when we're fighting. Please make me not faint and not eat them, as you made me not stink at the ball."

"Give me Lady's scarf, if you please, Mistress." I did, and she took a knife from the rows of cutlery, marched to the disgusting end of the table, cut two onions in quarters, and knotted them into the scarf. "Let's see." She tied the scarf around my head so that the evil bundle hung under my nose.

Ugh! Ugh! My eyes watered. The onions overwhelmed all other scents.

Couldn't she have just cast a spell?

She guessed my question. "The magic would have been too big, Mistress. I'm sorry. But I have made it so the scarf won't fall off and the onions won't spill out until you no longer need them. Small magic. Do you think you won't faint now?"

I wasn't sure. I might vomit.

The crowd laughed as I returned—the ogre version of a horse with a nose bag. King Imbert shrugged and went back to his seat.

Wormy stood at the edge of the arena, swaying a little. "Evie, I'll be back. I'm just dizzy." He started for the castle entrance.

I lifted the scarf. "Tell Trunk to give you auntwort tea." I lowered the scarf back in place.

Another knight, Dame Kezia, entered the arena, moving with the bounce of a born athlete. I spread my feet and bent my knees a little. She mirrored my stance. We circled each other warily. I waited. From watching me before, she must have expected me to hurtle at her. I decided to let her come to me.

King Imbert cried, "Notice the ogre's wiliness."

Dame Kezia waited, too, but I believed I could outlast her. She'd want to impress the king, and I knew I couldn't. Finally, her circles tightened. She was preparing to pounce, I was sure of it. As soon as I could get to her with my longer reach, I grabbed her upper arm, pulled her close.

I didn't smell meat and didn't tingle and was able to keep my senses. Dame Kezia stiffened with surprise. I seized her neck and waist and raised her over my head.

She writhed, kicked, arched her back, to no avail. If I'd wanted to kill her, I could have, easily, by dashing her to the ground and breaking her skull. Instead I carried her to the stands, where I set her down. I backed away and curtsied.

The master of occasions intoned, "Victory for the ogre."

Dame Kezia, recognizing her defeat, wobbled to the other contestants.

Princess Eleanor, Mandy, Mistress Daria, and Squire Jerrold applauded. After a blink, Prince Peter joined in, shouting, "Well done!"

Princess Eleanor cried, "Hurrah for Mistress Evie!"

I said, "Your Highness, I beg of you, instruct your master of occasions to say my name."

The king did so.

My next five opponents were as easy as Dame Kezia had been, but then I rolled on the ground with Sir Owen, a massive man, for a minute or two before I punched his ear and his chin and ended the fight. He recovered quickly when my victory was declared and I stood away—I hadn't harmed him seriously.

Of all I fought, Squire Jerrold proved hardest to defeat. He was fastest, cleverest, and relentless. We battled at least a full five minutes—punching, rolling, jumping up, pulling the other one down, pinning each other, squirming free—before I finally caught him from behind, my arms confining his, my legs scissoring his.

"I concede!"

I released him, and he bowed to me, the only one to do so, the true, courteous prince.

King Imbert stopped the demonstration. I removed the nose bag.

"This was discouraging," the king said, "but enlightening. No wonder we have so little success. We must be even more in awe of my heir for his accomplishment."

The heir bowed in his seat.

King Imbert said, "Is there anything that might have been done to defeat you, Mistress Evie?"

Everywhere in the kingdom, movement ceased.

I said the obvious. "In a real encounter, there might be no fighting. If they had enough members, a band would instantly persuade the humans into submission." Could I think of anything to help? What? Oh! Why had no one thought of this? "We should stop our ears. Wax! Soldiers should put wax in their ears at the first hint of us."

The silence continued for a moment. Then excited talk broke out. Princess Eleanor cried, "Hurrah for Mistress Evie, healer and tactician!"

King Imbert held up a hand. "Promising, if there's no trick in it."

Didn't he remember I'd saved his life?

Seemingly, he did, or he was more thoughtful than I'd seen before. He descended and bid me follow him out of the arena. The guards started after us, but he waved them away, saying, "She wouldn't dare."

When we passed the contestants' bench, Prince Peter stood to join us.

The king held up a hand. "I'll relate all to you."

"I'm eager to hear." Prince Peter sat again. I saw a frown, instantly erased.

King Imbert led me far enough from everyone that he didn't have to stand near me and smell me and we still wouldn't be overheard. He also half faced away from me. I was sure the sight of me troubled him, too. "Mistress Evie, I noticed an oddity in what you stated just now. You said *'we* should stop *our* ears,' and then 'at the first hint of *us.*' In the first you placed yourself as human, in the second as ogre. Explain, if you please."

My heart threatened to explode out of my chest. Lucinda, please! If I must keep this form forever, let the king understand the truth. Let me be protected.

I opened and closed my mouth like a fish in air. I swallowed. I choked. Tears of effort streamed down my cheeks. No words came, except, "I'm sorry, Your Majesty."

"I believe you are." He climbed back to the balcony and spoke again, this time for all to hear. "If my knights and soldiers can't hear the ogres, they won't be persuaded and there will be fighting. Mistress Evie, I ask you again, can you think of anything else to aid us?"

We were bigger, angrier, hungrier, less afraid, had fangs and poisonous nails. No.

Yes! "If the soldiers fight in pairs, they're likely to have more success. Ogres never cooperate." Forgetting my fangs, I grinned. "Even if cooperation occurred to them, they wouldn't be able to stick with it."

This was greeted with shouts and universal applause.

The banquet table had been cleared during the combat. Now, led by Trunk, a line of serving maids brought dinner out. The people in the stands and those in the balcony descended to partake. The townspeople spread blankets on the field and opened picnic baskets. The tower clock chimed noon. Four more hours.

When I backed away from the table with a full plate, Trunk followed. "Master Warwick is in the apothecary."

"How is he?"

"Sleeping."

Good.

Trunk scowled. "A *physician* tended to him." He pointed at an elderly man approaching the banquet table from the castle entrance. I remembered that, when I'd first treated him, King Imbert had wished for a physician named Sir Titus.

"Did he dose Wormy?"

"He called it a decoction."

"Did he say what was in it?"

"No. Master Warwick wanted to return here, but the physician told him to rest. I watched him sleep while I stirred and chopped and rushed about."

The master of occasions announced that the jousting would start in an hour. I loaded my plate again. I wasn't to joust.

But when everyone was settled to watch, he proclaimed

a change. "King Imbert has considered Mistress Evie's suggestion. We shall return to hand-to-hand combat, this time in pairs against the ogre foe."

Me.

The master of occasions announced the pairings. Wormy wasn't mentioned. Prince Peter and Squire Jerrold were to face me together. Had Prince Peter arranged that? I thought of Princess Eleanor's warning, but he hadn't known people would be paired. He couldn't have anticipated this.

I retied the nose bag. First to fight me were Dame Kezia and Sir Owen, who placed themselves on either side of me so that I could see just one or the other.

At once, they both attacked.

In a frenzy of fury, I pushed both away at once. Dame Kezia stumbled. I leaped on her but remained aware of Sir Owen. I heard a hiss. He'd unsheathed his rapier. Unfair!

I circled her throat with my left hand. She clawed at my arms, my face. Ha! Couldn't make me uglier. I tightened my grip. Her face began to blue.

I felt the air stir and knew Sir Owen had launched himself. Without looking, I reached up. When his body hit my hand, I used his momentum to hurl him over my head, backward to the dirt.

He lay still. Had I killed him?

Had he landed on his rapier? No. There it was, in the dirt, unbloodied.

Had I killed Dame Kezia? I let her go and stood. After a long half minute, she opened her eyes.

Sir Owen groaned.

I raised the nose bag. "Ogre ears are sharper than human."

Prince Peter stood. "Our turn."

So eager?

He descended to the arena, where Squire Jerrold joined him.

I lowered the nose bag back into place. Squire Jerrold crouched, tense, ready for anything. Prince Peter slouched, smiling. I remembered how lithe he was. He might be the one to watch, more than Squire Jerrold. And the squire didn't want me dead.

There we stood, the false prince paired with the true, against the ogre, also false—for a few more hours.

Let them come at me. I crouched, too. The humans fell silent, except in the stands, where a baby cried.

Prince Peter whirled like a top, surprising me, diverting my attention. Squire Jerrold hurled himself at me. The crowd cheered. The squire and I went down, rolling over and over, trying to pin each other. Prince Peter perfectly timed a kick at my head. I took the blow, and, brain reeling, grabbed his ankle, pulling him to the ground, both of them on top of me.

Defeat Squire Jerrold first; then Prince Peter would be easy. The muscles in my trunk, shoulders, and thighs bunched. I rolled them both over so I was on top, ignored Prince Peter, and rained punches on Squire Jerrold, but he twisted—

—and Prince Peter screamed.

Squire Jerrold and I jumped up and away.

A rapier lay on the ground. Blood spurted from Prince Peter's thigh.

CHAPTER THIRTY-SEVEN

MY GUARDS RAN into the arena.

In a high, shocked voice, Prince Peter cried, "I've been stabbed!"

He'd stabbed himself! Squire Jerrold wouldn't have knifed him, and my hands had been where everyone could see them.

I rushed toward Prince Peter, who would faint if he kept losing blood. Princess Eleanor's scarf would stanch the flow.

Two guards caught my elbows. The other two pointed their swords at me. Several contestants held Squire Jerrold, though he'd been standing still.

The physician bent over a moaning Prince Peter, pulled off his own ruffled cravat, and pressed it into the wound.

Princess Eleanor rushed down from the balcony and headed, not to Prince Peter but to me, halting just beyond the guards.

King Imbert descended too. "How bad is it, Titus?"

"Bloody, not deep," Sir Titus said. "He'll be fine in an hour."

"It's agony!"

"Hush, my boy," the king said. "You're making me ashamed."

Prince Peter groaned.

"Sire," Princess Eleanor cried, "Mistress Evie would never hurt anyone."

"I don't know about that. She didn't wield the rapier, but the two of them"—the king gestured at Squire Jerrold—"almost certainly conspired." He picked up the rapier and went to Squire Jerrold. "This is yours, I think."

Trunk let out a howl of despair.

This was the time, or past the time. I said, "If you execute him—"

"Prison is enough, Sire," Prince Peter moaned.

"Assassination," King Imbert said, "even when it fails, warrants execution. And no trial is called for, since hundreds—"

No! "Sire, if you execute him, you'll execute your son."

Silence.

Squire Jerrold stared at me.

"This is absurd. I have no son." King Imbert told a guard, "Run him through first and then the ogre."

I was glad Wormy wasn't here to see me die.

"Majesty!" Eleanor cried. "Don't!"

One of the swords that had been pointed at me now turned toward Squire Jerrold.

There was only one way. "Squire Jerrold—" Could I say it? Would Lucinda let the words come out?

The guard pulled back his sword elbow.

Nothing stopped me. "Propose to me! Ask me to marry you."

Surprise stopped the guard's sword.

King Imbert held up his hand. "I'm curious."

The guard waited but didn't lower his sword.

I didn't love Squire Jerrold.

He loved Mistress Daria, but he trusted me. "Mistress Evie, will you marry me?"

"Yes." Thought departed. The ground seemed to fall away.

I heard gasps.

I choked on stench. If *I* no longer stank, my clothes, which now hung on me, still did. I managed to keep my last meal from rising, but I had never felt so stuffed.

"Mistress Evie!" Princess Eleanor threw herself into my human arms.

I heard a satisfied sigh, even a musical sigh, which could come from only one source. There was the fairy, standing between Squire Jerrold and me, beaming.

I heard "Harrumph!" in Mandy's voice.

"Mistress Evie?" Squire Jerrold said. "Is that you?"

"I love a romantic, happy ending!" Lucinda cried.

"She was human all along?" King Imbert's face reddened and his chest heaved.

I feared for his heart. Sir Titus went to him.

"I'm all right." The king glared at the fairy. "You did this to her?"

Lucinda, don't make him an ogre or a squirrel!

The fairy seemed not to notice the accusing tone. "She found her true love! Because of me! I adore creating joy!"

The king turned to me. "What's this about him"—he waved an arm at Squire Jerrold—"being my son?"

"My father was a magistrate," Squire Jerrold said. "I'm not your—"

"His grandfather is Lord Niall, now calling himself—"

"The master is a lord?" Trunk cried.

"You're a fairy." The king turned to Lucinda. "Is this young man my son?"

322

Lucinda's eyes flicked away for a second. "Yes, he is. He is your son." She clapped again. "This grows better and better." She clasped my hands, and I was afraid to pull them away. "You're a princess!"

"I'm your son?"

The guards released Squire—Prince Jerrold.

"You're not my son if you—" He faced Lucinda again. "Can you tell me if he stabbed the crown . . ." He looked around.

Prince Peter no longer lay on the ground. He wasn't in the crowd around the arena, in the stands, or on the balcony. King Imbert dispatched the guards, who took off at a run, two toward the castle, two toward the drawbridge.

The king turned back to Lucinda. "Did my son stab anyone?"

Her eyes became unfocused again. "Certainly not!" She frowned. "How odd. A young man stabbed himself."

King Imbert embraced his son. "My child." Tears coursed down his cheeks. "My own child. My daughter." He reached to embrace me, then thought better of it.

I was about to be an ogre again. "Prince Jerrold, thank you for the honor of your proposal, but on further thought, I don't want to marry you."

Lucinda sputtered, "Why not?"

"Squire Jerrold loves Mistress Daria, and she loves him."

"Then why did you ask this one?" Lucinda asked him and pointed at me.

"Because I knew she would help me."

"No matter." Again, Lucinda seemed to do nothing, but the ground tilted, and I had returned to ogre form. "Soon . . ." She thought a moment. "Oh. Today. You'll be an ogre forever. It's out of my hands."

"She loves Master Warwick," Princess Eleanor said.

"The first one?"

"But he's vowed never to marry," I said.

"Because of you. You ruined his life." Lucinda vanished.

Had I?

King Imbert declared, "Mistress Evie, you must stay in Frell. I command it. You are under my protection and my son's after me."

Mother could come and live with me. That would be a great thing. "Sir Titus?" I said. "How is Master Warwick? Is he very ill?"

"No, not very. He is in distress. He may make himself sicker."

I ran into the castle.

"Follow her!" Prince Jerrold shouted. "Don't let anyone interfere with her, by order of . . . me!"

As the castle clock struck three, I raced through the entrance. Up the marble stairs. Now patients would come to me. If Wormy stayed in Frell, I could heal him until death parted us.

But he wasn't in the apothecary. The chamber was empty except for a young woman, who sat in the rocking chair, sobbing into her hands.

I had no time for her troubles, though I sensed a lake of sadness and an abyss of horror. "Have you seen Wor— Master Warwick, the young man who—"

She looked up and turned out to be dainty Mistress Chloris, her face brick red, tears streaming. "He . . ." But she couldn't continue. She swallowed, gulped, tried again, gave up, and sobbed harder than before.

I honeyed my voice. "There's comfort in a sympathetic ear." Both her sadness and her horror shrank a bit. I went on, promising relief.

Finally she was able to speak. "My Wicky was so sweet—"

She had her own pet name for him? *Her* Wicky?

"—and shy. I thought he'd never find the courage to propose." She tilted up her chin. "And I can be brave, so I did it." The tears started again.

He'd turned her down. Good! But where was he?

"Yes, that *was* brave—" I heard footsteps in the corridor.

They'd ruin my zEEning. "Wait!" I rushed out and waved back a crowd that included Lady Eleanor, Prince Jerrold, Mandy, the king, contestants, guards. "Halt! No farther."

As I rushed into the kitchen again, I heard Prince Jerrold echo my command. Once inside, I said in my sweetened voice, "Go on. Your Wicky just wasn't ready." And never would be.

She nodded. "That's what I think." She swallowed hard. "But now it's too late." Her sobs broke out anew, and I sensed a surge in the horror. "The fairy—"

Lucinda! Fear for Wormy made me almost unable to zEEn. "You can tell me."

She tried, opened her mouth, closed it, tried again. A vein in her forehead throbbed.

If Lucinda had turned him into an ogre, people would have seen him, and he'd be easy to find—so what had she done? I raced out to the corridor. Mandy would know.

Mandy must have whispered it to Lady Eleanor, who tried to tell me. "He's—" Her mouth worked. Her expression was tragic. She gave up. "I'll show you." She pushed through the crowd and ran back to the grand staircase.

I followed. Outside, in the outer ward, she pointed at the only tree that grew there, a tall spruce.

Lucinda had turned him into a tree? I'd happily propose

to a tree! But how would it say yes? And the spruce had been there before.

Lady Eleanor held out her hands about nine inches apart from each other.

Oh! Wormy was a squirrel.

He must be terrified.

How would I find him?

CHAPTER THIRTY-EIGHT

I WHEELED AROUND. "Prince Jerrold, please! We have to catch all the squirrels. Don't hurt them! Not a hair!" Poor Wormy! "Every squirrel. We can't miss a squirrel."

Why did that blasted girl have to propose?

Prince Jerrold issued another command. Guards, contestants, townsfolk—too many people!—ran for a shed that abutted the outer curtain. I rushed to the trestle table and grabbed the bowl of walnuts. Madly, I ran around the ward, scattering nuts, shouting, "Look, squirrels! Walnuts! Nothing better than walnuts!"

Back where I began, I saw a serving maid race into the castle and knew that Trunk had sent her for more nuts. I called after her, "Carpet the ground with nuts! Nuts everywhere!"

People milled about the ward, wielding long bird nets.

I cried, "Come to me, Wormy!" If Lucinda had done to him what she'd done to me, his mind and heart would be half squirrel, and squirrels were terrified of me. The human side of him, too, would be afraid I'd eat him by accident. "Don't worry, Wormy! I'll never eat squirrel again. King Imbert will outlaw eating squirrels. You won't be eaten." Was he nearby to hear me?

Where might he go?

He'd return to where he felt safest—a healing place. I dashed back into the castle.

As I ran up the stairs, a corner of my mind wondered how many minutes had passed since the clock rang three.

I scanned the walls, floor, ceiling, as I flew through the corridor. No Wormy.

The serving maid passed me, hefting a huge sack.

No Wormy in the kitchen apothecary, where, while Mistress Chloris wept, I even looked in the pots and in my biggest herb jars, and I swept everything off each surface in case he was hidden behind something.

Racing back out of the castle, I wondered if Wormy had contrived events—except for becoming a squirrel. Had he lured Mistress Chloris into proposing so he could refuse, so Lucinda would be angry and would—

—turn him into an ogre—

—and he could be with me?

Wormy! You idiot! How I love you!

How soon would the clock strike four?

Back in the arena, a makeshift pen surrounded by guards held a dozen or more squirrels. The serving maid tossed in walnuts. If a squirrel tried to climb out of the enclosure, a guard—gently—nudged it back in. People straggled out of the granary with more squirrels in their nets.

"If you please," I begged a guard at the pen, "pick the squirrels up one at a time so I can talk to them."

Prince Jerrold told the guard to do so.

The guard pulled out a squirrel, who trembled all over, whose moist brown eyes looked at me and away, at me and away.

Did Wormy still understand Kyrrian? "Wormy, will you marry me?"

In the crowd, a man laughed. When this was over, he'd regret it.

My words caused no change in the squirrel. I proposed to three more.

Trunk ran out of the granary with a squirrel in his net, crying, "Mistress Ogre, look at this one!"

His squirrel was trembling as violently as the others, but despite that and despite the net, it managed to bring its little squirrel hands to the sides of its head and then to its stomach, up and down repeatedly.

Headache! Stomachache!

"Lower the net, Trunk." I faced the squirrel eye to eye. "Wormy, will you marry me? Please marry me! As your healer, I advise you to marry me."

It stopped trembling and ceased touching its head and stomach. It couldn't speak, but it could nod. Why didn't it nod?

"Nod if you'll marry me. Please nod!"

It didn't. Why not?

"Wormy, I love you."

The castle clock struck once.

Oh, no!

Oh. "Not just to cure you of being a squirrel. I want to be your wife. I know that now."

The clock chimed a second time. The squirrel—Wormy—nodded.

And, as the third peal rang, the squirrel lengthened and broadened and became Wormy, whose words tumbled out, "Will you marry me?"

I roared, "Yes!" a blink before the final stroke of four.

I smelled lilacs.

Lucinda frowned dangerously at me. "Are you about to change your mind again?"

"Definitely not."

"Ah. Good girl. As always, I gave the perfect gift."

I became human again—again. Cheers erupted all around. Lucinda congratulated herself twice more and then vanished.

Despite my stink, Wormy kissed me.

I tingled.

EPILOGUE

PRINCE JERROLD CONGRATULATED us solemnly.

King Imbert echoed his son's congratulations and added, "What a fool I've been."

Wormy looked around the arena. "Are the exercises over?"

"Yes." As briefly as possible, I told him what had happened.

His eyes widened over Master Peter's stabbing. Though fearing the news might be too much for him after the shock of being a squirrel, I revealed Prince Jerrold's true identity.

But as soon as he heard, he knelt to him and pledged his allegiance, which none of the rest of us had thought to do. We all followed suit.

When we stood again, Mistress Daria said, "Mistress

Evie, you deserve every happiness."

Lady Eleanor crowed that she'd helped to bring about the happy outcome. "I told you he admired you!"

Trunk said, "It's a great day." He beamed at all of us, but especially at Prince Jerrold. Then he added, "Mistress O—Evie, you might benefit from ginger sheep's milk now, too."

If I were ever hungry again. I smiled around the arena. "My dear friends, I have to bathe."

I spent the night in a castle bedchamber and hoped the pigs weren't missing their ogre too much. In the morning, half a dozen patients awaited me in the kitchen apothecary, and I had hours of happiness tending to them, with Lady Eleanor assisting. Though she no longer set off my tingle, her company was pure pleasure.

Wormy came in the afternoon and we repaired to a deserted parlor to be happy in each other's company. I could no longer sense his feelings, but his glad face was revealing enough. We drew a sofa close to the fireplace and sat. I tingled, and I suppose he did, too.

He said he had spent most of the morning seeking Mistress Chloris. "I finally found her." He avoided my eyes. "She's very angry. I doubt she'll ever forgive me. Leading her on was the worst thing I've ever done."

"Does she really love you?" Of course she did. Who wouldn't?

"I don't think so. We knew each other for barely more than a week."

"Then she'll recover," I said, all healer.

He went on. "Evie, I should have told you this other thing long ago."

"What?"

"I should have told you before I proposed."

"What?"

His chest rose and fell in a big breath. "Evie, I wasn't always sick when I said I was. Sometimes I just wanted to be in the apothecary with you. I'm sorry."

That was his confession? I waited for more.

When no more came, I smiled. "But I cured you anyway, I, the healer who restores both the sick and the well."

The following day, at Prince Jerrold's command, the heads of my band members were taken off their pikes.

And Master Peter was found on the road to Ayortha. In his sack were his crown, two golden candlesticks, and a diamond brooch that had been lost at Lady Eleanor's ball.

The great sadness was that, because of Lucinda, Lady Eleanor still had to marry him. For her sake, King Imbert didn't punish him and even restored his knighthood. Lady

Eleanor's parents gave him the protection of their respectability. He became a merchant again and was encouraged to be often on the road—where Lady Eleanor never accompanied him.

Prince Jerrold's investiture as crown prince, a mere formality, took place as soon as the master—Lord Niall—reached Frell. Naturally, he didn't recognize me, but we were soon reacquainted.

I'd written to Mother and begged her to come, too. She entered the city in perfect health on the day of the investiture. I looked at her every other minute during the speeches to assure myself we really were together again.

A royal wedding between Prince Jerrold and Mistress Daria took place a month later, on a date and hour that, according to the gazettes of Kyrria, was crowded with other weddings—in hopes Lucinda would be too busy to attend. No speeches, just a quick joining of the two, not even a ball afterward. The fairy didn't appear.

Lord Niall moved into the castle, and Trunk became installed there permanently as chief cook.

King Imbert lifted his command that I remain in Frell, though he warned he might call me back occasionally to consult about ogres.

When Mother, Wormy, and I returned to Jenn, a delegation of townspeople apologized for their attempts on my life.

Using the proceeds of the purpline Mother had sold, I repaid the farmers I'd stolen meat sticks from. Since I still thought us—especially Wormy—young for marriage, he agreed to wait. Two years later, when we finally set our wedding date, Prince Jerrold and Princess Daria wrote to say they had hoped to come and bring their infant son, but, "of all people," as Princess Daria put it in a letter, Lady Eleanor's cook had cautioned against the journey, and Lady Eleanor had begged them to heed the warning. I understood that the attendance of royalty would have increased the likelihood of Lucinda's appearance—and, very likely, a dreadful gift.

However, Mandy and a pregnant Lady Eleanor did come. And, on an occasion-crowded day, the mayor married us—quickly, as we begged him to do.

Wormy said his vows: "Evie, I promise never to be entirely well and to try not to get entirely sick."

"As your wife, I swear to cure you of every ailment and infirmity. You are my most perfect patient."

We kissed and were wed.

ACKNOWLEDGMENTS

An ocean of thanks to my most responsive, most thoughtful of editors, Rosemary Brosnan, whose enthusiasm has consistently buoyed me up. My gratitude to the entire team at HarperCollins: Thanks to Ann Dye and Megan Barlog for bringing *Ogre Enchanted* to market and for delighting me by approving my title! Thanks to copy editor Karen Sherman for joining me in the engrossing weeds of English usage and for helping me give the reader a bump-free read. Thanks to art director Erin Fitzsimmons for the look of *Ogre Enchanted*, which may have presented a particular challenge. Especially grateful thanks to Olivia Russo for getting the word out and for her excruciatingly careful attention to details large and tiny.

A different ocean of thanks to my agent, Ginger

Knowlton, who, through all my books, stories, and poems, is always in my corner.

And my gratitude to long-dead Andrew Lang, whose rainbow fairy books and the straightforward adaptations they contain have fed my imagination from childhood to today.

More Enchanted Books by
GAIL CARSON LEVINE!